# Forbidden Chronicles
# of a Roman Centurion

## A Novel

# John Chaplick

Published by:
Southern Yellow Pine (SYP) Publishing, LLC
4351 Natural Bridge Rd.
Tallahassee, FL 32305

www.syppublishing.com

This is a work of fiction. Names, characters, places, and events that occur either are the products of the author's imagination or are used fictitiously. Any resemblance to actual persons, places, or events is purely co-incidental.

The contents and opinions expressed in this book do not necessarily reflect the views and opinions of Southern Yellow Pine Publishing, nor does the mention of brands or trade names constitute endorsement.

ISBN-10: 1940869412
ISBN-13: 978-1-940869-41-4
ISBN-13: 978-1-940869-42-1 EPUB
ISBN-13: 978-1-940869-43-8 Adobe PDF eBook
Library of Congress Control Number: 2015940317

Cover Design: Jim Hamer
Back Cover Shutterstock Photo Credits ©mishabender
Front Cover iStock Photo Credits ©standby

Printed in the United States of America
First Edition
June 2015

# Dedications

No book, including this one, was ever written by its author alone. I wish to express my deepest gratitude to those special people whose help and patience made *Forbidden Chronicles of a Roman Centurion* possible.

My wife, Avis Anne, who took the time to edit each draft of my manuscript and who managed to maintain a calm understanding while I sequestered myself away for far too long.

My two sons, Trevor and Kyle, and their wonderful families who have always encouraged me no matter what I was doing.

My editor and critic, Paula Stahel, who, gently and firmly, helped turn a raw manuscript into an engaging novel.

My friend, beta reader, and critic, Ginger King, whose experience as an accomplished actress on stage provided a new dimension to the dialogue in the book.

Reverend James (Pastor Jim) Yearsley who screened my original manuscript for doctrinal errors and offered encouragement for its publication.

Reverend George Clark, retired minister and seminary professor, and wife Sherie, Bible-study teacher, who helped cleanse my novel of historic factual errors.

My critique group members whose combination of objective assessment and warm encouragement helped me to develop my craft:

Tracy Bird, Golda Brunhild, Gene Cropsey, Kathryn Dorn, Shaun Darragh, Elizabeth Griffith, Michael Hanson, Bob Hart, Vaughn Jones, Jeff Stark, Shaunte Westraye.

Theresa (Terri) Gerrell, at Southern Yellow Pine Publishing, for her resourcefulness and persistence in launching this novel with maximum marketing effectiveness.

# Acknowledgement

*Forbidden Chronicles of a Roman Centurion* was inspired by Dr. William Lane Craig's publication entitled, *God: A Debate between a Christian and an Atheist*. With every effort to avoid any trace or semblance of plagiarism, I designed my novel to convert the Christian/Atheist conflict inherent in Dr. Craig's work into a story that recognizes the strengths and limitations of any religious commitment. It is my sincere hope that Dr. Craig, to whom I've sent a copy of the manuscript, and all readers, will accept *Forbidden Chronicles of a Roman Centurion* as an interesting fictional adventure novel that addresses, from a unique perspective, a central issue in our culture today.

# Preface

Thirty-four years had passed since they crucified Him. No one at that time could have anticipated that the apostolic writings about Jesus would subsequently be altered in the interests of expedience. The full extent of the *New Testament* forgeries might never have become known at all had it not been for an accidental discovery, twenty centuries later.

# Prologue

## Rome, A.D. 67

Centurion Maecelius's old wounds had begun to leak again. Dark crimson stains spread outward, a fraction of an *uncia* at a time, across the pale linen sheet like shallow streams seeking the path of least resistance. His coughs, which months before had been nothing more than occasional muffled interruptions of his speech, now convulsed his body. Arrius took the blood-speckled kerchief from him. He placed a fresh one in the large hand from which illness drained all power. Arrius turned away as if to ensure the centurion wouldn't see the tears forming in his eyes. He had served under Maecelius in Deiotariana Legion XXII through the Parthian expedition and the Jewish wars. Now his face betrayed an awkward reluctance to watch his leader die.

The centurion raised his hand and motioned to his subordinate. "Arrius, bring the pillow. Prop me up a bit. I want to explain how you should deliver my letter and this compendium of writings to my son when you join up with him in the Britannia campaign. You'll need to do it before he transfers out to Legion XX."

Maecelius waited while Arrius eased a pillow under his sagging shoulders and tendered him a cup of water. Maecelius knew the Britannia conquest would likely be successful now that Boudicca and her predatory hordes had been vanquished. He would have been the one to lead that campaign had his chest wounds not incapacitated him.

Arrius drew the writings and the letter from Maecelius's outstretched hand and laid them on the table next to his bed. "You need to rest, Maecelius. The more you talk the more you cough and the more you bleed. I'll deliver these as you requested, but it isn't worth discussing right now. And possession of them may get your son in trouble. I'm sure you're aware that after they stoned the man who gave this to you, he was beheaded in Rome for all the trouble he caused. An execution long overdue if you ask me."

Maecelius remembered the Jew standing on a stone bench to deliver his message to any who would turn to listen. Some were alarmed and walked away while the curious stayed to hear his strange words about there being only one true god. For Maecelius it seemed a vague and shadowy concept, far removed from the well-defined Roman deities. He'd watched the crowds gather around the outspoken Jew while the insults began and grew more vindictive until they turned into violence.

"Arrius, they stoned Paul because they hated him," the centurion replied in the tone of a teacher admonishing the errors of his pupil. "They hated him because they feared what he had to say. However, it was for violation of Roman law that they executed him, as I warned him they would if he continued to antagonize the judiciary."

"You knew this man?" Arrius's eyes conveyed more than sudden surprise that the man at whose side he had fought for so long could relate to a radical Jew.

"Not well, but, yes, I knew him." The words came slowly, like a confession that would be made only to someone who could be trusted with it. He could never disclose to anyone else acknowledgment of a relationship with someone like Paul, who challenged the foundations of the Empire.

"Were you friends?"

In an effort to ignore the look of alarm on Arrius's face, the centurion turned away, took a few sips from the cup, put it down, and slowly turned back. "No, not exactly. I had occasion to travel with Paul not long ago between Philippi and Thessalonica. I learned things I didn't know. He talked at length about a leader he called Jesus who spoke of his god in an impressive way.

"Arrius, you may not know this, but Paul came from a well-to-do family in Tarsus. They had Roman citizenship, as did he. I found him to be quite intelligent. Stubborn and opinionated, yes. Nonetheless, I concluded that much of what he said about Jesus as a teacher made considerable sense despite the unbelievable qualities Paul seemed to attribute to this man. Paul's Greek was fluent—even better than mine.

2

The judiciary delayed his execution because, under Roman law, a citizen cannot be executed without a trial."

Arrius shook his head. "Nonetheless, the Jew was still a criminal, Maecelius, as was this Jesus who was put to death at Golgotha."

The centurion continued as though he hadn't heard the remark. "From what Paul told me, I concluded that Jesus's death was ordered by forces other than his Roman captors. Paul seemed to fear for his own life, although he refused to disclose the reason. I surmised he'd been threatened by those same forces."

Arrius paused before he responded. "Well, in any case, the execution was well deserved."

Maecelius had seen more than enough criminals in his time. He'd even presided over the executions of a few. The one called Jesus was not a criminal; he was certain of it. The centurion's recurring recollections of the events, which had taken place years earlier, were incontrovertible proof. The difficulty would be in trying to explain that experience, or any part of it.

The Mediterranean summer sun baked the surface of the calfskin tent which now provided only shade as a measure of relief for its two occupants. Maecelius shifted to ease the pain. "I'm aware of the facts surrounding their executions. Still, there's something I must tell you. I've never revealed the contents of this letter to my son or anyone else." The centurion paused to cough up a mouthful of bloody phlegm and reached for another kerchief. "Many years ago during my first assignment in the Legion, I was ordered to oversee the burial of a man executed as a criminal. At the time, I considered it a menial task, well beneath the dignity of a Roman soldier."

Arrius raised his eyebrows in a gesture of curiosity. "You never mentioned that."

"No. Until now, I saw no reason to bring it up. Still, I remembered the incident and the strange events that followed." He struggled to repress another cough. "I had forgotten the man's name until my conversations with Paul. It was only then I realized the man whose tomb I was required to guard was the one Paul called Jesus. I've included a full account of the event in my letter, along with a summary of my discussions with Paul."

Arrius hesitated for a moment, as though he were reluctant to confront his superior on political or philosophical issues. His expression suggested an urgent compulsion to respond.

"May I speak frankly, sir?" Arrius asked.

Maecelius surmised that the account of his relationship with Paul was repugnant, even to the loyal Arrius. "Of course, and there's no need for that kind of deference to my rank. We've been with each other too long for that. I remember our days together when our legions moved into battle like a giant turtle under the protective shields of the cohorts. Do you recall the day you challenged my decision in Syria? You were right; and because I listened to you, the lives of a hundred Roman soldiers were saved. You spoke frankly then, and I've expected no less from you since."

"Please don't take this badly, Maecelius," Arrius began after another awkward hesitation, "but we both know your son hates Jews and has nothing but contempt for this Jesus. We're Romans, Maecelius. We have our own gods and they've served us well. We don't need one more. As to this document and your letter, I'll deliver them as you wish; but with all due respect, I believe your son is more likely to burn this thing than read it."

The centurion leaned back, shifting slightly again in hopes of finding some relief from his agony. He closed his eyes for a moment while he gathered his thoughts. Arrius's response disappointed him, but he could have predicted it. Many saw the wandering Jew and his followers as religious radicals trying to incite rebellion against Rome. The time for changing anyone's mind had long since passed.

Maecelius looked directly at his subordinate and spoke in a resolute voice. "My son will do as I instruct him. And so must you, Arrius. I want you to make sure I'm buried with my tunic, full armor, my gladius, and my field manual, which must not be allowed to fall into the hands of the enemies of Rome. And when you make the delivery to my son, be sure to include the resin."

"Resin?" The comment provoked a look of curiosity.

"Yes. The dictario is actually a compendium of writings on parchment sheets squared off, specially treated, and pressed so they can be bound together at the edges in the form of what Paul called 'pages.'

4

He assured me that these were of the best Egyptian papyrus when he gave the document to me, but resin is necessary for preservation."

Another spasmodic cough interrupted the conversation, and Arrius moved quickly to provide a fresh kerchief. The centurion's chest rose and fell in a strained, uneven rhythm. He paused to catch a wheezing breath and continued with forced determination.

"Without resin neither the pages nor the letter will last long in Britannia's damp climate. Paul went to great lengths to have the scribes copy the old teachings from the parchments. The copies included many of the letters Paul himself had written, along with those written by several others he called 'apostles.' The letter to my son is about more than the teachings. It provides some counsel as to his behavior as a soldier, including some combat maneuvers that have often saved my life and which he will find useful throughout his campaigns. My letter articulates the reasons he should study the contents of these writings, his own contempt for their authors notwithstanding. Therefore I want both documents protected, and you must so instruct my son."

Arrius frowned. "I will do as you say, Maecelius. The military instructions will be useful to your son. Still, I fail to see how he can benefit from anything written by a radical Jew. Anyway, you need to rest now. Try to sleep."

The centurion filled his waning thoughts with visions of the possibilities Paul's world could offer his son. Maecelius drifted in and out of consciousness as the late afternoon shadows turned to dusk. He did not live to see the next morning's sunrise.

# Chapter 1
## Wesleyan University,
## Middletown, Connecticut 2012

They had no faces. Students filled Professor Wykoff's class again this semester because History 125 was a required course at Wesleyan. In years past, his students always had memorable faces he could match with their personalities. Now they didn't, or so it seemed. He'd seen how they had changed since he began teaching. Perhaps the evolving culture modified their behavior…or failed to change his.

After they clicked on *submit* to transmit their final exams electronically and logged off, Samuel Wykoff watched them file out of his classroom for the last time. He no longer felt the sadness that used to creep uninvited into his emotions at the end of each semester. He waved an occasional "goodbye and have a nice summer," but his heart wasn't in it. The truth was he really didn't care. That he couldn't even remember most of their names only added to the hollowness of the gesture. He felt smothered by oncoming waves of guilt for not having tried to bond with them much at all.

"Come on, Sam," the call from the doorway behind him rang out. "Even history professors need to eat, and you're going to have lunch with me today whether you like it or not." The ebullient voice of theology professor Dr. Peter Clemens would have been recognizable even if they hadn't been best friends for the past ten years. The rest of the faculty thought it was nothing short of miraculous that they'd managed to maintain such a close personal relationship, in spite of their opposing, deeply felt, and often argued views on the existence of God.

"Pete, I'm glad you stopped by. I'm not really hungry. I need to talk to you about something." Sam never felt the need for pretense with Peter. Maybe it was the honesty between them rather than any kind of social connection. Since they did not agree on much, Sam reasoned it must have been trust and mutual respect that linked their diverse personalities.

Peter pulled out a student chair and settled into it. "Okay, is this about Martha?"

Sam erased the last of his lecture notes from the board, cast a furtive glance at the PowerPoint projector he never used, and perched on the edge of his desk. "No. I still miss her so much I can hardly stand it, but I think I'm holding myself together fairly well on that." He turned to Peter with an expression that blended discomfort with anxiety. "This is something else. It's so big I'm going to need your help. You know that graduate student I'm mentoring, the one who's been struggling so hard to finish his thesis?"

"Roger Denault? Your young protégé who's still trying to live up to his father's image?"

"The same. Well, he's in London on what I thought was part of a history research project. It turned out, much to my dismay, to be an archaeological dig. Roger's apparently made one hell of a theological discovery. He's uncovered some ancient Roman document which, he claims, could throw the entire Christian doctrine—as you Christians know it—completely out the window."

Peter raised his eyebrows. "Oh, come on. The whole doctrine?"

"Yeah. Look, personally, I don't give a damn, Pete. I'm concerned about the impact on Wesleyan University. I'm Roger's mentor, and if this thing turns out to be a hoax, it'll reflect badly on my department as well as the university. If it's real, the story will get out of control the moment the news media learn about it. You can imagine what all those indignant religious freaks will do."

Peter glared at him. "I don't know whether I want to hear this or not, Dr. Wykoff. Okay, in the interest of not passing up a good story, let's lunch at Downey House, and you can enlighten me. You can also tell me what's really bothering you. Was it this London discovery?"

"No. I was simply recalling happier days. Back when classes were smaller and I could seat my students around me in a semi-circle, it was always conducive to a rich mixture of serious discussion, varying points of view, and relaxing outbursts of laughter. We even joked about my unconventional dress…my 'fully depreciated' sports jacket, as they used to call it, my mustard-splattered shirt with no tie, and running shoes they said had seen better days. That's all gone now, I'm afraid. Regrettably, my little semi-circles were driven into exile by conquering rows of evenly spaced computer stations, all heavily armed with keyboards and video screens. Do you know what I mean?"

Peter nodded. "I think I get the picture."

Sam rose from his desk and paced back and forth in front of it. "After that, my students simply receded into amorphous shadows behind those screens, shielded from me by their damned technology. Even my Socratic method of teaching became obsolete, I guess. Nowadays they stroll into the classroom with their iPods, Blackberries, and other electronic mutations attached like growths at the end of their arms. I can't be sure anymore whether they're recording my lecture or texting back and forth on miniature keyboards designed to make whatever they're doing none of my business."

Peter reached behind a student's desk, picked an empty coffee cup up off the floor, and tossed it into a nearby wastebasket. "Sam, you've rebelled against the system since the day I first met you, and you're still a maverick. The fact is we live in a completely different world now."

Sam stopped his pacing and reclaimed his seat on the edge of his desk. "Yeah, I know. Martha used to chide me about being the last of the Renaissance men, an anachronism lost in the new electronic age. It was her gentle, wifely way of urging me to stick it out for the few years remaining until my retirement. Damn, I miss her! Next month would have marked our fortieth anniversary, Pete." Sam turned away for a moment and swept the back of his hand across his eyes.

Peter looked down as if to pretend he hadn't noticed, then looked up at his friend. "I think you need to get away for a while, Sam."

Sam seemed to ignore the comment. "We'd planned to celebrate it the same way we had the previous thirty-nine: a candlelight dinner, a glass of her favorite Merlot, and a lively discussion of a book we'd agreed to read especially for that event. Martha always read voraciously even after I stopped reading anything except an occasional professional journal. I'd read that one book just for her. Then that damned pancreatic cancer took her away forever. Don't know what I'll do without her. The best part of my life has already gone by." He pulled a handkerchief from his pocket and wiped his tears, unashamed.

Peter held his arms out, palms up. "What about your kids? Might they spend the fortieth with you?"

Sam stuffed the kerchief back into his pocket. "I don't think so. Jennifer's job doesn't pay enough to finance a trip out here from Los Angeles. Mike's busy on Wall Street making millions for large clients who already have millions. I don't want this to be an imposition on them. I can handle it. I just miss my Martha, that's all."

Peter stood and put his hand on Sam's shoulder. "I know, Sam. I know. I miss her too. Even so, you need to get past this and become you again. I still miss those inspiring lectures you used to give when Martha was around to provide motivation. You may not remember when I first visited your class that day several years ago. I sat spellbound while you mesmerized your students with your theory about the Civil War. I still recall their faces when you told them to stop thinking of it as a military conflict about states' rights, or even slavery. They gasped when you tossed your history book into the wastebasket and told them to think of the war as a cataclysmic cultural clash after which our country would no longer be perceived as *these United States*, but as *The* United States."

Sam smiled for the first time that morning. "Yeah, I remember. Those were the good old days."

Peter turned away and stared out over the empty desks. "I've always envied you. My own lectures, and even my sermons, always seem to come across as dry. At least that's what I surmise from the stifled yawns coming from my audiences and the absence of any post-presentation show of interest as my attendees flee to the exits." He looked up again and forced a smile. "Anyway, let's go have some lunch, and you can tell me all about this apocalyptic discovery in London."

Sam flicked off the light switch, cast a lingering glance around the room he once considered his own private fiefdom, and turned his back on a semester that had brought him one step closer to retirement.

* * * * *

Peter watched Sam wince at the smell of the food the minute they walked through the door of Downey House and couldn't stifle a grin. "Come on, Sam. The mediocre quality of the food here is more than offset by the collegiate ambience. You've often said, 'it's not unusual, even at the same table, for the ghosts of Renoir and Napoleon to dine together whenever the influence of history upon art became the topic of the hour.' Smile."

While he watched Sam chomp on his burger, Peter picked apart his sushi. He listened, with mounting anxiety, to Sam's description of an ancient Roman letter which challenged the validity of the New Testament in its entirety. Roger's discovery would have been frightening to any believer—but particularly to a theology professor who had never contemplated the possibility that one day his ecclesiastic world might be overturned.

Peter had always known that his classroom lectures, his Sunday sermons at the University Chapel, and his occasional appearances as a guest speaker at the Middletown Presbyterian Church were comfortably Bible-based. All of his core beliefs stood firmly on the rock-solid premise of a God-centered resurrection of a divine Jesus. Now, Sam's synopsis of what they dug up under the streets of London revealed a cataclysmic finding so ugly in its implications that the shock of it precluded any response for a few moments.

After a long silence, Peter pushed his half-eaten meal away and leaned back in his chair. He groped for some rational response to a completely irrational proposition. "Sam, first of all I can't imagine anyone even suggesting such an outlandish theory. Look, if what you say has any truth in it at all, then I think you and I together should have some direct input into both the translation and analysis of these documents your protégé has uncovered."

"What are you talking about?"

"Well, I mean the more I think about it the more certain I am that you should be involved from a purely historical point of view, and I from a theological perspective—plus who knows how many other archaeological and theological experts. This could be earthshaking, and I don't think we should leave it in the hands of a graduate student. Especially one whose competence is still somewhat suspect, to use your own words."

"So, what are you suggesting?"

"I hadn't thought about London until now, but that seems as good a place as any for a confirmed bachelor with the summer off. Besides, I've been there only once, and that was a long time ago, on my way to Oxford

11

as a young Rhodes Scholar. Right now, this discovery promises to make up in excitement whatever it must surely lack in scholarly content. I'm saying this trip is definitely necessary."

"I agree, Pete. Roger's a nice kid, but he's a bit immature, and leaving something of this magnitude in his hands is probably asking for trouble. That's the reason I wanted you to hear this. I think you're the one who should look into it, since you're the religious expert. I don't see any need for me to be involved. Besides, I have enough on my plate right here."

Peter paused to examine the lunch bill, paid it, and continued the conversation. "Sam, that's one of the reasons you should go. You need to get away from your grief and this incessant tendency to blame God for what happened. You told me you were holding it together well, but you're not. When I came into your classroom, I saw a dismal man, not the professor I used to know as a brilliant, upbeat scholar with a great sense of humor, his atheistic views notwithstanding. I think a little religious exploration in London might relieve your sadness. It might even spark a new perspective on your views about God."

Sam heaved a deep sigh. "Pete, I appreciate your concern, you know that. You also know that we've had this discussion before, and it always ends in the same place. Your religious arguments are based on a commendable, although questionable, conviction that this whole marvelously structured universe couldn't possibly have happened without some kind of supernatural intelligence."

"And what's wrong with that?"

Sam shook his head. "Well, I'm still waiting to see one single shred of evidence that this elusive deity of yours ever existed. Or that this character you call Satan ever existed. You know my theory on those. God is a well-designed myth to make people feel safe from dying. And Satan is another fabrication to allow the human race to blame something else for the sins arising from its own greed."

Peter frowned and shook his head. "Good grief, Sam, I hope you didn't talk like that in front of Martha during her last days."

"Of course not. She always believed the same things you believe, and I went along with them through to the very end. I sat on the edge of her bed, held her hand, mopped her brow, massaged her body, and dispensed her medication. I read to her and tried to keep smiling until the sedation finally took effect and she mercifully fell asleep. Then I trudged out to the living room, slumped down in the La-Z-Boy, and sobbed until my limbs shook. All the time, I couldn't help but wonder where that so-called benevolent God of hers was while she writhed in agony."

Peter leaned back in his chair, thought for a moment, and then responded softly, as if to circumvent the possibility that his old friend might take it as a counterargument. "If you really wanted to know where God was, you might simply have asked Martha."

"What?"

Pete ignored Sam's glare. "I think she would have told you God was right by her side, just like you were. If you weren't so opposed to the concept of God, you might take some comfort that Martha's with him now."

"Damn it, Peter, I love you but you're incorrigible." Sam threw up his hands and reached for his jacket. "Let's go. I've a pile of papers to grade. And, by the way, the ones I really blame are those incompetent physicians."

"Come on, Sam, you can't spend the rest of your life hating doctors for their failure to save Martha. That's over the top, even for you."

"I don't hate them for that. I despise them for it. What I hate them for is that they knew at the very outset they were going to fail. They even told us so. Think about it, Pete, and try to put yourself in Martha's place when they dumped that ugly diagnosis on her. Just think about it."

"Sam, I'll tell you what. I think joining me on this trip is the best kind of therapy you could possibly find. I really need you. Besides, Roger is, after all, your student, not mine. Come on, what do you say? Just think of how this whole thing could embellish your future lectures." Peter paused to give his friend a moment to mull it over.

Sam glanced around the room as though he were seeking a second opinion. After a long pause, he nodded. "Okay, maybe you have a point. Roger is my responsibility. A finding of that magnitude would have significant historical implications. In fact, I can almost imagine the possibilities: authoritative proof that millions, maybe billions, of Christians have had it all wrong for two thousand years. Let those high-tech students key that into their hard drives. Come to think of it, I like the idea. Okay, fine, Pete, I'll do it. On two conditions."

"Name them." Peter knew at least one of them would have something to do with Sam's contempt for religion.

Sam pointed his finger in the air and shook it. "First, there'll be no discussion about my contrary-to-doctrine beliefs. Second, you won't mention the word 'God' except insofar as it specifically applies to the documents we're analyzing. Deal?"

"Done." Peter drew a sigh of relief. Sam's conditions could have been more difficult. "I'll make the arrangements, and we'll be airborne as soon as possible. Not that I'm really looking forward to it. This whole thing looks like it might turn out to be a fascinating little piece of archaeology."

They shook hands and went their separate ways. On his walk across campus, Peter reflected on the dark little discovery which threatened to change his world. The more he thought about it, the more troublesome the whole idea became. On the one hand, the very process of probing into such an iconoclastic theory would be an exciting adventure in itself. On the other, the timing couldn't be worse. Christianity in the Western World was struggling to hold its own. Developments in technology, anthropology, and science in general seemed to be contributing more to the concept of a Darwinian world and commensurately less to the biblical doctrine of Creation.

What the Church Universal needed right now, he'd convinced himself, was to reach out more effectively to its constituents, particularly the younger generation, in order to gain much-needed credibility. What it did not need was some shattering revelation that would undermine the very premise on which Christianity was based. If the underlying theme of Roger's discovery turned out to be correct, public disclosure of it would likely name Peter as one of the proponents behind a scheme to discredit The Bible. As an academician, he'd be front page news. As a theologian, he'd be finished.

# Chapter 2

# London

The moment Sam and Peter reached the steps of the London Museum, the dark, swollen clouds that had threatened all morning burst—a torrential admonishment for forgetting to bring umbrellas—and left them soaked. Their frantic dash up the steps and through the front door only partially mitigated the consequences. Peter glared at Sam. "You and your 'only sissies use umbrellas.'"

Sam grinned. "Hell, a little water won't hurt you. We'd probably forget and leave the damned things here, anyway. Heads up, I think this little guy coming toward us is our host."

The thin, immaculately dressed man beckoned them in. He reached out tentatively, as if he didn't want to shake hands at all, but had decided that courtesy required it. "Welcome to London, gentlemen. I'm Dr. Nigel Patterson. Your young protégé is waiting in the conference room with my associate, Dr. Stickney. You can hang your wet jackets over there by Mozart."

They shook their jackets and draped them over the coat rack opposite a small stand with a bronze bust of the eighteenth-century composer incarcerated in a corner. While they followed Nigel down the hall, Peter made a noticeable effort to ignore Sam's wry grin.

The long, spartanly furnished conference room wrapped itself tightly around a dark mahogany table of almost the same length. The snug little setting conveyed a clear message that the space was designed as a workplace, not a lounge.

Roger stepped forward, offered a deferential smile, and greeted Peter and Sam as they entered the conference room.

"Roger, I hope this discovery of yours isn't as ugly as you made it sound," Sam said. He turned to greet Patterson's counterpart. "And you are?"

"I'm Dr. Courtney Stickney, Dr. Wykoff. Please call me Courtney. Nigel and I come, as what you Yanks would refer to, as a package deal." He launched his six-foot-four frame out of the chair and wrapped his hand hard around Sam's, in sharp contrast to Nigel's tepid greeting. "I'm a theologian, and he's the director of archaeology here at the Museum of London Archaeological Service. He affectionately refers to it as MOLAS. We're now officially Museum of London Archaeology, but we still go by MOLAS. We're glad you're here. This thing Roger has come up with seems to have all the earmarks of a rather frightening archaeological dig."

"Please call me Sam." The "package deal" looked to Sam like anything but a package. Patterson's trim frame and gaunt, pale face accentuated his tiny moustache. The combination put his outward appearance in sharp contrast to that of the large, ruddy-complexioned Stickney, who stood at least six inches taller and a good one hundred pounds heavier. Courtney's lumpy suit further exaggerated the difference between the two men. Sam gestured toward Peter. "I'd like you to meet my colleague, Dr. Peter Clemens, a long-time friend of mine even if he is a theologian. What exactly do you guys do here? I mean, how did you get involved in Roger's discovery?"

"The museum covers a wide range of archaeological services," Courtney said. "All our activities are conducted under Nigel's competent leadership. His speciality happens to be forensic archaeology, which deals with laboratory analysis among other things. I'm an archaeologist, as well as a theologian, here at MOLAS. I'm assigned to this project primarily because of its theological implications."

Peter shook his head. "Which are terrifying, if this thing has any truth."

Courtney nodded and then turned to Sam. "I understand you're Roger's mentor as he pursues his doctoral degree. Am I right?"

"You are, and I feel obligated to tell you I'm not at all pleased with his getting sidetracked like this on a venture which has nothing to do with his doctoral program as we've planned it."

Courtney put up his hand. "I can't even begin to address that issue. However, I think you'll forgive him when you see the likely impact of his discovery. What he's uncovered in this Fenchurch Street dig could conceivably change the future direction of almost every civilized country in this world, not to mention the Vatican itself."

The group settled into chairs around the table, Nigel at one end, Roger at the other, and Sam at Roger's elbow. Sam started the conversation. "So, what do you have at this point in your discovery process, Roger?"

The young graduate student's face tightened, as though he were facing an inquisition. He lowered his eyes, tugged at his tie, then fumbled while he tried to separate the documents in front of him into two piles. His elbow brushed one of them, knocking it to the floor. He reached to retrieve it and shuffled the sheets back into position. Roger continued to look down while he spoke, casting only furtive glances at his seniors, while he tried to hide his malaise.

Sam reached over and placed a gentle hand on Roger's shoulder. "Roger, relax. We're not here to punish you, just to find out what this is all about."

Roger looked up and tried to force a smile. "Well, for starters, we have an almost completely intact letter from a Roman centurion to his son, a soldier named Vinicius, whose remains we dug up quite by accident a few weeks ago. The letter's in bad shape, despite having been preserved in some kind of resin compound. The plan is to—"

"We're preparing it now for a multispectral imaging scan," Nigel interrupted. He paused to fidget with his moustache. "There's been considerable deterioration, as you might expect. We're walking a fine line here between what could be a significant find and a hoax that would damage the reputation of—"

"I think the reputation of the museum is safe," Courtney interjected. "This document doesn't look anything like a hoax from what I've observed."

Nigel fixed a steady glare on Courtney. "That remains to be seen. Anyway, I will not permit the latter to happen. Roger, why don't you update your superiors on just what part of it we can almost read and what part we can't?"

Roger nodded. His expression reflected a small measure of relaxation. "Yes, of course. Well, it looks like it's dated late in the first century, and we know that the writer was a Roman centurion in Legion, or *Legio*, XXII. His son apparently served in *Legio* XX, which eventually camped here in London, or *Londinium* as it was known then. Aside from some mundane instructions to his son, the centurion's letter appears to contain—and we can't tell for sure without the scan—some rather astounding disclosures about his own past experiences."

"Astounding? How?" Peter asked, his face drawn tight.

"Well, we think the narrative, or parts of it, claims that this centurion was one of two soldiers to have guarded the tomb of Jesus Christ after they took him down from the cross. Not only that but—"

Peter flew out of his chair. "He did what?"

"Yes, sir. I know it...um...it sounds pretty bizarre...ah, Dr. Clemens. We can't confirm it until the imaging brings out the narrative more clearly. However, we're fairly certain of it. The thing that bothers us is that we can't read what happened at the tomb because the words aren't very legible. Some of the narrative is in Latin and some in Greek. We're not sure why, but that complicates things a bit. We'll have to wait for the scan on that."

Peter glared at him. "Roger, do you actually expect us to believe this?"

"Let the lad finish," Courtney said. He leaned back in his chair and lit up his Meerschaum pipe. "You haven't heard the frightening part yet."

"Well," Roger continued, "we suspect that the letter may confirm those minority opinions that Christ's resurrection never happened. Moreover, the author makes repeated references to something that looks like it might be a book given to him by Saul of Tarsus, better known as the Apostle Paul. Our best guess, or I should say Dr. Stickney's best estimate, is that this thing is an original version of The Bible. Now the alarming—"

"Please be more specific," Peter interjected. "What do you mean by 'thing'?"

"Well, sir, I mean the print isn't clear, but the centurion uses the word 'dicta' something. We can't quite make out the last part of the word, but we surmise the centurion means the equivalent of the word 'dictum.' We're thinking it's a book. The alarming part is that an almost

18

illegible portion of this letter seems to suggest a completely different version of God and Jesus than appears in today's Bible. The specifics of that will show more clearly once the scans are completed. If this document can be found, it'll be the only one in existence and may reveal some hitherto unknown truths."

"What's so earthshaking about that?" asked Sam, who had been observing the dialogue with a calm amusement. "Weren't there twelve of those guys handing out Bibles back in those days?"

Nigel glared at him. "Overlooking, for a moment, your facetious sense of humor, Dr. Wykoff, and the fact that you seem to have confused disciples with apostles, I'll tell you what's earthshaking about it." As though he were agitated as much by the flippancy of the comment as its content, Nigel turned to address his next remarks to the group. "Neither this soldier nor his father could possibly have come into possession of a Bible, or anything else in book form. Back-bound books, as we know them, didn't exist when this letter was written, only parchments rolled up into scrolls to protect their contents."

"That's true," Peter added. "In fact, Codex manuscripts were the first biblical texts to be compiled in book form. As Courtney can probably verify, Codex Vaticanus, now located in the Vatican Library in Rome, was compiled early in the fourth century and contained the first complete copy of the Septuagint and the New Testament."

Nigel stroked his moustache again. "Yes, that was the first time that the twenty-seven books of the New Testament were collected in an approved canonical collection of Scriptures. This one is often referred to as the Codex Sinaiticus, but it's a fourth century compilation. So, frankly, I'm not sure whether the centurion's reference meant the New Testament as a book, or simply the Books of the Old Testament."

Peter offered a vigorous nod. "And that should, I hope, put an end to all this speculation. As to the imaging results, I frankly don't care what they turn out to be. I think we can dismiss the contents of this letter as undocumented fiction, with all due respect to the creative imagination of its author. Wouldn't you agree, Nigel?"

"Yes, I would. Still, I'd like to see the imaging results before I make a final assessment. And that, I'm afraid, will probably take the better part of—"

The conference room door swung open, drawing everyone's attention away from Nigel's summation. A man burst into the room wrapped in rain-and-mud-spattered overalls which concealed his build but couldn't hide his penetrating blue eyes, sharply chiseled facial features, and protruding chin.

"Gentlemen—" Nigel held out his arm to acknowledge the interruption. "Allow me to introduce Gordon Marston. He's a part-time historian and archaeologist I've asked to join this group for essentially two reasons. One, he brews the best tea in London, and two, he happens to be our foremost expert on the subject of the Roman army." He looked Gordon up and down. "You're a bit late. Don't you have a suit you could have worn for this occasion?"

The broad-shouldered man grinned while he struggled to extricate himself from his outer garments. "Yes, old boy. I actually have one and a half rather stunning outfits I could have worn. But they wouldn't have fared very well, slopping around in the dig under Fenchurch Street where Roger found this document. I felt it was worth another look for The Bible itself, since it may well trigger a monumental rewrite of what we thought was historic fact."

"Let's try to avoid speculating on this," Nigel snapped.

"The problem," Gordon continued without acknowledging Nigel's interjection, "is that the Roman residue lies at the bottom of this dig underneath all the subsequent centuries of medieval buildup. King Alfred's ninth century urban renewal virtually obliterated even the Roman roads. Thus, I didn't have any more luck in my search for that Bible than Roger did. Anyway, where do we stand on the spectral imaging of the centurion's letter?"

Nigel walked over to close the door, as if to assure that no one outside could listen in on the debate. "We're probably two, maybe three, weeks away from any readable output. Until we have some, the whole thing's looking more like a purely academic issue."

"Oh, how so?" Gordon asked as he leaned over a wastebasket and wrung the water out of his muddy overalls, ignoring Nigel's look of appalled disapproval.

Nigel paused to glare for a moment before he continued. "Well, the letter, or what we can make of it, references the centurion's presence at Jesus's tomb. To me, this sounds a bit fictitious, since no historical accounts have ever mentioned a soldier at the tomb. As a matter of fact, Gordon, that book, which you presumed to be a Bible, also strains the limits of credibility. Indeed, such a discovery would probably have set in motion your monumental rewrite were it not for the fact that the technology for back-bound books did not develop until the early third or fourth century. Therefore, I consider the existence of such a book impossible during the time this soldier's father lived. Dr. Clemens here has already written the whole episode off as a creative hoax. I'm about ready to do the same. I'd still like to see the final scans, however, before I do."

"You mean you think the centurion's account was a fabrication?" Gordon looked at Nigel as though he were challenging Nigel to pronounce his final verdict in so many words.

"A fascinating one," Peter jumped in. "Yes, I think we should put this dialogue to rest once and for all." He glanced at Nigel, appearing confident that Nigel agreed. "Look, it's common knowledge among biblical historians that almost fifty-four hundred copies of the New Testament writings survive today, most of them in Greek. No two are identical, and most of them have mistakes because they were transcribed, over the centuries, by scribes who copied manually. I think we can discount this whole affair as being highly—and I mean highly—implausible."

Gordon tossed his wet outer garments into a corner and reached down to straighten his trousers. He turned to face his colleagues with a broad, confident grin that seemed to derive its strength from the man's empowering sense of himself. "Ah, well, I can see you accomplished academics may be competent in your respective fields, but you obviously don't know much about the Roman army."

Peter frowned and his face tightened. "What does that mean?"

"I mean the author of this document held a fairly responsible position in Legion XXII. And if you knew anything about the strict military behavioral code that prevailed in the Roman army, particularly at his level, you would know that any such fabrication would be uncharacteristic. It would also have invited censure if discovered."

"A good point," Courtney spoke up, and tapped his pipe on an ashtray to empty the blackened residue. "I might add there would be additional punishment in store for any Roman soldier suspected of

21

authoring a document that might, in any way, be construed to confirm the authenticity of Jesus."

He paused, sweeping a glance at his audience while he refilled the Meerschaum.

"No," Courtney went on, "Gordon's right. This centurion would not likely risk his career, or his son's, on a fairy tale. He confided in his son an experience which he believed in so deeply that he was willing to risk the consequences. I'd say that the likelihood of anything in that letter being false is virtually non-existent."

They turned to look at each other. A silence fell over the room, broken only by the sound of Courtney sucking on his pipe to get a good light going.

Nigel ended the silence by calling attention to three barely legible photocopies of parts of the letter he'd spread out on the table. "Very well then, since it seems we're forced to go back and revisit this whole thing, let's take another look at these photographs I made before I sent the original back to imaging. The tomb part is so illegible it's not even worth discussing until after the final scan. Courtney, since you're the one who seems to find some credibility in it, I'd like you to focus on the references to the words the centurion used for 'book,' if you will. He seems to use the words *dicta* and *biblia* almost interchangeably. I'd like you to refocus too, Roger, since this apocalyptic discovery was yours to begin with. Unless both my Greek and Latin have gotten rusty, the word *biblia* means 'books,' as in the plural."

Sam stood and yawned. "Right, but can't it also mean Bible?"

"Possibly so." Courtney bent down for a closer look. "I see where Nigel's going, though. *Biblia* doesn't necessarily mean Bible. It more likely refers to a collection of books. That could mean almost anything but probably was a reference to the Books of the Old Testament. They were in scroll form, rather than back-bound form, and definitely in existence then and had been for centuries. The word *biblia* is derived from the ancient sea port of Biblyon, from which much of the world's papyrus, or paper, was shipped in those days."

Peter flew out of his chair. "Absolutely, and I can show you even further support for that. I'll call your attention to 2 Timothy, 4, where Paul writes 'When you come, bring my coat that I left in Troas with Carpus; bring the books too and above all the parchments.' That was a pivotal phrase in one of my sermons. It confirms that Paul himself was referring to the Books of the Old Testament. In parchment form, I might add."

"Correct," Nigel said as he brushed a speck of lint off his lapel, "but I meant that, since the centurion's letter uses the plural form, it couldn't mean only one book. I think the centurion was clearly referring to parchment scrolls, not likely a Bible as we know it. What are you staring at so intently, Gordon?"

Gordon repositioned one of the photos for better lighting and raised his hand to motion them to gather around him. "Gentlemen, I don't mean to interrupt the trend of this scholarly dialogue, but let me share my magnifying glass with you for a moment, and take another look. I think you'll find that the centurion actually wrote *biblio* not *biblia,* as in one book."

Roger leaned over for a closer look. "Yes, I believe he's right," he added. "As smudged as it is, it really does appear to be an 'o' rather than an 'a.' I guess I failed to notice the first time."

"We all did," Nigel added, "because the image isn't clear. Moreover, we were all focused on the centurion's reference to Paul's belief that he feared a plot to murder him."

Peter frowned. "I'm getting a bit confused here. What do you mean, murder?"

Nigel shrugged. "We're not sure, but it introduces another dimension to what we thought was biblical history. The scans will tell us more."

Peter shook his head. "Either way it's still a collection of parchment scrolls, not a Bible. At that time, I believe it would have required a descriptive phrase, not a single word, to describe such a document."

"Hold on a minute, you guys," Sam countered. "Let's step back away from all this theological rhetoric and look at this with some simple logic. The young man who possessed this thing was a Roman soldier." He raised his hands in the air. "How many soldiers have you heard of, Roman or otherwise, who'd carry a bunch of scrolls all the way across Britain while fighting one battle after another? No, gentlemen, I think this young man was carrying exactly what his father said he gave him—a book…one book. And if it's really an original version of all this stuff, and as valuable as you seem to think it might be, then I'd say we better

23

hustle our fannies out there and find the damned thing before someone else does. Once the media get wind of what I'm sure those scans are going to reveal, every treasure hunter in this hemisphere will be out there digging holes under Fenchurch Street, and everywhere else the Roman army went in Britain."

Peter rolled his eyes. "Sam, have you any idea how many thousands of square miles the Roman army covered in its conquest of Britain? Just where would you suggest we begin?"

Gordon grinned. "Peter, I think your question, in itself, indicates a reluctant admission that Roger's discovery might have some historic significance. I think I can answer it." He walked over to the wall and pulled down a map of Great Britain. "We're not going to dig any holes in the ground, and we don't have to track the whole Roman army. Only five or six of their legions invaded Britain."

Gordon pointed at the map, leaving tiny dots with his pen. He deliberately ignored Nigel's frantic efforts to hand him a pointer in order to prevent any further desecration of museum property. "Five Roman legions marched into one part or another of what's now known as the British Isles. *Legio* XX, or *Valeria Victrix*, marched through Scotland under Agricola, and eventually camped here in London, or *Londinium*. The soldier in question belonged to that legion. He died here in London, so all we have to do is track that one."

Gordon stopped tapping on the map, and Nigel breathed a sigh of relief.

"I can assure you," Gordon continued, "that, if this soldier lost the book anywhere along that trail, it wouldn't be underground. It would have been part of the debris that would have been left behind at any battle and, if it was deemed worthy of anything, it would have been scavenged and either destroyed later or turned over to a local church."

Courtney moved beside Gordon in front of the map. "Gordon, I can't dispute what you're saying, but even narrowing it down that far still presents a scenario that resembles the needle in the haystack story. Let me suggest another option. If Paul gave a Bible to that centurion, then he must have given others to the churches in the larger cities along his route." He shrugged his shoulders. "There aren't many of them left, so why not track Paul's itinerary and see what we can come up with? And by the way, I'm assuming we all understand that we're talking about the

24

New Testament here...or more precisely, an original version thereof, since Paul was the dominant contributor."

Everyone nodded except Peter.

"Okay, look," Peter said, shaking his head. "We can't be talking about the entire New Testament because certain parts of it weren't written until sometime between 50 and 90 A.D. So, Paul may have distributed a substantial portion of the Scriptures, but not the whole document. Even if we accept the remote possibility that some of these original Scriptures—or copies thereof—still exist, we're looking at one enormous task. I say this because if you guys really want to do this right, we'll have to exercise both options simultaneously. Otherwise, this task will take too long to complete. I don't think we have that much time before the media figure out what's going on. I mean, one team tracks Paul while the other tracks the battle sites of this soldier...what was his name again?"

"Vinicius," Roger replied.

Peter nodded. "Right, Vinicius. Now, do we know when this soldier died?"

"No," Nigel replied, "but the centurion's letter to him was written sometime between A.D. 60 and A.D. 69."

"How do we know that?" Sam asked.

"Well, nothing about this letter is unmistakably clear, but our forensics experts translated enough to be reasonably certain the first digit of what looks to be a date placed it within that period."

Peter put up his hand. "Okay then, let's do these searches at the same time. And I'd also recommend that you, Nigel, commission a couple of your diggers to have one more go at the site where this soldier's remains were found, just to make sure we don't overlook something right under our noses."

"As good as done," Nigel said. He glanced back at Peter with an arms-out-palms-up gesture of reluctant surrender. "We have one more problem, however. I'm afraid news of this has already leaked out. After Roger brought the letter to us, a member of our staff became over-anxious. Before we could stop him, he contacted two people he apparently thought could help decipher the writing. One was a priest named Trazerri. The other was some kind of expert on ancient inscriptions. They're both located somewhere near Paul's route. We'll have to stop and talk to them whether we like it or not."

Gordon slapped his forehead. "Damn it, the sot should have cleared it with you first, Nigel."

"I know. Believe me, it won't happen again. I've sworn the entire staff to complete silence on this. I'm embarrassed about it, and I've been in communication with the two people contacted by my staff. They assured me they'd never mention it to anyone."

Nigel motioned for Peter to stay behind while the others filed out of the room at Gordon's invitation to lunch. He waited until the room had cleared. "Peter, let me say this by way of explanation," Nigel said, as if to clarify what appeared to be a reversal of his original position. "I have mixed feelings. On the one hand, I sense the utter futility of it all. On the other, I must say I feel a certain excitement about the possible publicity benefits such a find would generate for MOLAS."

Peter frowned. "I didn't think MOLAS would want that kind of publicity."

Nigel scooped up a small pile of documents, pulled his briefcase from under the table, and stuffed them into it. He walked out into the hall, asked his secretary to bring in some tea, and returned to his seat. "Peter, if you'll sit down for a minute, I'll explain how things are here at MOLAS. I've been quite secure in my position as director of archaeological research for the last nine years. My tenure at the museum was never seriously challenged, until recently. My requests for excavation funding were rarely denied. However, archaeological digs are a bit like drilling for oil. The up-front costs are high, while the prospects for success are uncertain. This means my funding requests are subjected to tighter scrutiny. To complicate matters, compliance with local and jurisdictional regulations where a dig is concerned often ranges from difficult to virtually impossible."

"Are you saying your job is in jeopardy?" Peter asked.

Nigel paused to allow his secretary to place the tea on the table, then poured himself a cup. "I don't think so. However, the tangible products of my efforts over the last three years have been, off and on, significant but not inspiring enough to create any real public interest. There's been some gradually mounting pressure to replace me. I'm not terribly worried about losing my job, but a significant find like this would

26

solidify my position beyond any doubt. So, now that you know my motivations, what do you think?"

Peter slid his chair forward, leaned his elbows on the table, and paused to consider Nigel's confession. "Well, I'm still opposed to this whole charade. I see where you're coming from, however, and I would have to agree. A revolutionary discovery would put MOLAS and you both on the front pages of the media everywhere. I'm worried about what would happen if this whole affair turns out to be a hoax."

"Then we get credit for saving Christianity from an exciting, but potentially devastating, hoax. MOLAS wins either way, you see. Look, I know this whole concept runs against your grain as a theologian, Peter, but—"

"Yes, it does. I think we're playing with a nuclear bomb here. Frankly, I see more damage than good coming out of it."

Nigel nodded. "Well, that's one way to look at it. Let me offer a suggestion. I propose we make this a bloody damned adventure for the next couple of weeks while my forensics crew deciphers that letter. After that, we'll know one way or the other, and we can finalize our position on the whole thing then. What do you say, old chap?"

They both stood and shook hands. Pete forced a partial smile. "Since I don't seem to have much choice, you're on, Dr. Patterson. Sam and I are looking forward to working with you Brits. Let's go do it."

\* \* \* \* \*

By noon the next day, they had finalized the itineraries and added three more archaeologists from MOLAS to in-house research efforts. Nigel set up the two teams—one to track the journey of Paul and the other to follow the selected route of the Roman army. Members came from the museum's artifact services, geo-archaeology services, heritage management, and post-excavation services. Over the years, the museum had patiently witnessed a host of significant discoveries but none that filled its chambers with such electric excitement.

Both teams required another full day of preparation before deployment. Aside from accurate identification of the Legion's battle sites, Paul's itinerary presented a host of unforeseen problems. Nigel presided over their last meeting before the two groups set out on their respective journeys.

"Gentlemen, I don't wish to dampen the excitement of what we're about to do. However, I must, in all good conscience, inform you that this project will not be an easy one. Paul's journey itself will not be difficult to track, but assessing the probability of his having distributed Bibles at each location will be almost impossible. First of all, he didn't distribute anything at some locations, but chose to write to the churches there. Second, as Peter pointed out, the likelihood that any of Paul's writings still exist is remote."

Nigel lit up his laser pointer and fired the red beam at Antioch on the large map. "Paul made several journeys, of which the one I'm tracing here, I believe, will produce the greatest likelihood of any distribution. Paul began this one around 49 A.D., leaving from Antioch on his way to Derbe. He was born in Tarsus, but there was no biblical reference as to whether or not he stopped there on the way. From Derbe, he proceeded to Lystra where he and his traveling companion, Silas, visited Timothy." The red dot marked the trail. "There is no confirmation that any Bibles were distributed."

Nigel stopped to pour another cup of tea. He stroked his moustache once or twice and frowned while he rearranged them by positioning the tea in the center and the cream and sugar containers equally spaced on either side of the teapot.

He picked up his pointer again and continued. "From there, Paul stopped for a day or so in Troas before setting sail to Philippi. Controversy marked his stay there, as evidenced by the street riots. He moved on to Thessalonica where he met resentment from the Jewish community and had to leave quickly at night. Paul's journey took him next to Berea and then Athens, where he preached from the well-known Mars Hill."

All eyes followed the silent beam which slid easily across the map along a trail that everyone knew must have been tortuous in those days.

He paused to sample his tea. "Distribution in Athens," Nigel continued, "is still a matter of pure speculation. Paul proceeded to Corinth where he worked for a while and stayed with Aquila and his wife Priscilla. His last significant stop before concluding his travels at

Antioch was Ephesus. He later wrote a letter to the Ephesians from a prison cell in Rome."

Peter raised his hand. "Then maybe we should focus mainly on Ephesus."

Nigel returned the pointer to his shirt pocket and leaned against the podium. "No. I've concluded that, although Ephesus will probably constitute the most likely location for any distribution, the other cities are also important. The most serious problem is that most of the cities along Paul's route are now extinct, either destroyed by the ravages of war or buried under centuries of accumulated earthen buildup. Many of them are only partially excavated. So—"

"This exercise is looking more pointless every minute," Peter said.

Nigel shook his head. "Let's not give up before we even begin. Here's my recommendation as to how we should split into teams. The church research team will include Sam, Courtney, and Roger. Their assignment is to visit Antioch, Lystra, Ephesus, Corinth, Thessalonica, and Athens. The battle site team will include Peter, Gordon, and me. At this point I surmise, of the three of us, Gordon is probably the only one who optimistically entertains thoughts of actually finding anything of significance. Gordon, you're responsible for keeping our spirits up. Any questions?"

Sam raised his hand. "Yeah, I have one. Is it too much to hope that we'll find a Burger King somewhere along this pilgrimage?"

Except for Nigel, the group broke into a mixture of chuckles and outright laughter.

Nigel glared at Sam. "Yes, it is. I'm afraid you'll have to settle for whatever the local fare is wherever you happen to be. Very well, if there are no other penetrating questions, let's be on our way. I wish everyone Godspeed and my best hopes for a successful journey."

\* \* \* \* \*

Peter felt less uncomfortable with Nigel than he did at the outset but harbored some serious misgivings about Gordon. He waited until he and Nigel were alone in the conference room before he decided to share his concerns. He scanned the room. "Nigel, is there any coffee?"

"No. We drink tea here at MOLAS," Nigel snapped. "You look like you're waiting to ask a question."

Peter pushed the tea tray away. "I am. Look, I'm not in a position to critique the composition of our teams, and I agree that we need Gordon's expertise on the Roman army. And yet, he seems sort of, well, anti-religious. I mean, I was left with the distinct impression that nothing would please him more than discovering evidence that would impair the credibility of The Bible."

Nigel nodded. "Gordon comes across that way sometimes. We take it with a grain of salt."

"Well anyway, I'm fine with Courtney," Peter said. "I sense he has strong Christian values, combined with a sincere academic interest in this mission. Gordon, however, is another matter. I have to be honest. I question his objectivity in this endeavor. You've apparently known him for a long time and are, of course, in a better position to judge. How do you feel about it?"

Nigel leaned over the table, replenished his cup of tea after he straightened the milk and sugar containers again, and settled back in his chair. He pushed a pile of papers aside to make room for his cup, stacked the papers in neat order, and paused to smooth his moustache before he responded, as though he were deciding whether to answer the question at all.

"Peter, quite frankly I've never discussed Gordon's religious convictions with him. However, I can assure you he would never deliberately bias a research project for any reason. He's a secondary school teacher who should be teaching at Oxford, but can't because he doesn't have his doctoral degree. Gordon's never had to worry about money. The Marstons of London trace their wealth as far back into English history as anyone can remember. In fact, he even married into money. So, with all that, I suppose there's never been any pressing motivation to, as you Yanks would say, 'hustle.' "

Peter gave a nod of grudging acknowledgment. "Okay, I'll accept your judgment. Is that sugar you're dumping into your tea?"

Nigel sipped his tea, winced, and added another lump of sugar. "I know what you're thinking, Peter. Yes, some Englishmen actually do use sugar. Anyway, Gordon's never come right out and told me what I'm about to tell you, and you must not repeat it. I believe he desperately wants to teach at one of the more prestigious universities and knows there are only two avenues open to that objective. One, earn his doctoral degree, which he doesn't want to take the time to do. Two, produce a distinctive academic breakthrough of unquestioned significance, which he would thoroughly enjoy doing. And which, I shouldn't have to add, would almost certainly be accomplished if this venture of ours actually produced the kind of findings we now suspect it might…regardless of which way the findings go."

Peter rose from his chair and fixed a skeptical glare on Nigel. "And given that objective you still think he can be impartial?"

"Completely. I'd trust Gordon and his work under any circumstances. I'll admit I understand your concerns. And now that you've called Gordon's objectivity into question, let me suggest that your impatience to get this whole affair closed down back there in the conference room might spark some concern about your own impartiality. So, as the court magistrate would say, how plead you?" Nigel managed one of his rare grins as he pushed the teapot invitingly in Peter's direction again.

Pete laughed. In a gesture of apparent surrender, he poured a cup for himself. "All right, guilty as charged, I guess. Now, tell me candidly, do you really think we have a snowball's chance in hell of finding anything?"

"Absolutely. We have five competent professionals and a bright graduate student conducting this search."

Peter shook his head. "I think you're an optimist."

"Is that so? Define optimist, Peter."

"Okay. It's a camper who wakes up in his tent at night to the buzz of a swarm of mosquitoes around his head and assumes that they're simply looking for a way out."

Nigel forced a chuckle. "Now that has to be an expression only a Yank could come up with. You know, I think we'll be successful, if for no other reason than that Gordon is a bulldog in his typical relentless search for anything he sets out to find. Although he doesn't talk about his instincts, Gordon always trusts them. You and I both share some reservations about this venture. However, the interesting fact is that we don't have to find an entirely intact version of the New Testament writings."

"What do you mean?"

"I mean all we need to do is uncover any form of ancient documentation that confirms the existence of writings that differ in their contents from those in existence today. That, in combination with what I presume the imaging scans will show, should be enough to confirm what the centurion's letter alleged. We'll have the scan results in a few weeks. In the meantime, what say we put our reservations aside and give it a good go? By the way, don't be too surprised to find that Courtney isn't as clinically detached as you seem to think he is. Remember, he and I both need to come up with something historically significant enough to keep MOLAS in the public eye, and in the good graces of our funding sources. Are you comfortable with all that?"

Peter shook his head again. "No. I'm picturing myself at the pulpit of my church sometime after the dust settles on this God-forsaken witch-hunt. I can see opening my sermon with something like: 'Good morning, congregation. I'd like to begin by saying we won't be using our Bibles anymore because they're all obsolete now. So listen carefully while I take a wild guess at what Jesus would have said if he'd really been Jesus, and don't worry about God. He retired after the seventh day and left the whole thing in our hands.' So, right now, Nigel, I'm afraid my thoughts are darkened by menacing forms of the antichrist dancing while he defecates on the Holy Bible."

Nigel's chuckle came naturally this time. "Peter, stop worrying, and let's hope for something better than your dark thoughts. I'll see you tomorrow. Get a good night's sleep. I think both our teams will need it."

# Chapter 3

## Antakya, Turkey (Formerly Antioch)

A light breeze from the Nur Mountains cooled the moist evening air in a lingering spring that stubbornly refused to make way for Antakya's hot, dry summer. Sam, Courtney, and Roger welcomed the end of a frustrating day by enjoying the popular meal of kebab brought in from the Harbiye district. Served with spices and onions in flat, unleavened bread, the combination made their mouths water. They followed it with a hot cheese kadaif-based sweet pastry and Turkish coffee. Courtney and Sam ate with a fierce determination while Roger paused to examine each bite before making the commitment to ingest it.

"Courtney, is this real coffee," Roger asked, "or just caffeinated mud from the Orontes River?" He grimaced as though he wasn't sure whether he should have swallowed his first mouthful or spit it out.

"Roger, my good lad," Courtney replied, "I'm pleased you've become comfortable enough with us to drop the 'Doctor' formality. As to your question, you've just experienced the world's only true coffee. Other blends pale in comparison and are little more than watered down imitations. I thought you Yanks loved it that way, and that's why you don't drink tea. And by the way, it's now called the Asi River."

Roger nodded. "Well, we like our coffee, but there's a limit to how much sludge we can tolerate. If this stuff is the true measure of coffee, then I think I prefer tea."

"Good grief, boy," Sam blurted out, "never make a confession like that to an Englishman. You'll ruin our country's reputation."

"Too late," Courtney said. He lit up his pipe and paused to savor the rich aroma of pure Turkish tobacco. "As the designated theologian of this team, I've already made a permanent mental note of it. At the first opportunity, I intend to insert it at some appropriate place in that diary you've been writing, Sam. By the way, what exactly have you been writing?"

Sam dipped a pastry into his coffee and bit off a corner of the dampened morsel. "I've decided to record the events of our travels. Roger is doing the same. If this venture goes the way I hope it will, I may be able to enlighten my fall classes with a long overdue rewrite of two thousand years of erroneous history. No offense intended, padre."

"And none taken, my friend. Now, let me ask you a question. Do you believe what that priest told us today?"

Sam wolfed down the rest of his pastry while he contemplated the question. "Yes, I do. That is, assuming that the guy who was translating for us did it accurately. The priest had no reason to lie. He openly admitted he'd never seen an original version of The Bible, but I couldn't help being impressed by his certainty that our search was not without merit. He seemed sure an original had been sequestered by one of those churches along Paul's itinerary. And his rationale made sense. The Catholic Church—and every other Christian church for that matter— might have a reason to want that version dead and buried. Did you notice that he seemed alarmed, even a bit frightened, when Roger summarized the contents of that letter?"

Courtney reached for a biscuit and smothered it in something that looked like butter. "I did. Still, until the scanning is completed we have no assurance the centurion's reference to what appears to be a completely revolutionary concept of God and Jesus will actually turn out to be one. If not, your apocryphal revision of theological history becomes nothing more than a bad dream. As to the existence of this sequestered version you mentioned, there's an inconsistency in your logic. If all of Christianity wanted such a document abolished, why would one still be preserved intact? Therefore, why would we look for it?"

Sam grinned. "Money, Courtney. Can you imagine how much money and bargaining power such a document would be worth during those interim centuries, let alone today? The monetary value of every other document in the world, including the Magna Carta and the Declaration of Independence, would seem like pocket change by comparison. Not to mention the publishing value of history's biblical reconstruction. Think about it."

34

"The money I can understand," Courtney said as he reloaded his Meerschaum, "although I think you've grossly overestimated the amount. What I'm not seeing is how a new biblical presentation of Jesus, or even God, would change anything. Your flaw is that you're still thinking in a three-dimensional secular framework. In the fourth dimension, the Divine God is still divine, regardless of any alterations in the way His relationship with Jesus, or mankind, happens to be chronicled by us."

The remark caught Sam off guard. He had based his most effective arguments against the existence of a supreme being upon the presentation of the concept in biblical doctrine. He'd never considered a different perspective and didn't welcome Courtney's apparent effort to wrench him away from his lifetime convictions with some vague truth drifting beyond his grasp.

Sam shifted in his chair. His thoughts wandered back to Martha. He knew he wasn't ready to debate the issue in the fourth dimension…whatever Courtney might have meant by that. Ever since Martha's death, he'd felt a heavy, leaden hollowness that manifested itself in a chronic discontent which always seemed to impair his enjoyment of the moment. It was as though his life with Martha had been a dream that existed outside of time and could never be recovered.

"As you wish, Courtney," Sam said in a tone of concession. "You think about it in your way and I'll think about it in mine. What are your feelings, Roger?"

Roger followed his mentor's lead and gave up on the food screening. He smeared his own biscuit as though he'd decided that, if Courtney hadn't choked on it, maybe it would be safe to eat. "I think I'll let you two settle the theological issues while I build my thesis. I'm basing it on whatever we find about history and religion on this journey, plus what the imaging scans ultimately produce about the relationship between the Apostle Paul and that Roman centurion."

Courtney patted him on the back. "Not a bad idea. Any other thoughts on how you're going to develop your thesis?"

"More or less, but it's a little premature to limit the scope of it right now. I think there's always been a sort of interdependence between history and church doctrine, but this whole experience will help me articulate it in a way that's never been done before."

"How so?"

"Well, for example, Emperor Julian's attempts to make the city of Antioch a commercial rival to Constantinople ran into trouble when the city's Christian population violently opposed the pagan worship of Greek figures like Adonis and Apollo that he had mandated. The city subsequently went into decline, accelerated by the great earthquake of 526, after which it became the conquered victim of one dynasty after another."

"And so?" Sam interjected with an air of academic challenge.

"Well, I think I could expand the example geographically and include such events as Emperor Diocletian's 303 A.D. decree that all Bibles be destroyed. The church had grown from a small mystery cult into a power on nearly equal terms with Rome itself, so the Roman Catholic Church banned all reading of The Bible. During the Dark Ages, following the demise of the Roman Empire, the early Christian writings nearly perished. They owed their survival almost entirely to the devoted monks who preserved them in the scriptoria rooms of stone abbeys scattered across Europe and Asia Minor. The church tried to retain its hold on political power by stifling the spread of education. I could go on and on, but you get the picture."

Roger glanced quickly at his mentor as if to seek some preliminary sign of endorsement.

Sam stared out at the Asi River and said nothing.

Courtney nodded approvingly and waited several moments for Dr. Wykoff to share his thoughts.

Sam offered a non sequitur without turning or interrupting his gaze, as though he hadn't been listening. "Did you guys know that most of the remaining traces of the great Roman city that was built here are now at the bottom of that river and that modern construction has almost wiped out the rest? You know, we bury even the most insignificant humans under aesthetically appealing little monuments offering testimony to their existence. Yet we allow great civilizations to lie under centuries of accumulated sediment with, at best, only decaying junk to mark their graves." A hint of sadness in Sam's voice suggested he couldn't bring himself to accept the gradual disappearance of remnants that once defined the magnificence of the Imperial Roman Empire.

"More than that," Courtney added, "even though Antioch was once the cradle of Christianity, her churches are gone. Paul's converts were the first to be called Christians. This city was one of the largest in the world after places like Rome and Alexandria. Alexander the Great is said to have camped here briefly, although no proof exists that he actually did. At any rate, it's been a long day, gentlemen, don't you think?"

Courtney stood and paid the waiter. He felt an unwelcomed mixture of excitement and apprehension. The day before, the prospect of rewriting two thousand years of history had seemed little more than an academic "what-if" that could be easily drowned in rhetoric. Now, the prospect had become reality, and it frightened him. "You may be right about the money and all that, Sam," he said. "And if you are, Roger will be more famous than his father. Maybe even a Pulitzer Prize winner, like his dad. In fact, we'll all be either the heroes or the villains of modern history. You guys can think about that while I try not to. Either way, I'm going to get some sleep." He nodded in the direction of the hotel. "I'll see you tomorrow."

\* \* \* \* \*

The Church of Saint Peter on Hurriyet Caddesi stood aloof from its dry, barren surroundings as though it didn't want to be associated with them. It served a small but active Christian community in Antakya and had become a place of pilgrimage for both Muslims and Christians. Akben Dar greeted Sam, Courtney, and Roger with an almost imperceptible bow. His words of greeting were polite, but his forced smile signaled some discomfort at their visit.

"Welcome to Antakya, gentlemen. Please sit down. Your London colleague—I believe his name was Patterson—told me you'd be coming." He pulled a silk handkerchief from the breast pocket of his suit, a drab-looking garment that appeared to be in worse shape than Sam's old sports jacket. He paused to clean his glasses. "I was surprised, both at the nature of your search and that MOLAS has allowed it at all."

He paused again to replace the glasses and adjust them on the bridge of his pinched, bony nose. "Now, tell me why you think that such a document could still exist after twenty centuries? And why would you believe that any of the churches along your itinerary might have preserved a copy?"

To Sam, the man's air of confidence seemed contrived, and the smugness of his remarks did little to mask what Sam perceived to be an underlying defensiveness. Sam glared at him. "Why not?"

Courtney raised his hand as if to abort a pending argument before it began. He paused to extract some notes from his pocket before he responded. "The churches along our itinerary existed in the cities in which the Apostle Paul preached. We have reason to believe he distributed the first versions of the New Testament along his route. We know that none of the original churches still exist. We had hoped, however, that at least one copy of those writings might have been handed down over the centuries and might be in the possession of a currently existing church."

Akben leaned back in his chair and folded his hands in his lap. "Why would you think that to be possible?"

"Well, it would seem logical since the churches during those twenty centuries preached the gospel as promulgated by Paul. We assumed they couldn't have carried forward the liturgy all those years without reference to some kind of Bible, original or otherwise. We know that all of the Christian Bibles extant today are simply reproductions, copied over hundreds of times from the Codex Sinaiticus and Codex Alexandrinus versions from the fourth century."

Courtney folded his notes and returned them to his pocket. "I hoped that you, a theologian, would see our point. The cities along our itinerary—or I should say Paul's itinerary—are the only places in the world likely to have a preserved version of the original writings distributed by Paul. The Vatican has already disavowed possession of any. If we don't find anything on this journey, then we're probably out of luck, because any Bibles that might have been preserved were most likely turned over to the Catholic Church and would have been destroyed long ago."

A deep frown accentuated Akben's pause and seemed to have wiped away the man's pedantic airs. He looked directly at Courtney. "I must tell you I'm appalled at what you're setting out to do. I beg you to call off this dangerous quest. It's difficult for me to believe that men as academically accomplished as you would even consider turning ecclesiastic history into a Pandora's Box for the naysayers of this world."

Sam spoke up before Courtney could open his mouth. "Hell, man, it's precisely for that reason we've agreed to the necessity of the search. As an historian, I'm personally committed to it. What are you afraid of?"

Akben's glare met Sam's. "Unless you're blind, it should be obvious. The Bible is the only known medium through which the word of God has ever been communicated to the world. If you convincingly discredit it, Western civilization collapses."

"What in the hell are you talking about?" Sam raised an already angry voice to the next level. "We're referring to one damned book, here. Okay, you Christians aren't going to like what we find. I get that. What I don't see is how Western civilization became involved?"

Roger put his hand to his mouth as if to stifle a gasp. Courtney turned to deliver a reproachful glare at Sam.

Akben leaned over, drew a Bible from a file drawer, and slammed it on the table in front of Sam. "Civility itself emanates from biblical focus on the God-recognized value of the individual, particularly the weak and poor. This 'damned book,' as you called it, describes a covenant between God and humankind, and among humans themselves. It demands a behavioral code based upon a higher standard—one clearly articulated by Jesus."

Akben appeared to be waiting for some kind of response, but charged ahead as though he really didn't have the patience to hear it. "Don't you see? Once the credibility of that covenant is destroyed, it won't be long before our social structure breaks down, leaving a moral vacuum. The rich and powerful will raise materialism to a new level. Moral behavior will become little more than an outmoded convention. Economies will erode, followed by the breakdown of our system of laws and government. In the ensuing chaos, democratic governments will evolve into dictatorships, much like the ancient fiefdoms."

Courtney put up his hand again and leaned forward. "Gentlemen, I think we get the picture."

Akben withdrew The Bible, returned it to the drawer, shot another angry glare at Sam, and continued as though he and Sam were alone in the room, engaged in mortal combat. "Let me state this in another way. When we fall away from God and turn against His commandments, our blessings will be withdrawn. In the end, the antichrist will offer us a covenant of a different kind. So, what I'm saying, Dr. Wykoff, is that this little book you're seeking to discredit is the only bulwark between Western civilization and the apocalypse."

An awkward silence fell over the room. Akben managed a forced smile, almost as an apology for having been so harsh, and continued. "At any rate, I can't help you. No document in my possession now dates back more than fifty years. And if I had found such an historic document, I would have turned it over to the Vatican. Perhaps you will be more fortunate at your next stop which, I understand, is Madenşehri, near the place formerly called Derbe, and then on to Lystra, yes?"

"Yes," Courtney said, returning the man's reluctant-appearing smile with a contrived one of his own. "We're hoping to find some existing church that might have been the recipient of such a legacy."

"I don't suppose you have any suggestions?" Sam asked between clenched teeth.

Akben shoved back his chair and stood without responding, a signal the meeting was over. "Once again, I implore you not to do this. If you're determined to continue this vile mission, I have only one suggestion. Be extremely careful as you proceed. There is much danger where you are going. I'm sorry, I'll terminate this discussion. I have a busy day ahead, and you have a long, precarious road in front of you."

Sam, Courtney, and Roger looked at one another with expressions of disappointment, thanked the priest for taking the time to see them, and left in silence.

\* \* \* \* \*

Roger's junior status earned him the job of designated driver. His duties required him to follow the map, fill the tank, and book hotel reservations at each stop. Dining accommodations along the way were agreed to be on an as-available basis, with the stipulation that the three travelers would not eat at any restaurant or café where one or more of them couldn't tolerate the menu. Thus far, that situation had not presented itself, much to the openly admitted surprise of Courtney, who had already expressed his belief that the culinary tastes of most

Americans rarely extended beyond hamburgers, french fries, and Coca-Cola.

Roger broke the silence as soon as he wheeled the car onto the main road and watched Antakya recede in the distance through the rearview mirror. "Sam, you looked like you thought that man was crazy. What's your take on what he said? Do you think he's off the deep end?"

"No. I think he's simply a classic illustration of what can happen when religion is carried to its logical, and unfortunate, conclusion."

"Well, like him or not," Courtney shot back, "I have to admit he has a point. Intended that way or not, the New Testament goes a long way toward establishing a behavior code that holds our social infrastructure together. That means there's a large body of people who will not to want to hear what Centurion Maecelius had to say. More to the point, the church is probably not going to stand by and allow any discrediting of a biblical message that has constituted its source of power for the last two thousand years."

"Okay, how about spelling that out a little more directly, my good English friend," Sam said.

Courtney paused, rubbed his eyes, and glanced at the map, as if to assure himself that Roger hadn't started on the wrong road. "As long as we appear to support the contents of that centurion's letter, the greater the threat we become to whoever might want our search shut down. I suspect our colleagues doing the scanning back in London may be in jeopardy as well. I've already left them and the other team a message on their cell phones to that effect."

Roger took his eyes off the road and threw an anxious-looking glance at Courtney. "How could that happen so quickly? We're on a search with about a one-in-a-million chance of success. The scans could easily show nothing at all. The news media know nothing about this, and we've barely begun. How could anyone possibly figure out what we're doing so soon?"

"Roger, watch where you're going," Courtney admonished him. "You're swerving. Anyway, news that threatens large organizations usually travels fast. A potentially significant discovery like this one doesn't need an international press release to find its way to the right people."

"Are you saying this large organization is some kind of underground Mafia," Sam asked, "or are we talking about the Catholic Church here?"

"I mean the Church Universal. We're talking about a conglomeration of denominations that has more power, cash, and real estate around the world than either your Mafia or any government. They have much to lose at a time when they're currently struggling to hold on to their membership. The last thing they need is a sudden error message in their doctrine. Even doubt can be as devastating as unassailable fact."

Roger refocused his attention on the road but continued to press the issue without turning his head. "How could the Church be so sure we'll find anything? Or even that the scans will contradict doctrine?"

"They don't have to be sure, Roger. The possibility that we might disclose something is enough to make it worth their while to simply eliminate everyone connected with this project. Don't think for a minute that I don't share your fears. I do."

"Okay, as head of this little team's theology department, what are you suggesting we do?" Sam challenged Courtney, without seeming to pay any attention to the course of the vehicle.

"Well, so far I can't see any compelling reason to change our plans or our itinerary. Are we all in agreement?" Nodding heads confirmed unanimous consent.

"What troubles me a bit right now," Roger said, "is that if it turns out someone wants so badly to have this project aborted, maybe we should back off."

"This is too big to back off," Sam snapped, ignoring the unassailable logic of Roger's concern. "I don't care whose ox we gore. If this turns out to be what we suspect, the world needs to know about it."

Courtney chuckled. "And the publishing royalties you and Roger will get from it won't hurt either. Right?"

Roger raised one hand in a gesture of objection. "I can't speak for anyone else, but right now my only objective is to retrieve enough relevant information to build an acceptable doctoral thesis."

Sam and Courtney turned to give him the kind of comforting smile that comes from knowing the pressure he was under to meet his famous father's expectations.

"I have a feeling you'll find plenty of it on this trip, lad." Courtney gave him a reassuring pat on the head, then slumped in his seat to take a nap.

It wasn't long before the refreshing breezes of the morning surrendered to the afternoon heat that had begun to envelope the Turkish plains. The Fiat's air conditioning system had become a noisy burden to the engine. The little four-cylinder workhorse sputtered and snarled indignantly, as if to lodge an official protest against performance expectations that far exceeded the terms of its original contract. By unanimous consent, the group agreed to make Derbe the last site visitation of the day before they proceeded to the village of Madenşehri for food and lodging.

\* \* \* \* \*

Even before they stepped out of the car, Derbe turned out to be a disappointment. Waves of tall, dry grass bowed respectfully under soft summer breezes that swept unimpeded across empty fields. With the exception of flying insects and a few small birds, they saw no sign of life anywhere. Sam walked to the edge of the road. He stared into the nothingness, as though he'd come to the end of the world with a mezzanine view of a burial ground that covered centuries of lost history.

"Well, if Paul preached here he couldn't have had much of an audience," Sam announced as he gazed out over the large hill of grass and the few remaining stones. "This place looks like what's left of a one horse town on a Texas prairie."

The disappointed look on Roger's face confirmed his agreement. "If the ruins buried under these mounds could only talk," Roger said. He swept his gaze over undulating sunlit fields of yellow, reminiscent of a Van Gogh painting, "Just imagine the tales these hills could tell. Like Sam said, it looks about as barren as an abandoned shantytown."

"Now, yes," Courtney said. "However, in ancient times Derbe was one of a very few Christian cities in existence, and it offered a refuge for traveling believers. In 300 A.D., the Roman Emperor Diocletian burned and buried the great church that Paul visited here. By his order, the city was destroyed. There's a ton of history lurking here, all waiting for archaeologists and historians like you, Sam, to set it free." He turned to

Roger. "Maybe even a copy of that Bible of yours is under there, Roger. Why don't we check in, get some dinner and a good night's sleep? We've a big day tomorrow."

\* \* \* \* \*

They found the meal tolerable and the dining atmosphere marginally acceptable. Still, they agreed the whole environment seemed crude and not particularly to their liking. The language barrier became more of a problem the farther they progressed from larger towns, where at least some broken English was spoken. The three of them dined with a minimum of conversation, each seemingly deep in the labyrinth of his thoughts.

Roger broke the silence. "Every stop we make along this journey is either going to bring us closer to our objective or confirm its ultimate futility. Centuries of war, devastation, and tons of accumulated sedimentation have probably destroyed whatever evidence the Catholic Church failed to obliterate. What'll we do if we keep running into one dead end after another?"

Courtney smiled. "You've asked the same question every archaeologist in the world has asked at the start of a dig. Look at it this way. You're not making a random search for something of such little significance that, if you failed to find it, you would have wasted time that you could have better spent doing something else. You're actually searching for something of monumental importance. Better yet, you're doing it with evidence, provided by the centurion's letter, that what you're looking for might actually exist."

Sam grinned at Courtney. "You really believe that, don't you?"

"Yes, and I'm hoping we'll get lucky. Whether we do or not, the letter you uncovered remains as indisputable documentation that what we're looking for is real. That centurion's Bible either still exists, or once did, regardless of whether we find it. Archaeologists are optimists by nature, and you should be too."

"He's right, Roger." Sam pushed the remains of dinner aside and gave his protégé the look of a professor gratified to find that one of his students had finally provided an opening for a meaningful class discussion. "This is anything but a random search, and the stakes are higher than any of us can imagine. So keep your chin up. With two teams of experienced people, fully competent in their respective fields, we're bound to uncover something."

Roger turned a quizzical expression to Sam. "Not to appear presumptuous, but what are you hoping to get out of all this? I mean, assuming we actually find something that confirms what the scans are likely to show."

Courtney struggled to stifle an emerging grin, as though he were anxious to see if Sam would continue his assault on Christianity.

"Well, it isn't money, in case that's what you were thinking," Sam said, glancing furtively at Courtney. "Obviously I'd like to drag this whole religious farce out into the open where it belongs. More importantly, I'm also hoping we can finally wake the world up to the need for a heightened comprehensive focus on the historical impact of excavation. You mentioned what results could be achieved if only the underground contents of these mounds could talk. Well, as an historian, I can tell you there are places like this all over the world with secrets waiting to be told."

"What about you, Courtney?" Roger asked, in a tone that sounded like his own faith in the mission depended on a reaffirmation of its purpose. "Are you concerned that our findings might bring down the wrath of the world?"

"I'm concerned, of course, Roger. A lot depends on precisely what that Roman centurion actually saw, and what he wrote in that letter. We won't know the answer until we see the scans. In any case, based on what we know already, this is likely to become an archaeological discovery of overwhelming long-term significance. Immediate reaction to it will be irrelevant. However, keep in mind that our findings might not be as iconoclastic as you think. They might just as easily go the other way and confirm, once and for all, that this universe and everything in it didn't just emerge by cosmic accident."

Sam frowned without saying anything. He remained silent throughout the rest of their journey to Madenşehri, his thoughts drifting back to Martha. The clearer his images of a life lost forever, the more intense his grief, until sleep provided a misty veil of relief.

# Chapter 4

## Lystra (Gökyurt)

The vote turned out to be unanimous. Sam, Courtney, and Roger rejected the fish and rice menu at Madenşehri, and walked out. They climbed into the Fiat and motored to the village of Gökyurt, where they found an acceptable breakfast of kasar cheese and sausage. Sam ordered a round of coffees. He did it partly because he wanted to cash in on the investment he'd made in learning to tolerate Turkish coffee and partly to watch Roger's manly efforts to choke it down.

The penetrating aroma of the dark beverage revived Sam's impulse to offer a late response to the remarks Courtney had made in Derbe. He downed a swallow without wincing and readdressed the issue. "Okay, Courtney, tell us again what kind of Bible we're looking for. As I understand it, Paul was a New Testament guy who preached here when this place was called Lystra. So, how different do you expect an original Bible to be than all the versions that are out there now, passing themselves off as the true word of God?"

Courtney washed down the last bite of his breakfast with a slug of coffee that still looked to Roger like Mississippi mud. "Sam, old boy, I've spent a good deal of time wondering how anyone who lives and breathes on this planet could possibly attribute that luxury to anything but the grace of God. Thus, you must surely appreciate the irony of my role in our quest for the unholy grail. Your colleague, clearly appalled by our decision to proceed with this search, undoubtedly dreads what we might find. I don't share that fear. The Holy Bible is the word of God. The possibility that we may uncover a serious challenge to its present format is exciting, but not relevant to the existence of God."

Sam shook his head. "You keep referring to this thing as the word of God. So, here's my question: Even if you accept the bizarre theory that there ever was a 'god,' how do you know that The Bible we're looking for actually represents his word?"

"Yeah, I guess I had the same question, Courtney," Roger chimed in. "I mean I believe in God, but I've always wondered how The Bible came to be accepted as his word."

Courtney closed his eyes for a moment as if to ponder the question in more depth. He opened them and split his attention between Sam and Roger. "Okay, you need to understand The Bible's background. We don't have anywhere near enough time for me to do justice to this, so I'll do my best to give you both a brief lesson in biblical history. It kind of goes like this: The fourth century A.D. Codex manuscripts were the oldest known formal compilations of all the previous writings which date back to Greek translations of Hebrew writings in the third century B.C. Of these writings, the Tanakh contained the five books of Moses, or the Pentateuch."

That Courtney paused in the middle of his dissertation to order another coffee brought looks of surprise from his breakfast companions.

He ignored them and continued. "Jewish scholars, known as Masoretes, tried to create a standardized text called the Masoretic Text, which became the basis for subsequent translations of the Old Testament into Western languages. The Old Testament represented the revelation of God up until the time of the years of Prophetic Silence, between 400 B.C. and 5 B.C. The Latin Vulgate, compiled by Jerome in 404 A.D., was the most famous translation of the Scriptures from Greek to Latin and became the official Bible of the Roman Catholic Church for the next 1,000 years."

Sam's brow furrowed. "So how did all these Codex writings take the form of a Bible?"

Courtney leaned back and cupped his hands behind his head. "The Christian Bible includes the same books as the Tanakh, representing the Old Testament plus twenty-seven specifically Christian books known as the New Testament, which focused on the teachings of Jesus and his followers. The monks, acting as Christianity's official scribes during the Dark Ages, subsequently translated all of this. In fact, if it hadn't been for their tireless efforts to record and sequester the Scriptures away from harm during that period, the Western World wouldn't have a Bible now."

47

The waiter placed a brown-colored pastry in front of Sam, who stared at it as though it didn't bear any resemblance to what he had ordered. He winced while he turned it over in his hand to examine it. He pushed the gooey offering aside and turned to Courtney. "So, if all the sequestering was successful, then what's the problem?"

"The problem," Courtney continued, "is that everyone has assumed all these years that the monks translated all the Scriptures accurately. The Dead Sea Scrolls, discovered in 1947, confirmed that assumption. The scrolls mirrored, almost word for word, exactly the writings of the Old Testament as they appear today. However, in spite of all that, there has been serious doubt expressed about the accuracy of the New Testament."

"Why am I not surprised?" Sam said in what sounded like a low growl.

"Well, the centurion's letter appears to confirm those doubts, suggesting that, either through mistranslation or deliberate alteration, the New Testament in existence today substantially compromises the true teachings of Jesus—and even the concept of God as we hold it."

He scooped up the biscuit Sam had rejected, and took a bite. "So, by finding an original version of the New Testament, or any pieces of it, we will either support or refute what the multi-spectral imaging scans of that letter show when our folks in London get them finished." Courtney leaned back, devoured the rest of the soft brown pastry, and grinned. "Get the picture?"

Sam reached up and clasped his hands behind his head. "Yeah, I guess so. Roger, are you okay with all this?"

"I'm fine with it, Sam. My only question is what if we don't find any part of the original versions of what Paul and the other apostles actually wrote? Because, in that case, even if that centurion's letter really says what we think it says, who's going to believe it?"

"I'm afraid he has a point, Sam," Courtney said, stroking his chin. "In which case we'll have to let the world decide for itself. At any rate, the world will always be confronted by a factual document written by a Roman soldier who personally knew Paul. This was a soldier who put himself and his family at great risk by writing the letter. True, he could have misunderstood Paul, but he had absolutely no reason to lie. It's going to be almost impossible for the leaders of the church, or anyone else, to sweep that one under the rug. In any case, regardless of what the

48

true semantics of that letter turn out to be, I still believe that the fundamental message of The Bible remains the same."

There was no response. They paid the bill, climbed into the car, and began the short hop to Konya.

Sam turned to Courtney. "Now don't take this as representing any belief on my part in this benevolent God of yours, but I'd like to hear your fourth dimension idea again. You know, the one you laid on me the other night after I'd had too much Turkish wine."

Courtney and Roger smiled and exchanged glances, as if in unspoken recognition that the condensed history lesson had apparently raised the bar on Sam's interest in religion. Both seemed to sense the anger Sam locked within himself. Peter had told them a little about Sam's background, and that his anger stemmed from a deep inner conviction that God had purposely allowed his wife to suffer and die prematurely. It was only through Courtney's gentle regard for his feelings that Sam Wykoff appeared to have derived some relief from his demons, as though, somehow, he understood that Courtney had offered to share his burden.

"Sam, it was nothing more than a simple reminder that you, like many non-believers, tend to conceptualize God within the constraints of your own frame of reference, limited by only that which you've learned through your personal experiences. The problem is that your experiences have all taken place in your three-dimensional world of time, space, and scientific thought. Or, I should say, whatever scientific thought happens to be currently accepted, since it seems to revise itself periodically."

Before he responded, Sam glanced down at the map, to check that Roger was still on course. "Are you saying that, in order to know God, I have to abstract myself into this fourth dimension?"

Courtney shook his head. "No, I'm not saying that at all, although I think that expanding your frame of reference a bit wouldn't hurt. All you really have to do is step back a bit and examine the concept of creation more objectively. For example, the very fact that you can recognize that you exist separately and distinctly from all other creatures should tell you something. That you exist in this specific time and place, as opposed to any other time and place, should suggest that such a phenomenon is not likely to have happened through pure random chance."

49

Courtney leaned over the back of the front seat, tapped Roger on the shoulder, and pointed to a spot on the map marking the next turn. Roger nodded as Courtney slumped back into his seat and continued his explanation. "There has to be a determining force, otherwise all living creatures, including yourself, would be interchangeable through time and space, and without the ability to recognize that fact. So, it's not just your uniqueness that's pivotal, Sam, but also your recognition of it."

Sam raised his hand. "Yeah, but you're ignoring genetics. Isn't that the random chance factor you're talking about?"

"No. Genetics are simply a conduit through which the phenomenon takes place. Genetics would represent a common denominator regardless of whether living creatures are distinct as to time and place, or interchangeable. And that's precisely why there really is no conflict between Darwinism and the Christian doctrine of Creation. In other words, it doesn't matter whether you believe in evolution from the primordial slime, or Adam and Eve in the Garden of Eden. Either way, propagation of life requires a common denominator initially provided by our Creator. You can call it DNA, a living cell which science has never been able to reconstruct from scratch, just plain sex, or anything else."

Sam turned away for a moment, shook his head, then turned back to face the man who had become the dispenser of doctrine he didn't believe but could no longer ignore. "Damn it, Courtney, you must be smoking something in that pipe that could get you arrested. Okay, look. Some years ago, I attended a lecture given by a guy who called himself a biblical creationist or something. He said your God created the world in six days, with all living creatures already in mature form—no evolutionary stuff. I guess that eliminates the 'Who came first, the chicken or the egg?' controversy. So, how do you get all that to square up with the known fact of evolution?"

Courtney pondered the question a moment before he offered a response. "Okay, the debate between biblical creationists and world-view evolutionists has been going on for some time without any real consensus. The evolutionists criticize the creationists for stubbornly interpreting the Book of Genesis literally. The creationists blame the evolutionists for a conveniently allegorical interpretation of God's word on grounds that it allows them to avoid any strict accountability to it."

"Then I'd say that's a problem in itself," Sam countered.

"No, not really. The problem is that the Book of Genesis presents creation of the world, and all living creatures, as a six-day product, but remains silent as to all the supporting components which might have made for an easy reconciliation. Consequently, both sides have left each other no choice except to agree that God is, in fact, master and creator, while they continue to disagree on the specific chronology."

Sam's thoughts clung to the edge of the concept for a few moments before he leaned back and allowed the hum of the engine and the gentle rocking of the vehicle to lull him to sleep.

Roger smiled at Courtney. "I think he's dreaming of Martha, don't you?"

Courtney returned the smile. "I'm sure he is."

* * * * *

The Fiat's undersized engine coughed and sputtered in protest of the first steep grade it had encountered since the start of the journey. Although the roadside traffic advisory showed it as a steep hill, the thirty-degree slope seemed more like a small mountain. The ensuing struggle between rugged topography and four-cylinder engineering finally ended with the exhausted little car claiming a marginal victory at the top.

Roger turned to confirm that his mentor had awakened enough to appreciate the effort it took to reach the summit. "Sam, take a look. This view of the valley below is awesome."

Sam yawned and moved his shoulders back and forth to loosen them. "Yeah, almost makes the effort worthwhile, but I don't think this car has it in it to do this again."

"Roger, put it in a lower gear going down," Courtney cautioned, as they began the descent. "You don't want to put too much stress on the brakes."

"I did," Roger said, "but it doesn't seem to be helping much. We're still going too fast, and the road is getting narrower and winding more." His growing anxiety became evident in the high-pitched sound of his voice.

"Well then, pump the brakes every now and then," Sam responded in a soft voice, while he wrapped a comforting arm around his young protégé's shoulder.

A few seconds passed before Roger's mounting tension morphed into an expression of outright fear. The vehicle continued to accelerate. "Damn it, Sam, the brakes aren't working," he shouted. "Help me!"

Without hesitation, Sam swung his left foot down hard on top of Roger's, pressing the brake pedal to the floor. When nothing happened, Sam pulled the handbrake up in an effort to reduce speed, while Roger struggled to keep the vehicle on the road. Aside from the smell of burning metal, nothing changed as the car continued its downward plunge, veering alternately off the edge of the road and back on again.

Sam tried to ignore the tightening in his chest and reached around Roger to grasp the wheel. With the brakes gone, he recognized the Hobson's choice confronting them.

If he turned the wheel hard enough to keep the hurtling vehicle on the twisting road, it might flip over. The result would be an almost certain fatal roll down the hill that fell away into a valley of intermittent rocks. If he turned the wheel gently enough to prevent a roll, the car would miss the next turn and continue straight away down the hill, with little likelihood of maintaining an upright posture.

With no time to solicit group consensus, Sam took it upon himself to select the latter course of action. In silence, he offered up his first ever prayer to the God he'd always claimed didn't exist. He ignored the next turn and guided the Fiat off the road. The car began an erratic, bouncing descent, during which Sam focused intently on following the path of least destruction. Throwing its occupants from side to side, the unstable little vehicle careened off one boulder after another in a helpless plunge toward the bottom of the hill.

Tree trunks whipped past the windows like enormous spears thrown down at the car by giant hunters trying to impale a desperately zigzagging little animal. Whether by miracle or driver skill, the Fiat avoided the worst of the larger obstacles. It bounced over rocks which exploded the tires and ripped the undercarriage into a mass of twisted metal. After what seemed like an eternity of sheer terror, the vehicle, now a mass of ugly dents, skidded to an upright halt in the muddy approach to a shallow stream.

Its bruised occupants exhaled sighs of relief while they stared speechless at one another. For a few moments, no one could think of anything to say. Sam summarized the whole thing as a damned lucky roll of the dice. Courtney proclaimed it an act of divine providence. Roger sat glassy eyed, in the manner of a rescued victim still unsure exactly how the rescue came about.

None of them could remember how long they stayed there in post-traumatic shock before two men wearing dark green trousers and light green shirts, with red and blue insignia on their collars, approached them. Like policemen of any other country, these representatives of the Turkish Jandarma Trafik were required to file a complete report of the accident after they ascertained the condition of its participants.

They arranged to have the vehicle towed to the nearest town and told Courtney it would be several hours before a replacement could be available for rental. The first item in the police report cited the mechanic's conclusion that the accident was no accident. The brakes and gear mechanism had been tampered with by someone who knew just how long they would function properly before the car's downhill motion would require the driver to apply excessive pressure on them. The second item pronounced there would be no investigation on the fuzzy premise that there was no logical place to begin one, given the vehicle's itinerary.

"Damn it, I don't care who did this," Roger said, with an assertiveness that surprised everyone. "I'm not quitting. What do you guys make of this mess?" He sat down and stared at the report.

Courtney took the report from him and shook his head. "Well, I can tell you this. Whoever did it wanted us completely out of commission, one way or the other. And that means this little search of ours has attracted someone's serious attention. This may be a grim portent of what's in store for us if we continue. Anyway, I concur with Roger. Let's move ahead with it. Your thoughts, Sam?"

Sam paused while he made a futile effort to wipe the dust off his clothes. "Agreed. The best way to shove this whole thing back in their faces is to keep on trucking."

"Good," Courtney said. "It's unanimous then. By the way, nice driving…both of you guys."

\* \* \* \* \*

Konya looked old from the moment they drove into it. Even the people looked old. It seemed like the kind of place whose inhabitants had

53

lived there forever, not by choice, but because they hadn't the resources to leave and no other place to go. Those who could be seen moved about slowly. Some didn't move at all, as though they were frozen in time. The village looked trapped somewhere between the ancient history it left behind and a future in which it didn't belong. Its shabby streets snaked between crumbling buildings splotched with a kind of green mold.

Roger brought their replacement rental car—a younger and more eager Hyundai—to a stop in front of a church that looked as though it had been constructed in a previous millennium. A survivor of the ravages of time, it now seemed to have taken its rightful place as the architectural patriarch of the village.

An old priest stepped out through the front door of the aging structure and managed an awkward walk down the cobblestone path to meet them. He forced a difficult smile and extended a fragile hand to Courtney. "Good morning, I'm Father Trazerri. Welcome to my church, gentlemen." He glanced at the dark reddish-purple marks on Courtney's face. "You fellows appear to have suffered some bruises. If I may ask, were you in an accident of some sort? "

"In fact we were," Courtney said. "A matter of brakes that failed. We managed to survive, thanks to the driving skills of my colleagues here, Dr. Samuel Wykoff, and his student, Roger Denault. I'm Courtney Stickney, Father Trazerri. I don't know how much Akben told you about our mission, but—"

"Yes, I've been made aware of it," he snapped. "Please come inside, quickly. I'm sorry, I don't mean to seem rude. You see, ever since Father Santoro was murdered by Muslims, this part of the world has been a dangerous one for Christians. We are, as I'm sure you must know, a declining population here." The old man threw a cautious glance over his shoulder, as though his next comment would be a dark secret he didn't want to share with anyone other than his visitors.

With a swift, almost imperceptible, movement of his hand, the priest loosened his collar and gestured for them to follow him through the arched oaken door leading into the church. His graying hair and uneasy shuffle marked the man's advanced years. Sunken cheeks and dark circles under his eyes suggested an accumulated fatigue that made him appear much older than Akben Dar had said he was.

54

Sam surmised the man's life had been a difficult one compared to his own relatively comfortable existence. His thoughts flashed back to Martha again, evoking an uncomfortable feeling of compassion for the old man and a renewal of his own grief which refused to relinquish its hold.

Aside from a small courtyard landscaped with a stone statue of Mary Magdalene, a bird bath, and a variety of colorful shrubs, everything about the church looked drab. Its exterior, in desperate need of repair, did little to prepare them for the explosion of color that took them by surprise the moment they entered. A clearly Roman and Byzantine décor presented itself in a kaleidoscopic array of brilliant red, yellow, and orange hues splashed on the walls and ceiling. Their contrast with the quiet white of old marble columns made the sanctuary look more like a mosque than a church.

After Courtney paused a few moments to take in the imposing surroundings, he began the dialogue as comfortingly as he could, an obvious attempt to ease the priest's apparent anxiety. "Father Trazerri, we've uncovered an historic document that makes it imperative for us to be here. We hope to locate at least some remnants of the Apostle Paul's contributions to what subsequently became the New Testament. We have reason to believe that portions of his, or other writings, might still be found. It's our intent to search within the confines of the churches currently existing in the general area of those now extinct churches once visited by Paul."

The priest nodded as though he understood.

"We realize most of the churches along Paul's route, such as the ones in nearby Lystra, have long since been destroyed or buried. We had hoped that religious leaders like you, in surrounding areas, might be able to direct our search more precisely."

The old priest remained silent until all three of his visitors were comfortably seated in his study. In subdued contrast to the vibrant sanctuary, the modest little study offered no pretense to be anything other than what it was. If the priest had any personal belongings, he'd hidden them well. Old books filled the shelves. Nests of piled papers cluttered the desk, and a large crucifix dominated an otherwise bare wall.

For a few moments, it looked as though the priest might not respond at all. Then he leaned forward with both hands in his lap, paused to gather his thoughts, and spoke in a low, solemn tone. "Gentlemen, what I'm about to tell you puts me at grave risk. Guarding it has weighed heavily on me for many years. Although I've never actively sought to disclose it, I've often wondered how I would react if pressed to do so. Now, it seems I am. When I first learned about your discovery and that you would be visiting here, I made up my mind to tell you nothing, as would be my perfect right to do."

He stood, looked up at the crucifix, bowed his head, and sat down again.

"You look tired, Father," Courtney said. "Would you prefer that we do this another day?"

"No. Please let me finish while I still have the inclination to do so. During the last few days, I came to realize such an action would only extend the burden of my silence. What I'm about to tell you has tormented me ever since that fateful day that caused me to wish I had never been born. Until recently, my fear of disclosing the events of that day has always outweighed the agony of my silence. This is no longer the case. The hell to which I feared I might be sent in my afterlife has already come to me in this one."

The priest raised himself ungracefully from his chair and paced back and forth. His movements were deliberate. The old man seemed to be struggling with his thoughts before deciding to release them.

Sam leaned forward. "Are you all right, sir?"

"Yes, thank you. What finally prompted my decision in favor of disclosure was the irrefutable fact that Muslim extremists will eventually eliminate Christianity and all its churches in this part of the world. So, in some strange way I feel that, before I die, I must share with someone the suspicions which I've dutifully guarded all these years. And perhaps it was the will of our merciful God that we are brought together at this time in my life, that I might finally shed this terrible burden."

Sam opened his mouth to speak, but Courtney raised his hand to stop him, allowing the priest to continue uninterrupted.

Trazerri returned to his seat and lowered his head. "Before I was ordained, I served what you might call an internship in an old church in the town of Selçuk bordering the Aegean Sea, not many kilometers from here. In ancient times, as you probably know, it was northeast of the city of Ephesus, where the Apostle Paul made several visits. I was a junior

56

apprentice. Many of my first tasks were rather menial, including the one which I have spent a lifetime regretting."

"And what task was that?" Roger asked before Courtney's scowl shut him up.

"I was ordered by the priest who supervised my activities to go down into the basement, scrub the stone walls, and sort all the junk I found. He said he would decide what to retain and what to throw away. While I was scrubbing the wall, I noticed that one of the stones was in crooked. After I took it out to fix it, I realized that particular stone was there only to conceal a compartment. Curious, I stuck my hand in and discovered an old goat-skin pouch containing twenty or thirty pages, obviously torn out of a book or binding of some kind."

The priest reached into his desk drawer for a small crucifix and closed his eyes for a few moments while he clutched it close to his chest. After he murmured some inaudible phrase, he opened his eyes and returned the crucifix to its place in the drawer.

"The pages," the priest continued, "surely must have been originals written in the ancient days. I am certain, to this day, they were. They had been preserved, although not very well, with some kind of powdery substance, and they were still legible, albeit terribly fragile. I recognized the writings as those of Apostles Paul and of Timothy who, you might remember, was a protégé of Paul."

He lowered his head for a moment, and Sam could almost feel the aching in the old man's bony shoulders. The priest began to sob uncontrollably in a guttural tone, so deep Sam feared the man's lungs could not sustain it much longer. Sam reached to lay a consoling hand on Trazerri's shoulder. Finally, the tears stopped, and the priest mustered up the courage to continue.

"I cannot begin to describe the shock I felt when it became clear to me that these Scriptures described a completely different Jesus—and even a different God—than is portrayed in The Bible from which I have since preached and, indeed, which exists throughout the world today." He lifted his hands in the air and drew them back down to cover his face with them.

Sam opened his eyes wide and leaned forward. He spoke as gently as he could. "What did you do? And in what way were the writings different?"

"And where are those pages now?" Courtney interjected, with a mixed expression of amazement and anticipation.

The priest turned away for a moment to pull himself together, paused, then turned back to face them. "I brought my discovery to the attention of my superior, who flew into a rage and chastised me severely. He threatened to have me banished from the priesthood, and even to have me excommunicated, were I ever to disclose to anyone what I had found. Then, after he calmed a bit, he sat me down and explained that, in the year 449, the Church of Mary in Ephesus held a Second Council, but that its controversial acts were never approved by the Catholics."

"I presume that was the notorious Robber Council," Courtney said.

Trazerri nodded. "It distributed many Bibles, probably including the one from which the pages I discovered had come. The contents were condemned by the Roman Catholic Church. My head priest explained that the pages I found had been stored in the basement of that church by all the generations of priests who preceded him.

Courtney frowned. "Why?"

"My priest wouldn't say. I believe, however, they were to be used, if necessary, as leverage against the Vatican. That priest eventually died and, over the years, I rose in the ranks of the Church. I finally ended up here, where the Bishop says I will stay until I retire. Throughout the years, my preaching has always been clouded by the belief that I'm teaching a false gospel written by the Church, rather than the real one as originally authored by the apostles. I could tell by the way the three of you looked at me you sensed my suffering. Now you know why."

"Where do you think those pages are now?" Sam persisted. He was reluctant to press an already distraught old man, but determined not to relinquish what might be the only viable key to the mystery that seemed to shroud their whole venture.

The priest took in a deep breath and exhaled slowly. His confession had apparently provided enough relief from his suffering to ease some of the tension which had contorted his face. Like the prisoner allowed out into the sunlight only briefly before being returned to his cell, Father Trazerri paused to glance out the window before he continued.

"Dr. Wykoff, I really don't know. They may still be in the basement of that church if my head priest decided to continue his predecessors' policy of preserving them. However, I rather suspect that he never

58

actually knew they were there until I discovered them and, in his anger, he probably destroyed them."

"I don't mean to press you, Father," Courtney said softly, "but can you tell us exactly what those pages contained that was so different?"

"Please understand," Father Trazerri replied in a tone that sounded apologetic, "I'm not trying to be evasive. You must remember the incident occurred a very long time ago. Mercifully, one of my few accomplishments in this life has been my ability to submerse the whole memory deep within my own agony. In this way, I have almost entirely suppressed what I saw. I truly can no longer recollect the exact nature of those passages. I can only tell you I am certain that, at some point during the first three centuries of the Common Era, someone rewrote the passages of the New Testament. I don't know about the Old Testament, but I'm certain the—"

"Excuse me, Father," Courtney said. "Why did you just now use the expression 'Common Era'? I thought that term reflected the Jewish rejection of the concept of a divine Jesus and was used in lieu of the Christian expression that means in the year of our Lord."

The priest smiled for the first time. "Exactly, Dr. Stickney." A look of relief spread across his tortured countenance. "And with that you've summarized, most concisely, my answer to the question you asked."

At the end of a prolonged silence during which the three visitors looked first at one another and then back at Father Trazerri, Sam walked to the window and turned to address the priest. "Father, I'm not a religious man, so please forgive my ignorance in these matters. Did I just hear you imply that those documents, presumably original Scriptures or copies thereof, portrayed a Jesus who was something other than divine?"

The priest's face tightened again. He stood and opened the door to his study, signaling that the conversation had reached an end and it was time for his guests to leave.

"Gentlemen, I have much to do today and I'm already behind. So I'll bid you adieu, and wish you every success in your mission. By the way, I understand you intend to visit Ephesus next. Do you still intend to travel to Corinth, Thessalonica, and Athens after that, as Akben Dar informed me?"

"Yes, that's our plan, Father," Courtney responded.

The priest paused, as if struggling to decide whether to share what he was thinking or whether it would be best left unsaid. He turned away briefly, then turned back to face them, having apparently opted for disclosure. "I would suggest a different plan, if you will permit me. After you visit Ephesus, the remainder of your journey would be much better guided by a careful reading of Revelation, the last book in the New Testament. I would advise that in your travels you avoid the domain of Satan and then consider most carefully the number seven."

"I'm not sure I follow you," Sam countered with a pronounced frown. "What's wrong with our itinerary after Ephesus? And what has Revelation to do with our mission?"

"And why the number seven?" Courtney asked.

The priest shook his head. "Gentlemen, the research I have done has already added physical suffering to the mental agony I've borne since that terrible day. I will discuss it no more. It's in your hands now, and I can only beseech you to allow Revelation to guide your travels. Only then will your venture have any chance for success. Please, let us bow our heads while I offer a much needed prayer…for all of us."

They stood silently with heads bowed. Father Trazerri spoke in a voice almost hoarse from the strain of his confession. "Our Heavenly Father, please guide and protect these men as they continue on their journey, for their mission is a dangerous one. It is your nature to forgive sinners for the wrongful acts they commit. I have come to realize that my sin of silence, all these years, has been the worst kind, being one of omission. Now, in a final effort to relieve my guilt, I have passed that sin on to these three men. They must carry its burden until they find the truth, which will then serve as the only atonement I can offer. I pray in your Holy Name, asking forgiveness for all of us. Amen."

After a half-hour of small talk, they reached an unspoken consensus that there was nothing left to say. The three visitors thanked their host and left. Sam turned for one last glance at the priest, who waved goodbye before he closed the door.

Courtney put his hand on Sam's shoulder. "We need to be on our way, Sam. What are you staring at?"

Sam shook his head. "I was just wondering how different the old man's life might have been if he had simply ignored the loose stone."

* * * * *

The Hyundai Courtney had rented to replace the Fiat meandered through the hilly countryside toward the town of Selçuk, which surrounded the remains of the ancient city of Ephesus. Sam pointed out the window to places where armies had fought and conquered. Survivors had built cities in which cultures thrived, declined, and eventually disappeared. Now, thousands of years later, the vehicle's occupants could see only remnants of partly excavated aqueducts, temples, and topless columns standing naked, robbed of their ancient grandeur by unforgiving centuries. The historian in Sam could almost hear the ghostly remains of ancient structures whisper: "We survive as symbols of an old world that taught yours everything it knows. Explore what we were if you want to find out who you are." Sam's thoughts became his own architectural metaphors for his dreams. He imagined complete excavation of all historic sites, so ancient, so set apart from the twenty-first-century, and yet so much a part of it.

Faced with the unavailability of English tea and the uncomfortable ingestion of local coffee, the three travelers found an acceptable compromise in Coca-Cola, which offered the advantage of being accessible almost everywhere. One hand on the wheel and the other wrapped around his Coke, Roger found himself the object of his mentor's glances.

"Roger, I'm assuming the caffeine will prevent drowsiness and promote concentration, now that you've elected to drive with one hand instead of two."

"Yes sir. I'm completely on top of it here. No worries."

"Good."

Courtney reached over from the rear seat and tapped Sam on the shoulder. "Sam, I'd like to ask you something. I almost thought I saw you humbly praying back there with Trazerri. May I take that as a slight mellowing of your stance on religion?"

Sam yawned and stretched his arms and legs as far as the cramped space would allow. He turned to face the man whose depth of logic had challenged him in a way that he'd not been challenged before. "Well, the more I thought about it, the more I kind of felt sorry for the old gentleman. And if I could ever cajole myself into thinking that prayer

61

was anything more than a waste of time, I guess I'd probably pray for him. Think about it yourself for a minute. Here's a guy who's committed to preaching the gospel as he was taught it, but spent a lifetime struggling to suppress his suspicion that what he was taught was wrong."

Courtney nodded. "Right. I think we all felt the poor chap's pain."

"Then," Sam continued, "he believes so strongly in his creator that he prays to be forgiven for what he's done. Maybe you and the priest see something in your fourth dimension that I don't. Anyway, I have to respect him for his devotion and his courage. Don't read anything into that. I haven't changed any of my views on those biblical fairy tales, like the parting of the water, no matter what the scientists said about wind. These all seem to come under the mantle of heavenly promulgated Scripture. Now here's a question for you. What do you make of that comment about Revelation…which I assume is a biblical reference of some kind?"

Before Courtney could answer, Roger turned the wheel sharply to the left in order to keep the car from missing an unmarked turn. The Hyundai made the almost-ninety-degree curve successfully. Roger's Coca-Cola didn't. It slipped from his hand and came to rest in Sam's lap. Without saying anything, Sam handed the can and the remains of its contents back to Roger, glared at him, and pulled out a handkerchief to sop up as much of the drink as he could from his trousers.

"Damn, I'm sorry," Roger blurted out. "I'll keep the thing in the cup holder from now on. I'm really sor—"

"Forget it," Sam said. "Accidents happen. We're glad you saw the turn in time. For the record, I've found that when you're driving, it's better to take a drink only when you're on a clear straightaway."

Courtney grinned, shook his head, and handed Sam a towel he'd "borrowed" from their last hotel. "Sam, I'll let your comment about fairy tales ride for now. The Old Testament represents an historic chronicle which has always had its challengers. The New Testament, on the other hand, is a relatively more recent chronicle of historic events. It was written about a religious leader with whom a much larger body of people can identify, and documentation of his existence is clear. Even so, it has its share of skeptics."

Sam forced a half-smile. "Ahhh, so I'm not the only one who questions biblical validity."

"Perhaps not. Nevertheless, the underlying intent of the New Testament is to provide a foundation from which all people can better understand God and further develop their own relationship with him. Yes, Revelation is the last book of the New Testament. I'm not exactly sure just what the priest meant, but I'll give Revelation another good reading as soon as we get to Selçuk."

"Courtney," Roger said, "I know you said whatever we find wouldn't change your belief in The Bible's underlying message. So, what if the imaging scans turn out to verify what that priest said about the Scriptures being altered by the church? Do you agree with Akben Dar's contention that our publication of it would lead to the eventual collapse of Western civilization?"

"I'm afraid I do, Roger, although I don't think it would happen all at once. I believe our entire social structure would radically change once the scan results hit the street. Since the Scriptures represent the only historic chronicles in which God revealed himself to us, their credibility is of vital importance. If the centurion's Bible we're looking for, or any parts of it, should reveal a different version of God, then the world's perception of him will change dramatically. Like Peter, I'm not looking forward to a religious forgery which may very well throw this world into chaos. Hang on a minute, my cell phone is buzzing." Courtney turned away to grope, first in one pocket then another, to locate the persistent little instrument.

The minute seemed to go on and on until Courtney shouted, "Good grief, no!" One look at his ashen face and both Roger and Sam recognized the color of bad news. They waited anxiously for an explanation.

Courtney clicked off and stuffed the instrument back into his pocket. "That was one of the scanning crew in London. Someone broke into the museum and tried to steal both the scans and the equipment. One of our guys was still there working late and managed to get help. He broke up the intended theft but was shot in the process. He's alive, but apparently in pretty bad shape. Guys, I'm afraid we've stirred up a hornet's nest." He bent forward, his face in his hands, as though he felt responsible for what happened.

Roger shook his head. "Courtney, this is the second attempt to abort this project. So, I'll repeat my original question. What do we do now?"

Courtney raised his head and slapped his knees with both hands. "Well, that depends on what you and Sam want to do. We have several options. One, we abort our search for the original Scriptures. We do this on the assumption that the imaging scans in process will soon tell us all we need to know. Otherwise it wouldn't have been necessary for anyone to want to steal both the scans and the electronic equipment. Or, two, we can press on as before on the assumption that we will need the confirmation that Trazerri is convinced still exists somewhere. And I believe we will, regardless of what the scans show."

"Why do you say that?" Roger asked.

"Because by A.D. 397, when the Synod of Carthage confirmed as canonical the twenty-seven books of what is now the New Testament, it was simply recognizing that those books had already been in use and read by the churches for three centuries. At least some of those books must have appeared as originally written, prior to any alteration. We need to find one of them, or at least parts of one, to either confirm or refute what the scans produce."

"Have you heard anything," Sam asked, "from Patterson and his team who are supposed to be scouring the battle sites?"

Courtney nodded. "He sent me a text message yesterday. So far nothing."

Sam gave a thumb-up gesture. "I vote we keep going."

"Agreed," Roger said.

The Hyundai continued to close the distance to Selçuk. While Sam stared out the window, his reflections on the London incident triggered another possible avenue of assault on Courtney's seemingly impregnable religious fortress. "Courtney, tell me this. If your God is the benevolent power you say he is, then why would he allow the kind of evil we encountered with the tampered brakes and now, this attack in London? For that matter, why would he allow my Martha, and others like her, to suffer so horribly?"

Courtney managed a faint smile, as though it wasn't the first time he'd been confronted with the question. "Sam, God is not the author of evil. Once again, you're coming from a very limited perspective. You're asserting the premise that, since God has no morally sufficient reason for permitting evil, he must therefore have some morally sufficient reason to protect his world from all evil."

Sam raised his eyebrows. "Well, hell, Courtney, doesn't he? I mean if the guy's supposed to be God the father, as you Christians claim he is, doesn't he have an obligation to protect his so-called children from disasters?"

Courtney shook his head. "No. I know it's difficult for you to understand this, particularly after Martha. So, try to expand your horizons a bit. Any event taken out of historical context, and examined by itself in a vacuum, is bound to lead to the same kind of erroneous conclusion that you've just reached. However, if you look at God's kingdom over the span of thousands of years, you'll see that, despite all the individual incidents of suffering, war, and disease, the human race is far better off today than it was two or three thousand years ago."

"So, what the hell does that prove?" Sam snarled.

"Well, consider this. I remember reading statistics which show that in the year 100 A.D. non-Christians outnumbered Christians by a multiple of 360-to-one. Today, I believe they outnumber Christians by only seven-to-one. I think you'll agree those numbers represent a fairly positive statement about the advancement of the kingdom of God during a period in which he had to endure a number of evil doings. I'll state this another way. God gave all of us the capability to make our own decisions, or what the philosophers would call freedom of choice. So, I'm sure you must realize that the gifting of such capability precluded any subsequent micromanagement by God."

Courtney's logic rang out with such impact that Sam felt compelled to nod in reluctant acknowledgment, his own grief notwithstanding. "Yeah, I see your point. I don't much like it, but I suppose I get it."

They made the rest of the journey in silence. Sam could think of no meaningful counterargument, and Courtney said nothing, as though he was content to allow Sam to mull the whole concept over for a while.

# Chapter 5

# Deva (Chester)

The second battle-site team of Nigel, Gordon, and Peter had no
difficulty identifying the general vicinity of Legion XX's Britannia
campaign at Chester. A more precise delineation of the battle's
boundaries would have been preferable, but it was impossible to obtain
even with the aid of GPS technology.

Peter scanned the site from the rear seat of their Mercedes and shook
his head. "Gordon, I hope you meant it when you said we won't have to
dig anywhere."

Gordon shook his head. "Digging would be pointless. Two thousand
years of sediment lies on top of anything we'd want to find."

Peter scratched his head. "So, where do we go from here? You've
been studying that fistful of notes, Nigel, for the last half hour. Is the
answer to my question in there somewhere?"

Nigel nodded. "I believe so. The map indicates that the town of Deva
is less than a mile from here. It's our best hope of retrieving anything
that might have been abandoned by Legion XX. We've probably already
spent far too long combing through Gloucester and Colchester. As you
Yanks are prone to say, 'we've struck out.' Or something like that."

"Chin up, Nigel," Gordon said. "The Yanks would also tell you the
game's not over until it's over. Right, Peter?"

Peter smiled. "True, but although I admire your perseverance, I have
to agree with Nigel. The game may not be over, but this is the ninth
inning. If we don't uncover something tangible here in Chester we're out
of luck. What I'm having trouble coming to grips with is that all the
documents we looked at relating to Legion XX's battles pointed to
Colchester as the most likely spot for salvage. Even Gloucester seemed,
at least theoretically, to offer some hope."

Peter ran his finger along the itinerary marked on the map. "Look, see what I mean? We know Legion XX fought in both those places. I'm not getting why we came up empty there in terms of finding something relating to the centurion's son, Vinicius, or any of his belongings. I mean, the stuff we saw in those archives was interesting but not at all relevant. Maybe we'll just have to face the truth—we've been wasting our time out here."

Gordon turned the Mercedes into the unpaved parking lot of the little museum adjacent to the battle site. "Cheer up, lads," he said. "I think I've figured out the problem. I apologize for taking so long to solve this puzzle. Think back on the dates of those battles in the context of the time when this soldier must have lived and fought."

Nigel frowned. "I'm not following you. We're talking first century for all of these events, are we not?"

"Yes, but a hundred years is a long time compared to one soldier's life. And this is where I should have been more astute. I mean, the Colchester campaign went from 43 A.D to 49 A.D. The Gloucester expedition came in 50 A.D. We all knew this when we started."

"So, where's this going?" Peter challenged him in a tone of unmistakable frustration.

"My point is that Nigel has already explained that the forensics people placed the centurion's letter to his son somewhere between 60 A.D. and 69 A.D., right?"

"Yes, approximately."

"Well then, this chap's son couldn't possibly have been at the Gloucester or Colchester sites when those encounters took place. Since he was probably in his twenties or thirties when he received the letter, he wouldn't have been old enough to fight a battle in the forties or early fifties."

Nigel raised his eyebrows and grinned. "Ah, you're right. Yet, he could easily have been in the Chester showdown in A.D. 87. I'm beginning to see where you're going. Well done, my friend."

They climbed out of the car and entered the small, neatly arranged museum. The one-story building offered half of itself as a visitors' information center and half as a small local museum. A bit too large for the one function and too constrained for the other, the 200-year-old structure seemed to be openly protesting its twenty-first century conversion from its original status as the town hall.

Her face buried in a book, the curator didn't notice the three visitors until Gordon reached over the counter and tapped her on the shoulder. Her head snapped up, she put her hand to her face, and dropped the book on the floor. "Oh, you frightened me," she gasped. "I didn't see you come in. I'm sorry. I'm Robin Dunstan. Who are you?"

Gordon made the introductions and Robin listened attentively while he explained the purpose of their visit. Nigel looked more relaxed now that the historic timing mystery was cleared up. He glanced around the lobby as though he were looking for either his usual pot of tea or a restroom, whichever popped into view first.

Peter couldn't take his eyes off the curator. The short, borderline-plump girl with dark brown hair swept back in a bun smiled at him. Moderately attractive by any measure, but not beautiful, Robin's charm made the sum of her assets seem greater than the whole—at least to Peter. He suddenly felt embarrassed that his first reaction had been a sense of relief when the absence of a ring suggested she was unmarried. Gordon and Nigel pretended not to notice Peter's captivation.

"Gentlemen, our little town has naturally grown accustomed to tourists over the years," Robin responded in a soft voice. She acknowledged Peter's admiration with a knowing look. "Until now, though, we've seen no one with such unusual objectives in mind." In an apparent effort to make her movements unobtrusive, she straightened the collar of her blouse with one hand and reached down to adjust her plaid skirt with the other.

Peter took a brisk step forward, not wanting to miss an opportunity to engage her in conversation. "Miss Dunstan," he began, not entirely sure he really wanted to start his relationship with her by talking business, "we fully appreciate how remote the likelihood is of our finding anything dating back that far into antiquity. Even so, we had hoped that perhaps someone, or some organization, might have recognized the historic importance of such documents and made an effort to preserve at least parts of them. Right now we're simply seeking any small clue that might lead us somewhere." Peter tried to look hopeful, but there were no other visitors in sight and the place had all the earmarks of another dead end.

Robin put a finger to her forehead in a gesture of contemplation, and Peter imagined her sorting through years of accumulated curator memory. While he watched her, thoughts of how he might come back and reconnect with her after this was all over raced through his mind. He'd fallen in love once before—or thought he had—with a young, single girl in his congregation. He'd allowed the moral constraints of his pastoral role to block any further efforts to pursue the matter. Long after she disappeared, he learned that she had shared his feelings and had left the church in order to avoid what she thought might have resulted in a scandal that would hurt his career.

"The only document I think could possibly help," Robin said, "is an old military diary we have. It was drawn up some time back in the fifteenth century by an historian who apparently stumbled on some original records and wanted to summarize them before they rotted. We keep it locked under glass in the next room with a number of other artifacts. I'm afraid it shows only page after page of dates and notations. We're quite proud of anything dating back prior to the fifteenth century, of course, but it probably won't help you much if you're looking for first century documents."

"Miss Dunstan," Gordon replied, "do you happen to know whether or not those original records you referred to might be locatable somewhere?"

"No, they're most likely gone forever. Our little museum was lucky to come by that diary. I'll unlock the case and you're welcome to review it. I'll ask only that you wear these cotton gloves and be extremely careful turning the pages…they're quite fragile."

The document looked more like a road atlas and was bound between two badly preserved leather covers. Gordon's first comment was that the diary should never have been allowed to remain so long without proper treatment. Nigel's whispered response about incompetence on the part of the curator didn't sit well with Peter. He sprang to her defense with a few remarks of his own, observing that the document had deteriorated long before Robin had become its custodian.

Approximately one hundred twenty yellowed pages contained, as Robin had said, a chronology of handwritten dates and places, supported by the author's notations. The document consisted of its author's summary of Legion XX's bloody victory over what appeared to be fierce

Celtic opposition in the area. Gordon noted a complicating factor in that the pages covered not one, but two, separate battles, years apart, plus some seemingly irrelevant history of the town.

In an effort to save time, Nigel and Gordon decided to work back-to-front, focusing on the battle notations only and ignoring everything else. They based the strategy on the assumption that the most recent notations would likely be the best source of data about items left behind by the soldiers. After two hours of tedious investment, which produced nothing of any relevance, Peter finally suggested they go back and review the notations relating to the history of the town, to which Nigel reluctantly agreed.

Fifteen minutes later, Gordon's shout confirmed the wisdom of the decision. "Tally ho, boys!" he cried out with unconcealed excitement. "Take a look at this."

Peter squinted as he ran his finger over the notation. "All I can see is a scribbling that looks like the word debris or something."

"Read on," Gordon urged.

"Okay, I see it now," Nigel acknowledged. "It looks like the word book or books."

"No, it's actually the word booty, or spoils of war," Gordon corrected him. "And if I'm reading this right, it looks like the booty was distributed mostly to the inhabitants of the town and the rest to a church. Do you agree, Nigel?"

"I do. The bad news is there's no description of the booty. Although, what we're looking for might have been among the items given to that church."

"Yeah, but there's no description of what church it was," Peter lamented.

"Doesn't matter now, guys," Gordon said. "Whatever church it was is long gone. Since there are only two churches in this area, one of them either has it as a hand-me-down or we're at the end of our road." He turned to stare at Peter, hunched over the manual. "Peter, what are you doing?"

"I'm taking a photograph of this page and a few others. Don't you guys believe in the power of documentation?" The telescopic lens protruded inconspicuously, while the little Sony clicked several times. A

70

six-hundred-year-old handwritten record of a two-thousand-year-old event found itself captured in a high-tech twenty-first century database.

Nigel grinned for one of the few times Peter could remember. "Well, well, a camera. Not bad for a Yank who couldn't remember to bring an umbrella to London. Okay, I suggest we start with the smaller of these two churches. Agreed?"

Heads nodded, and they thanked Miss Dunstan on their way out. Peter threw one longing glance over his shoulder while Nigel, taking his turn at the wheel, pointed the Mercedes toward the spot on the map marked by Gordon's penciled circle.

Their enthusiasm didn't last long. They found the little stone church in an advanced stage of deterioration, boarded up and obviously long since abandoned after what appeared to have been a fire. The acrid aroma of burned wood still assaulted their nostrils.

Gordon pinched his nose. "Phew. I wonder how old this thing is and what it could tell us if we had access to its records."

Nigel ran his hand gently over one of the cornerstones. "Well, my guess is that it's only three to four centuries old. Therefore, the real question is what could its predecessors tell us?"

They stared at it in sullen silence.

Peter finally broke the hush. "Looks like one down and one to go. This is becoming a trail of empty sites."

Gordon nodded. "Righto. I'd say this congregation went looking for greener pastors." Nigel's wry grin signified at least a superficial appreciation of the humor, while Peter's frown conveyed his disapproval.

"Sorry about that, old boy," Gordon said. "No offense intended."

Peter shook his head. "That's all right. These things happen now and then to churches everywhere." He knew it had been an innocent pun, well enough intended. Still, it dredged up in his mind a sequence of flashbacks to the dwindling attendance he'd been experiencing at his own sermons. He'd not been oblivious to the fact that the customary six-hundred-level attendance at the large Middletown Presbyterian Church curiously dropped to four hundred or less whenever he appeared as a pulpit fill-in during the regular pastor's absence.

Peter remembered passing off the observation as coincidental the first few Sundays. Then, as the attendance gaps continued to grow, the ghosts of empty pews came as an unspoken rejection of him as a worship leader. Gordon's untimely humor only made it more difficult for him to expunge unwelcome memories.

Nigel sighed. "Well, let's not waste any more time crying over spilt milk. We need to move on to the other church and hope for better results. It's larger, been there not quite as long, and my directions show it's only about five kilometers from here."

In stark contrast to the broken remains of the first one, the surviving church seemed to stand triumphant, as if savoring some kind of victory over the other. Almost twice the size of the burned-out building, this one's heavy grey stone construction, imposing cornices, and prominent belfry made it appear even larger. It looked old and Peter wondered how many thousands of sermons had been delivered within its walls during the last few centuries.

The thick door squeaked when the scruffy old caretaker opened it after they'd knocked for what seemed an interminable length of time. His scowl spoke out in silent discomfort at their presence. "No one's 'ere 'ceptin' me, guvnor. Ye come in the middle o' the week, an' as ye can see, I'm bloody busy," he growled, and moved to swing the heavy oak door closed in their faces.

"We understand, sir, and we certainly don't mean to intrude." Nigel spoke in a soothing tone and placed his foot strategically to prevent any further closure. "Perhaps we might talk to your pastor?"

"'E ain't 'ere. The vicar don't come in 'til Saturday. Now if ye'll let me be about me business, I got work to do."

Gordon shoved his large frame through the doorway, pushing the little caretaker aside. "Excuse me," he commanded. "I'm Dr. Coleridge, your vicar's superior from London. My associates and I were commissioned by the church to conduct a thorough review of the operations of this parish. In that capacity, I now officially instruct you to make available to us all the records of this establishment, while we make a full exploration of the premises. I want all rooms opened without further delay."

Appalled at the sudden, outrageous lie, Nigel and Peter stood speechless, watching the frightened caretaker grovel in apologetic servitude. He motioned them to follow him to the basement.

"Where in the bloody hell did you come up with that?" Nigel whispered as they traipsed after the contrite little man, whose bent-over posture suggested a severe case of osteoporosis. "Do you realize this is equivalent to breaking and entering, and quite possibly burglary?"

"Nigel, if you can think of a better way to search for clues to antiquity," Gordon said, "I'm ready to listen. In the meantime, I'll examine the records while you and Pete search the rooms for any relevant archives that might turn up something. Keep in mind that this is our last possible battle site, and if we come up empty here, our venture is over."

Nigel frowned. "Very well, but there's going to be one enraged vicar when he learns what we've done. I wouldn't be surprised if we had the Church of England down on us before this is finished."

"Not to mention Scotland Yard and the distinct possibility of our doing some jail time," Peter added.

Peter looked around and saw a vibrant church, as alive as the other was dead. Outreach activities were evident everywhere. Committee meetings and their typed results were posted in the narthex. Hymnals, Bibles, and an array of religious stories lay marked with bookmarks left by their most recent readers. Arts and crafts, in different stages of completion, cluttered the tables. Corkboards, mounted on almost every unused wall surface, became art galleries displaying the works of children from Pre-K to Primary. As to what they were looking for, however, their three-hour search of the premises turned out to be as unproductive as Gordon's futile review of the church records.

"Okay, I've one last idea before we move on," Peter offered up as the three frustrated travelers and one still-trembling caretaker gathered in the narthex.

"Well, on behalf of our superiors in London, the rest of this delegation would be pleased to hear it," Nigel responded, as though he recognized the need to maintain the appearance of a legitimate investigation.

"Ah...yes. Well, given the importance of this audit to our London office," Peter continued, "it's imperative that we examine the premises of the other church, regardless of its cordoned-off condition. Of course, our warrant contains authorization to remove the barriers to entry. After we're through, we'll leave a copy of it with the caretaker here."

"Ye'll find nothin' there, gentlemen," the hunched-over little man snapped. "It's been empty for some time now. An' good riddance to it, I say. It took 'em long enough to get rid o' them heathens."

"What do you mean heathens?" Peter asked.

"Them as worship the devil is what I mean. An' I ain't sayin' no more. I done said me piece."

"Well then, we'll be on our way, and we thank you for your help," Gordon said. The caretaker's scowl made it clear he didn't want them to open the other church, but his silence offered an unspoken acknowledgement that there was nothing he could do to stop them.

\* \* \* \* \*

The pervasive odor of old smoke and burned wood filled their nostrils again, even before they entered the sanctuary. Gordon removed the boards and barriers that sealed the empty little church. Nigel commented on the strange absence of any property condemnation signs or other postings warning against trespassing. It was as though the building was socially quarantined by some popular consensus that didn't need an explanation.

Gordon scanned the interior. "Look at this mess. If that outer structure hadn't been made of stone, it too would likely have burned to a crisp. We're going to have to crawl over blackened rafters and oak beams."

Nigel and Peter shook their heads and made their way through the sooty remains of a recent fire. Nigel grimaced each time he tried to sweep off the soot accumulating on his perfectly tailored suit. Rows of sturdy wooden pews, without cushions or any other items conducive to comfort, stood scarred but defiantly firm in their upright positions. The remains of a pulpit lay crumpled in its final death struggle beneath a charred wooden Celtic cross, which had fallen when the beam from which it was mounted collapsed.

"Good grief." Nigel's voice echoed through the narthex. "Wouldn't you think someone could have stopped the blaze before it gutted the place?"

After a long pause, Gordon muttered, "I'm not so sure anyone intended to stop it." He ran his hand along the wall and then the floor.

"I'm no expert on fires, but I had to take a course on the subject for a job I had a long time ago. I know just enough to be dangerous. Judging from the way it appears that those flames spread, I'm almost certain this fire was no accident."

Peter looked disgusted. "Why in the name of the Lord would anyone want to burn down a church?"

"Well, whatever the reason, I doubt it was done in the name of the Lord," Gordon responded. "It looks like the basement is where it started. Come on, let's take a look. Help me move that hatch covering the entrance. It looks like it weighs a ton." He grabbed one end while Nigel and Peter reached down for the other. Despite Gordon's size, strength, and the strained efforts of his companions, they could only manage to drag the bulky thing far enough to unblock the entrance.

"Careful," Gordon warned, "the stairs are stone, but they're cluttered with junk. Watch your step and stay close behind me. I've only the one torch that was in the car, so step where I step and do it slowly."

Peter frowned. "Torch?"

"Flashlight, for you Yanks."

The almost vertical stairway led to a hardened-mud floor cluttered with debris and several precariously hanging beams that made exploration both difficult and dangerous.

"Gordon, I'm not well acquainted with church construction in England," Peter ventured as he kicked loose debris aside, "but isn't it unusual to erect a building so precisely and then leave a dirt floor?"

"Normally yes, but if you'll look over here I think you'll find the reason. You can see there's been a lot of digging going on. They've filled it all back in, but some heavy excavation has taken place. It's almost like a deep well, and I don't think the digging's been recent. Apparently someone buried something with the intent that it never be exhumed."

"Guys," Nigel interrupted their focus, "I think I've discovered what the old caretaker meant about the heathens. Take a look at the inscription carved on what's left of this fallen beam. I'll rub a little more black ash off, and you can see it more clearly. It was apparently carved in the beam a long time ago. Correct me if I'm wrong, but it looks like it reads 'In Alignment With The All, We Stand In Partnership With Humanity, Spirit and Matter.' Anybody understand it?"

"Yes," Peter replied. He slid his hand along the inscription. "It's a Druidic expression. This congregation was apparently practicing some form of Druidism. That's incredible in this day and age."

Gordon put up his hand. "How about clarifying that a little."

"Well, I did some extensive research on Druidism for a paper I wrote when I was studying at Oxford. You guys may not believe this, but if Druidism hadn't been practiced here centuries ago, we wouldn't be searching for that Roman centurion's Bible now."

Gordon frowned. "What are you talking about?"

"Okay, look. This ancient practice dates back to the time of Abraham. The remarkable thing about it is, when Druidism appeared here, it became so entrenched it kept the ancient Britons from lapsing into polytheism. In a way, it became the precursor to Christianity in this part of the world because it reflected the essence of a supreme being. This figure presented himself as a trinity named Beli, Taran and Esu…or Yesu, as the Britons called it."

Nigel swept more soot from his jacket with one hand and smoothed his moustache with the other in a nervous-looking gesture. "I think I'm almost following you, but I still don't quite get it."

Peter paused and closed his eyes as if to consider a better way to explain a far-fetched concept. "All right, think of it this way. Their trinity was looked upon as creator of the past, savior of the present, and re-creator of the future. Thus the Britons never adopted paganism, but rather always worshipped one God. That Celtic cross we saw in the sanctuary…it was also a Celtic Druid symbol. In fact, the non-violent conversion of pagans in Ireland was made possible largely through the use of symbols like that cross the pagan Druids had long held sacred."

Gordon scratched his head. "And so?"

"Sooo, Druidism might conceivably have been a forerunner of Christianity. Moreover, without it, the Britons, who we're hoping preserved something of Paul's documents—or the centurion's—would never have bothered to salvage them had they not practiced the kind of worship reflected in The Bible. Thus, we wouldn't be here looking for remnants."

Nigel's frown turned into a mild grin. "By George, Peter, I can only say this theory of yours requires one jolly good stretch of the imagination!"

"True," Gordon said. "Then again, this entire exercise of ours requires the same stretch."

"Very well, then how does all that make these people heathens?" Nigel asked. "It looks to me like nothing more than a slightly different form of Christianity."

"Well, not quite," Peter said. "You see, Christianity assumes that all creatures are subordinate to God and that only humans have divine purpose. Druidism assumes that all creatures—all forms of matter—are spiritually equal in partnership with the supreme being and are not subservient to him. And thus, the Druids would argue that conventional Christianity not only unjustly sacrifices our own individual purpose, but denies responsibility for it by placing it in the hands of an abstract being."

"So what are we really looking at here?" Nigel laid the question directly before them. "Is this simply an isolated local feud that ended Christians one and Druids nothing, or are we on to something?"

"I'm afraid it's more than that," Peter said. He pulled out his camera to record the beam's charred inscription.

With their attention focused on the photo session, they failed to detect the movements of the four large men above them. Even as the dark figures lifted the huge oak hatch cover and positioned it directly over the basement entrance, there was no sound. The men eased the hatch into place so precisely that it formed a seal to prevent the passage of air into the basement. They pounded a few nails into place and were gone before their three prisoners below realized what was happening.

Gordon was the first to hear the hammering. "Hold it. Someone's up there doing something to our hatch." He raced up the stairway and heaved his considerable frame against the underside of the hatch in a futile effort to budge it. "Damn it. I can't hit it hard enough to loosen it. Someone's nailed the lid shut on our only exit." He'd broken into a sweat and some hard breathing after three lunges.

Nigel's face turned ashen. "Gordon, I think we're wasting our time on it. That hatch must have been as heavy as a truck, and now it looks like it's sealed us in for good. Someone's planned on our running out of oxygen down here, and if we don't find another way out, the plan's going to succeed."

"Well, we'd better find it pretty darn soon, because our flashlight battery's not going to last forever, and neither is our air," Peter said.

77

"And I'm afraid my cell phone's not working because of the interference of these thick walls," Nigel added, as he jammed the failed instrument back into his pocket.

"Right now, I'll welcome any suggestions," Gordon said, slamming his fist into the unyielding hatch in a gesture of frustration.

Peter picked up a long iron pipe that looked like it had once been part of the plumbing system. "This is a long shot, but if we can locate the weakest part of the church floor above us, maybe we can punch a hole in it. It won't get us out, but it'll let air in."

"Very well, do it back and forth across the ceiling, and see if you can hear a hollow sound, or some sign of structural weakness," Gordon advised. Nigel nodded.

While Peter slammed the pipe, Nigel made an effort to take shallower breaths. He alternately wrung his hands and fidgeted with his moustache. Gordon paced back and forth, his eyes scanning the walls of their subterranean mausoleum for some sign of structural weakness. They took turns jamming the iron pole back and forth into the wooden ceiling in six-inch increments.

"Does anyone have any idea how long we can last down here?" Peter asked, his voice betraying his growing apprehension. "I'm sure you realize the more effort we exert, the faster our oxygen supply diminishes."

Gordon cocked his head in contemplation. "Well, with three people in approximately sixty-four hundred cubic feet of space, I'm guessing somewhere between twelve and seventeen hours."

Nigel stopped his fidgeting and turned to Gordon. "You've already figured that out?"

"No. I said I'm guessing. I've done this kind of calculation a number of times before, but only with a rather complex mathematical formula in front of me. Without being able to remember the formula, I can only guess, based on all the times I've done it before in a mining job I once had. I think my guess is pretty accurate."

"What if we keep shouting?" Nigel asked. "Think anyone will hear us?"

"Not bloody likely, and we'll only burn up our oxygen faster," Gordon replied in a tone of dejection that summed up their state of mounting despair. He turned to see Peter down on his hands and knees in a corner. "Peter, you look like you're praying. Divine intervention wouldn't hurt, but I think we're going to need more than prayer here. I suggest you come on out of that corner and take your turn again with the pole."

"I'm not praying. Come over here. The flashlight is dimming, and I stepped on an indentation in this mud floor. Give me a hand with this dirt. It may be our way out of here."

After a few minutes of scraping and scooping, Gordon stood and shook his head. "Forget it. I agree there's something down there, but the dirt's too deep and too hard. We're wasting valuable time. We need to be going up, not down, anyway. Let's get back to the pole-jamming."

What remained of the little flashlight's muted glow had begun to flicker its way out when Gordon's pole-prodding suddenly produced a small outpouring of dirt and wood chips. Two perfectly shaped little rectangular blocks of wood dropped squarely on his head. He stopped to brush the grime out of his hair and check for more evidence of structural weakness. Peter lunged for the charred little wooden blocks, as though he was anxious to find out, before the light completely expired, why two neatly formed objects could have been there in the first place.

"Hey you guys, I think these have some kind of writing on them." Peter's voice reflected a mixture of curiosity about the blocks and mild encouragement at the discovery of an apparent weak spot in their underground prison.

"Forget the damned blocks, and let's keep punching away on that spot," Gordon shouted.

Two more hours of exhausting labor produced a foot-wide hole which admitted sunlight, oxygen, and one more of the little blocks, which Peter stuffed into his pocket. With more furious prodding and pounding, the hole grew wider. Dirt, dust, pieces of charred flooring, and a few more of the mysterious blocks tumbled down on them during the next hour-and-a-half of their sweaty labors. After another two hours, the hole became an exit, and they wriggled their way up into the blackened sanctuary.

They wasted no time clambering out of the charred debris into the churchyard where they paused to soak up the late afternoon sun and take a deep breath with a renewed sense of appreciation. They stopped to conduct a brief examination of the workmanship performed on the basement hatch. They agreed it was impossible to make any meaningful diagnosis, other than their consensus that some determined people wanted their mission discontinued.

"My first choice for someone to blame would be that damned caretaker," Gordon snarled. "I'd like to return and pay him back right now."

"Forget it," Nigel said. "That would be like attacking the person whose house you just robbed for calling the constables. We don't need to publicize our little felony at that church."

"Well then, I think we need another visit to that nice lady at the museum," Gordon said with a grin. "I think Peter should go, since he's the expert on Druidism, don't you?"

Nigel laughed. "Absolutely. Especially since he was obviously smitten."

"Look, I think he's starting to blush a bit," Gordon said. "Perhaps she can tell him more about this church and those puzzling little blocks. I mean, after they've established a warm relationship, of course." They grinned at Peter's rising level of discomfort.

"All right, you guys, knock it off. I'm actually more interested in asking if she knows anything about that indentation in the floor. And why someone was so anxious to bury us there. We need to know more about everything that happened in that church. You can stop grinning any time now."

They poked around for a while longer for more of the blocks before they left, then rented a separate car for Peter to go courting. Nigel dusted off his jacket, gave his shoes a quick wipe with one hand, and his moustache a tug with the other. He shook his head and expressed his concern that their masquerade was probably no longer a secret.

\* \* \* \* \*

"I'm glad you came back, Peter." Robin said. She smiled in the same seductive way that attracted his attention in the first place. "Did you find what you were looking for?"

Peter knew the art of endearing responses had never been part of his DNA. On the other hand, he wasn't completely lacking in romantic feelings. He recognized the opportunity for some clever repartee such as,

"Yes, I found it the first time we met." As soon as the thought crossed his mind, he dismissed it as trite, and therefore an unbecoming way to begin a serious relationship. Nor did he feel this was the right time to discuss their near suffocation experience.

"Ah...yes and no," Peter said. "I mean, we've discovered that the boarded-up church represented a Druidic congregation. We hoped you could give us a little more information about its history and how the fire started." He could have kicked himself. Nice going, dummy, you just blew a perfect opportunity. Let's have a little more suave the next time.

"Sure, I have the clipping here in the drawer. It happened almost a year ago, and ever since then, some archaeology group from Scotland has been trying to buy the land the church sits on. It's kind of been the talk of the town, but so far nothing's happened."

"Why did they want to buy it?" Peter asked, trying not to sound anxious.

"They never said. Or at least they never made it known to anyone other than the local authorities. Here's the clipping. I kept it on the chance that some legitimate archaeological exploration might take place there. I'm not holding my breath. May I get you a cup of coffee? I'd normally say tea, but I've learned that most Americans don't enjoy tea as we do."

His missed opportunity had, thankfully, resurrected itself. A slight distortion of the truth would now be necessary in order to capitalize on it. "Tea would be fine, Robin. I've never been a coffee drinker. We don't get good English tea very often back in the states." He kept his head down while he said it, not so much to read the clipping, but more to prevent eye contact that might betray the lie.

Peter found the article typically newspaperish in both content and format, until one of the author's observations toward the end caught his attention. It was a casual and unsubstantiated speculation that an ancient Roman armory was rumored to lay a dozen or so meters beneath the church. Peter's thoughts raced to connect the past events with the rumor. An armory would explain the Scottish interest in the property, as well as the "booty" reference in the fifteenth century battle-log his team had reviewed.

"Robin, would you make me a photocopy of this article, please?" He could hardly contain his enthusiasm.

81

"Certainly. You look rather excited. Was there something in the article that would help your search?"

"There might be. If you'd have dinner with me, I'd like to ask you more about it. I mean…what I mean to say is, the article is of great importance to our search, but having dinner with you is most important to me."

Robin smiled then glanced away as if to hide her pleasure. "I understand. And yes, I'd love to. I know a delightful little restaurant that serves great English stew and the best tea in Chester. Have you rented a different car?"

"Yes. Gordon and Nigel needed the other to get around and find a hotel for us tonight. May I pick you up at six?"

Her seductive smile appeared again as she nodded, and he knew that waiting until six o'clock would be difficult.

* * * * *

The little restaurant turned out to be more like a pub than a restaurant, with only a few customers. A young couple locked in an amorous embrace sequestered themselves away in a corner. An elderly man hid behind his newspaper with wisps of smoke from his pipe wafting up from his sanctuary. The shepherd's pie meal was everything Robin said it would be, and Peter managed to hold back his questions until they finished their ale and the plum pudding dessert.

"Robin, I need to know whatever you can tell me about the fire in that church. It wasn't an accident, was it?"

"No. There was hostility all over town about the kind of worship going on there. Like many of the folks here, I never attended services there because of the ugly rumors going around. Finally, angry townspeople took matters into their own hands, although no one knows exactly who lit the fire. As to the little blocks you found, I have no idea what they were about. I never attended any of the Sunday services there. Did you say the blocks had biblical verses inscribed on them?"

Peter waited until the waiter had delivered two more mugs of dark, Irish ale and had walked away. "Yes. I only found a few of them. The inscriptions were in Latin, and I translated them. The sentences weren't complete because of the fire damage, so I couldn't draw any meaningful interpretations. I'm bothered most, though, by the newspaper article's reference to a Roman armory under that church. Do you know anything about that?"

"Not really. They say the basement is basically mud with reinforced walls and ceiling. Although I've never seen it, I suppose it could have been an underground storage facility for almost anything. Maybe that's what the Scottish delegation was after."

They raised their mugs in a toast to the future success of Peter's mission. Peter turned the conversation toward Robin and her family history. Through the ale and laughter, he discovered they had far more in common than he'd anticipated. Her father had even been a pastor himself for many years before he died.

Halfway through the second mug, Peter decided to skip the usual formalities and launch directly into a subject which, he feared, could either cement or obliterate their still-embryonic relationship. "Robin, if you don't mind sharing this with me, I'd like to know just how your father delivered his sermons. Well…, I mean I've been experiencing some…ah…difficulty connecting with my own congregation. As you can see, I'm having trouble articulating this. What I mean to say is I'm always looking for better ways to—"

"Never mind," Robin said with a comforting smile, "I think I know what you're trying to say. Dad had the same problem his first few years. His parishioners were falling asleep during his services, and he couldn't figure out what to do. Worse than that, they were leaving his church one by one."

Peter slapped the tabletop with his hand. "Yes, exactly. So, what did he do?" The words came out before he could stop them. He knew right away that he'd allowed his frustrations to force out the beginning of a confession before he could collect himself and abort it. His uncontrolled display of excitement had turned into a non-retractable blunder, and he felt embarrassed.

"Nothing," Robin replied, apparently ignoring his embarrassment as though the emotional display had been logical. "The whole thing kind of turned around naturally. He took a trip to Africa, developed a new perspective on people, places, cultures, and on religion itself. When he returned, his sermons were much more interesting. Plus, he became more skilled at relating them to the specific needs of his parishioners."

"Like how?"

"Well, for example, he sent some of them on mission trips. I was really happy for him. I think he realized his sermons focused too intellectually on biblical passages and hadn't reached the hearts of his congregation. Scriptural interpretation is good, of course, but the way he had done it wasn't making his flock feel good about being his flock, if you know what I mean. You look kind of stunned, Peter. Is this sort of what's been happening to you?"

Peter turned away, unable to look at her for a few moments. He recoiled at the realization that he'd laid bare his failures to the one person he wanted most to impress. Now, thanks to his clumsiness, she saw him for what he was. The sinking feeling he'd so often experienced in the pulpit suddenly came back again. It wasn't the first time he'd begun to feel that the church might not be the right calling for him. Oh well, all was probably lost already on the romantic front. He might never see her again anyway, now. So, he might as well use the rest of the evening to solicit whatever her father had taught her about effective sermon presentations.

Peter pushed aside the third mug of ale the waiter delivered and leaned forward as though he was about to whisper his sins in the seclusion of a confessional. "Sorry to take so long to answer your question, but yes, this is what's been happening to me. How did your father make his presentations so much more interesting...if you don't mind?"

"It wasn't that he made them more interesting, Peter. It was that he suddenly became more interesting, with a much broader outlook on everything. I think sometimes a significant event in one's life does that. Do you know what I mean?"

He nodded after a thoughtful pause. "Yes..., I believe I do. I've always believed a pastor's role is to bring his parishioners closer to God. The Bible is their path to him. Any deviation from the Scriptures simply sets them off on the wrong path, and I still feel that way."

He stretched his arms out, palms up, in a gesture of exasperation. "Somehow I just can't bring myself to be a Sunday morning entertainer. I'd feel like a barker at a sideshow. I've always pictured a pastor who did that to be kind of like a used car salesman trying to peddle religion with nothing down and easy monthly payments. I'm reasonably certain

I'm here for a more meaningful purpose than that. There has to be some other way to make God's word meaningful to believers and skeptics alike."

"There is, Peter. Look, my father ultimately came to realize what his parishioners really needed was a rich blend of sermons that were relevant to their daily lives and meaningful enough to draw them into the church. My father provided that, together with religious and social activities fulfilling enough to keep them there."

"And how did that work out?"

"Quite well. My father's church grew, and the attrition rates dropped to less than one out of five. You can do it, Peter. I know you can."

The more they talked, the more Peter came to realize he was gradually falling in love with her. The conversation and laughter went on for several hours before he remembered that the next day would be a working one for Robin and a challenging one for him and his colleagues.

He caught the waiter's attention, tossed down a third of the last ale, and paid the bill. "Look, it's late and we should be going. Robin, I hope you've enjoyed our evening as much as I have. I'll take you home and then rejoin my colleagues…assuming I can find where they're staying. I can't begin to tell you how much I appreciate all you've told me about your dad. He must have been quite a guy. I would have liked to have met him."

They'd walked halfway to the car when Robin stopped him and spoke with a directness that caught him off guard. "Peter, I'd like it very much if you'd stay at my house tonight. That way you wouldn't have to search for the motel in the dark. Besides, there's so much I want to share, now that I've found a wonderful person to share it with. I'm really glad we've met. And, by the way, my dad would have liked you very much."

She reached up, pulled Peter toward her, and kissed him. The sudden sense of warmth he felt came like an explosion that, somehow, made up for all the years he'd given up romance for his church work. He'd once before refused an invitation to spend the night with an attractive woman because of his ministerial obligations. There were no such encumbrances this time, and at that moment, Dr. Peter Clemens didn't care whether or not he and his two colleagues ever sorted out the mystery they were chasing. In fact, he really didn't care about much of anything except the possibility of spending the rest of his life with this perfect woman. His colleagues could wait.

\* \* \* \* \*

They slept in separate rooms after Robin's firm pronouncement that she didn't do one-night stands. Peter awoke to find a hot cup of coffee and a muffin on the nightstand beside the bed, along with a note clearly indicating that she'd seen right through his scam about preferring tea. Although he knew very little about her by all objective standards, Peter was now certain he and Robin could be companions at every level: serious confidantes, playmates, lovers, comrades, adventurers.

He wasn't sure how or why his circumstances had suddenly changed so favorably. He suspected, somehow, his creator must have had a hand in it. By the time he'd dressed and begun to drive around the town to find Gordon and Nigel, he remembered he'd left his cell phone off. He turned the dormant instrument on to find the first of two messages poking fun about preachers led astray by pretty young women.

The second one struck him hard enough that he had to pull over and stop the car by the side of the road. Nigel's frightening summary of the attempted theft of the scanning data and equipment from MOLAS in London brought him sharply back to reality. It conjured up a sobering thought that their mission must be a threat to someone and raised the bar on the significance of their search. When he finally found his colleagues eating breakfast at Morley's Pub, it was Nigel who spoke first, without making any effort to conceal a wry grin.

"Well, Peter, we don't know which topic should come first…the dreadful news about what happened in London, or the shady account of your un-preacher-like adventures last night."

Gordon grinned. "Yes, old chap, we've come to a choice between two possible explanations. One, you're a very slow listener, so it took you all night to digest what that delightful woman had to say about the fire. Or two, you never discussed the fire at all, but shared a bed with her and had a marvelous time, as is suggested by the healthy color in your cheeks."

Peter didn't even try to stifle a smile. "Guys, in truth, you're half right. I had an exquisite time with Robin. We also discussed the fire and

86

this newspaper clipping which, if you'll note the passage I underlined, will throw a new light on our mission." He handed Nigel the article. "And by the way, she also invited me to give the sermon as a guest speaker at her church the next time I happen to be in town. Of course, that will be as soon as possible. Now, are you at all impressed by that invitation?"

Nigel and Gordon exchanged glances, each seemingly waiting for the other to render a verdict. Gordon volunteered. "Well, she couldn't very well ask you to take confession after last night, now could she?"

"That's right," Nigel said, to continue the harassment. "We presume she's expecting a sermon on repentance or maybe something about the wages of carnal sin."

Unabashed, Peter grinned. He welcomed the jibes as a tribute to what he was sure was his first step toward becoming a more interesting person. He pulled up a chair and waited for their reaction to the clipping while he ordered a cup of tea, as if to rectify, at least partially, the lie he had told Robin.

Gordon leaned back in his chair, folded his hands around the back of his head, and turned to make sure he had their attention. "All right," he began after a long pause, "bear with me while I try to connect the dots on this one. First, we uncover the remains of a Roman soldier. Then we find a yet-to-be-fully translated letter from his father, stating that the Apostle Paul gave the father an original version of what we all presume must have been the New Testament. Indications, also not yet verified, are that it differs from the version currently in existence. Still, we don't find this original version."

The waiter approached and Peter held up his hand to stop the dialogue until the man had delivered the tea and left.

"Later, I get a text message from Courtney that he's found a frazzled old priest who claims he actually saw the remains of the original version, which the priest claims had been altered. Next, we discover a fifteenth-century rewrite of a battle log. The contents of it open the possibility that the original Bible, allegedly given to the centurion by Paul, might have been lost by the centurion's son, during a battle here in Chester. As if that's not enough, we learn our people in London fought off an attempt to steal the centurion's letter as well as the scanning equipment containing all the data."

"Do we know any more about that than we did before?" Nigel asked, as he smoothed his moustache.

Gordon shook his head. "No. I'm assuming everything's still secure there. Anyway, as of this morning, it seems we have an old newspaper clipping speculating that an ancient Roman armory exists beneath a burned down Druid church. So—and this is a real stretch—could the ancestors of those Druid worshippers have dug down under the church and found, in that armory, the original version of The Bible, exactly where that battle log implied it might be? And, if they were conducting their worship services from this forbidden Bible, could that be why the townspeople sacked their church and kicked them out? That having been said, what's your take on it Nigel?"

"I'd say it bloody well leaves us on the brink of a discovery that just might shake up the whole damned world. I won't deny I was skeptical about this blasphemous exercise when we first began. Its premise seemed too bizarre to be credible. Nonetheless, there have since been enough mutually supporting events to preclude mere coincidence as an explanation. I think the final dot in our sequence would be some defensible finding that might relate what's happened here in Chester to this Bible we're trying to find."

"Can we convince MOLAS to do some excavating under the church to see if there actually is a Roman storage there?" Peter asked. He looked directly at Nigel, the one person in England he knew to be best qualified to answer the question.

Nigel nodded. "We could, but it would take so long to get through the Treasures Act and the local ordinances that it wouldn't be feasible. It would be especially difficult in our case, because we have nothing more than a highly speculative editorial in support of the existence of any real artifacts. The authorizing agencies look for some kind of historical documentation before they allow anyone to finance the digging of large holes in the ground. That's probably what has kept that Scottish enterprise out of Chester."

"Okay, then," Peter persisted, "why don't we interview some of those Druid people and see if they can shed some light on this whole mystery. I'll bet Robin could round up a few of them for us. She knows the town. I'm guessing the ancestors of these people must have handed down a legend or two that might be helpful."

Gordon and Nigel looked at each other without saying a word. Peter surmised their long silence suggested the idea might have some merit.

"By Jove, I believe our itinerant pastor may have hit on something," Nigel exclaimed, nodding vigorously, "although I never imagined we'd have to interview Druids."

"Fair enough," Gordon said. "Then let's get to it, and we'll all visit that nice lady at the museum."

\* \* \* \* \*

Miriam McDarren welcomed them with a handshake and a warm smile. Peter found the gesture surprising. He'd assumed that none of the evicted members of the Druid congregation could possibly regard outsiders kindly after what had happened to them. With a wave of an arthritic hand, she motioned them to follow her in as she awkwardly shuffled behind a walker toward her parlor, so modestly furnished it looked like the decorator might have been the same one who did the MOLAS conference room.

The well-worn carpet and threadbare furniture coverings clashed with an outdated wallpaper design vigorously enough that one could describe the relationship as adversarial. Tightly drawn window curtains, stylish during the 1930s, conspired to keep sunlight out and a musty odor in. Apparently sensing her visitors' discomfort with the darkness, Miriam moved to open the curtains. Daylight flooded the room for what Peter surmised must have been the first time in years.

Despite her limited mobility, Miriam managed to serve them tea and biscuits with such grace and affection that none of them seemed ready to initiate an interview that might offend her. As it turned out, Miriam launched into the discussion herself.

"Robin called and told me you were looking for some information about our church. I would have refused your request for an interview except that she helped me once when no one else would. I felt it was time to return the favor." With barely noticeable difficulty, as though she'd trained herself to conceal all but a faint trace of her arthritic pain, she settled into a now-extinct kind of armchair.

"Thank you, ma'am," Peter answered, deciding that his knowledge of Druidism would support his self-appointment as the lead person in such a dialogue. "We need to know the history of your church. And, if I might add, we are truly sorry and appalled about what happened." He sampled the biscuit and washed it down with a sip of tea.

"Yes," Gordon added, "we were curious about a number of things, particularly why it happened and what might lie beneath the church. We noticed some excavation had already taken place there."

Nigel inhaled the aroma emanating from the hot tea, took a sip, and smiled, as if to offer a silent announcement of his official approval as an authority on the subject. "We'd be particularly interested in what you could tell us about the basis of your worship," he said, returning the cup to the center of the table next to his chair. He took a few seconds to rearrange the positions of the teapot and the cream and sugar containers on the serving tray. Symmetry having been achieved, Nigel stroked his moustache and turned back to Miriam. "I mean the documents from which your worship services drew their content. Were they salvaged from the fire?"

Miriam offered a warm smile. "You certainly have a lot of questions. Then again, it seems your generation always does. As Robin must have told you, I'm eighty-nine years old. I suppose that makes me what you people would call the town matriarch. You might as well know that most of what I can tell you is not really written anywhere. Our faith is based mostly on teachings handed down to us by our ancestors who, in turn, were taught by their ancestors, and so on. As I'm sure Robin must have told you, our sanctuary was destroyed out of ignorance, not because of anything we did wrong. In fact, services were conducted in our little church for over 200 years with very few incidents. Then one day, for no apparent reason, Vicar Chelmsridge decided we were some kind of threat to Christianity and incited the townspeople to drive us out. Well, he—"

"Excuse me, Miriam," Nigel said, stroking his moustache. "Would that be the pastor of the other church just down the road?"

"Yes, and as I was about to say, he's not going to succeed. We're here to stay, and we plan to rebuild as soon as we can get some decent local legislation passed."

Peter leaned forward closer to her. "Miriam, these worship documents you said don't exist anymore—what were they, and where did they come from?"

"Oh, I can assure you they existed at one time. It's just that our ancestors knew full well, the moment they uncovered it, that our Holy Writ was an ancient document. They knew it told the true story of Jesus, not the one the Roman Catholic Church wanted everyone to read."

She shifted uneasily in her chair. "Our ancestors also knew it would be unpopular and subject to loss, destruction, or outright theft. So they transcribed it, one verse at a time, onto little wooden blocks which they inserted into the beams, floors, side walls, and into various crevices in the church. Of course, the writing was on the inside of each block, with the blank side outward. The blocks were removable with a specially constructed metal wedge, and only the Guide had access to it. Each successive Guide—we called them pastors so as not to raise suspicion of any kind—would be the only one who knew the exact location of each verse."

"Miriam, was there any written backup for the blocks?" Peter asked.

"No, the Guide would conduct our worship services based upon a sort of legendary recollection of the original Holy Writ which our ancestors destroyed right after the Scriptures were transcribed onto the blocks. He always had recourse to the wooden transcriptions if he needed a specific reference. Of course, no one ever anticipated that our little church would become the victim of interdenominational arson."

Gordon followed Peter's lead and leaned in closer to her. "Where did this Holy Writ come from?" he asked. "Weren't the transcription blocks Peter found part of the original set?"

Peter showed her the ones he'd stuffed into his pockets.

"Yes, most of them were burned beyond recognition, but we saved a few. I'm glad you found a few more. The Holy Writ was unearthed some two hundred years ago by a mining crew digging for copper and lead. They dug up a basketful of Roman army artifacts and things from under what is now our church, and then left after the mine panned out."

"Was the writ an original?" Gordon asked.

The old woman drew a deep breath, with an audible wheeze. "No. Legend has it that a monastery was built over a Roman armory sometime in the fourth century. During construction, a monk found the writ and copied it. What a holy document was doing in a Roman armory no one ever knew. Anyway, the monk was reprimanded and ordered to destroy both documents. He burned the original, but couldn't bring himself to

91

destroy the elegant work he'd done to produce the copy. He buried it with his signature on it. During subsequent centuries, the monks were driven out, and the monastery fell into ruin. Nothing happened after that until the miners came in and started digging."

"So the miners found the writ," Peter said. "Then, how did your ancestors end up with it?"

"Our ancestors recovered from the excavation what must have been a copy of the writ—at least that's what their handed-down writings said. They then built the church on top of the filled-in hole. The miners took the artifacts, but didn't see anything about the Holy Writ, or the other documents, that they could sell. So they just left them there…a testimony to ignorance and human greed for which, in this case, our congregation is thankful to this day."

"Was this in book form, Miriam?" Peter asked the question, not certain he wanted to hear the answer.

"Well, the copy was. I'm not certain about the original. No one is, although I'm sure our ancestors could have told you. My grandfather once told me it was also referred to as The New Covenant in earlier times, but we always knew it as the Holy Writ."

Gordon sprang out of his chair and knelt beside her, his eyes wide. "You used the term 'other documents.' What other documents, Miriam?"

"Oh, mostly records of food and supplies received. The only item worth keeping, I guess—aside from the writ—was that old military manual my great-grandfather was so fond of. He sequestered it away for fear we children would do even more damage to it."

Gordon leaned forward, as though he were about to kiss her knee. "Miriam, do you think we might possibly take a look at that manual and the wooden blocks that survived the fire?"

She nodded. "Well, I suppose so. I'll get them for you. We always knew where our great-grandfather hid the manual, but we never let on."

She worked her walker across the room, scuffing as she went. She reached behind a cabinet and retrieved the manual, together with a shoebox full of blocks. A moment before they would have slipped from her bony hands, Miriam placed them on the tray of her walker. "Our Guide was more or less driven out of town by the local authorities after the fire," she said, "but he entrusted the blocks to me as matriarch of the church. He didn't really trust anyone else, and I don't blame him. The other members of our congregation are aware of my meeting with the three of you, and they've given me authorization to do and say whatever I feel appropriate. I don't think they'd mind my showing you what few blocks remain after what's happened. Here, I'll refresh your tea while you examine them."

Miriam handed Gordon the manual, so worn and faded that Peter decided to concentrate on the blocks and let Gordon struggle with the contents of the mutilated document. She shuffled back and forth with the tea and biscuits. Then waited patiently for an hour-and-a-half, while Nigel and Peter huddled over thirty-five badly scorched blocks, studying each one intently before Peter photographed it. Their discussions were brief. Nigel deferred from time to time to Peter for authoritative interpretation.

The old woman leaned back in her recliner and dozed off and on for five or six minutes at a time. Her woolen stockings slid ungracefully down over the tops of her old-fashioned leather shoes. Over the years, Chester's cold, damp climate had taken its toll on her wrinkled skin, which now seemed to hang loose, revealing the weight loss that had occurred gradually since the fullness of her prime, years ago.

Childless and long since widowed, Miriam was not a pretty woman. The timeworn photograph of her on the cabinet under the clock offered convincing testimony that she never had been. Yet the warmth of her personality seemed to fill the room, and Peter couldn't help glancing at her now and then, regretting that she was not, nor ever would be, a member of his congregation. He made a mental note to preserve her in his sermons.

After he'd finished photographing the blocks, Peter turned to Nigel. "Well, the only line of verse that seemed any different from Scripture, as we know it in the current version of The Bible, was that one about the 'partnership with God'... as far as we can tell, right?"

"Agreed," Nigel responded. "What bothers me is the lack of any further explanation and, in fact, the absence of all the other verse-blocks. Miriam, how do you interpret the partnership reference? Have you ever compared this writ to any of the currently accepted versions of The Bible?"

Miriam shook her head and waved her hand in front of her face. "We never put much faith in The Bible that's been handed out over the centuries. Of course, I see nothing unusual about the reference you cited. We believe God wanted all creatures on earth to be in unity with him, without any ethnic, denominational, or hierarchical distinctions."

"Are you aware of any other copies of this document?" Peter asked

Miriam put her hand to her chin and tilted her head slightly to one side as she pondered the question. She responded slowly. "I don't think so. My grandfather once told me that his grandfather had told him the monk's copy was the only surviving one. I'm afraid that's about all I can tell you, gentlemen. It's getting late, and I have some things to do. Then my afternoon nap, which I'm sure you can appreciate in someone my age."

Peter smiled at her. "Of course, Mrs. McDarren. We understand. And we can't thank you enough for your kindness in bearing with us on this. Before we go, may I take a few snapshots of that manual?"

"Go ahead. Just treat it gently, it's very fragile."

Gordon handed it to Peter. "Photo the pages where I inserted pieces of paper to mark them," he said. "My Latin's not bad, but yours is probably better. Check and see if I've missed anything important. I find it hard to believe what's in this thing."

Peter shook his head and threw a quizzical glance at Gordon. "How did this document manage to survive so long?"

"It didn't. This one's a copy…done manually, of course. In fact, it's probably a copy of a copy."

"Why would anyone want to copy it?"

Gordon cocked his head while he thought for a moment. "My guess is that the writ was not the only document the sly old monk took pride in copying. Both probably came from the same place. You have to remember that transcription was a delicate craft in those days. Skilled transcribers took pride in their product. Preservation of their work was important."

Peter's camera clicked repeatedly over the manual's military narrative. It spoke of the high honor of defending Rome along with the requirements that a soldier must be of Roman citizenry and a certain height. Slaves, women, and eunuchs were barred from military service, and centurions were feared by their men. The manual went on to discuss the art of siege, warnings about barbarians outside the gates of the city, and the importance of a good fit for the soldier's helmet. The narrative stressed the importance of the organization and structure of the legions. The list went on.

Peter returned the document to Miriam and turned to face Gordon's broad grin. "What did you see that's critical, aside from the contents?" Gordon asked.

Peter thought for a moment. "Well, it clearly belonged to Legion XX, but I didn't see any proof that this was the manual that belonged to the centurion's son, if that's what you mean."

"True, but I hope you noticed that this document is in book form." He glared at Nigel.

Nigel threw his hands in the air. "All right, jolly good and hail Mary. I take back what I said. Damnation, if the Romans were smart enough to construct a city-wide plumbing system, then I suppose they could have developed some kind of papyrus good enough for book-binding. Or, maybe they could do more with calfskin vellum than I thought they could. Anyway, it was a copy, the original format of which will never be known. We'll let the photos be a MOLAS discovery by itself. Let's bid this delightful lady goodbye and be on our way."

Peter raised his hand. "Hold on a moment. I have one more question. Miriam, I'm curious about this spiritual leader you call a Guide. What exactly did he do each Sunday? I guess what I mean is, how did he hold his congregation's attention? You know, I mean keep them coming back each week?" He felt clumsy again and knew that she must have noticed it.

She laughed. "Well, Peter, there was never any question about their coming back. Full commitment was required. Our Guide always completed the triangle for them, and they looked forward to that every week."

Peter frowned. "I guess I'm not following you. When you say triangle, what do you mean?"

She smiled and reached out to touch his hand. "I mean that our Guide addressed the three corners of their existence. For example, he once used Jesus's parable of the prodigal son's departure from his father to explain Adam's departure when he fell from grace in the old book of the writ. Then our Guide completed the triangle by encouraging his congregation not to make the same mistake of wandering off on our own in our daily lives. Do you see what I mean?"

95

Peter nodded and smiled. "Yes, I believe I do. You're saying he brought the Old Testament together with the New Testament, and then both of them into the consciousness of his congregation in a way they could relate to their daily lives."

"That's exactly what he did, Peter. Except we don't use the terms Old and New Testament the way you do. I'm pleased you understand."

"Thank you, Miriam McDarren." Peter shook her hand. "We'll be on our way, and please accept our best wishes for the reestablishment of your church."

Gordon threw up his hand. "Whoa! Hold on a minute. We've come all this way to track a Roman soldier's possession that might change world history. We're finally talking to a lady whose church is sitting on top of a Roman armory where this thing might be, and you fellows want to simply walk away?" He turned to face their hostess. "Miriam, we need you to tell us where in this town we can find a contractor willing to help us dig down under there."

Peter shook his head. "Gordon, I don't think that's a good idea. Nigel already told us—"

"I said it was a legendary tale," Miriam snapped, with face drawn in a way they hadn't seen before. "There's no armory there."

Gordon spread his arms out, palms up. "Miriam, you just now referenced all those artifacts. There has to be—"

"There's nothing down there you would want, young man." Her lips tightened and her eyes narrowed. "It's a place best left as it is."

Gordon frowned. "I don't understand, Miriam. Right now there's no doubt in my mind that—"

"Forget it, Gordon." Nigel grabbed Gordon's arm, nudged him toward the door, and smiled at Miriam. "Thank you, Mrs. McDarren. We'll be on our way."

With a gentle assist from Peter, Nigel escorted a frowning Gordon out the door and waved a comforting goodbye to their hostess.

Nigel's question, as soon as they climbed into their car, didn't surprise anyone. "Gordon, what in bloody hell were you trying to do back there?" He fired up the engine and turned the car onto the road.

"I was trying to salvage this whole expedition, which was on the brink of a dead end until this piece of fabulous good fortune fell into our laps. I think we have a rewrite of two thousand years of erroneous theological history on our hands, here."

Nigel glared at him. "So, exactly what do you propose we do about it in a way that's legal?"

"I'm suggesting that we ignore the damned legal restrictions, go back into the basement of that church, dig further down, and find out what in the hell that old woman's trying to hide. This is too damned important for us to get bogged down in local ordinances. I don't think we'll have to drill down very far. Look, you two know as well as I do that this may be the only way we can substantiate what we all are convinced the centurion's letter will reveal. As you Yanks would say, Pete, let's not blow it now."

Peter threw Gordon a skeptical glance, which looked more like a reproachful frown. "Aren't you at all concerned about the destructive effect this damned thing would almost certainly have upon Christianity?"

Gordon grinned. "I'm an historian, Pete. If correction of an historical mistake of this magnitude happens to undermine the biblical concept of Providence and the hereafter, so be it."

Peter and Nigel shook their heads and looked at each other in silence.

"Oh, damn it," Nigel blurted out. "Let's do it. I think he may have a point."

Peter grinned. "Okay. I've never been in jail before. It'll be an experience. Hell, my congregation might just enjoy a pastor who's an ex-con."

Gordon grinned. "Peter, try to think of it as being in good company. Even our hero, the Apostle Paul, spent some time in the lockup."

Peter smiled back at Gordon. "Okay, we'll follow your lead."

# Chapter 6

## Deva (Chester)

Equipped with a rented BT-121 twenty-one pound portable auger hole digger and several shovels, Gordon and his two-man crew launched their assault on the soft dirt floor of Miriam's church. Out of his own pocket, Gordon paid the rental fee plus the commission required to compensate the rental outlet owner for hauling away the church's heavy trap door that had almost sealed their fate several days before.

Drenched in sweat by noon, the three took a fifteen-minute break. They leaned against the dirt wall, downed their fish and chips, and sated their thirst on iced coffee.

Peter mopped his brow and let out a despondent-sounding exhale. "Gordon, by my rough estimate we've managed to transplant at least fifty cubic feet of earth from all these holes we've dug and piled them up in a corner. I'm beginning to think Miriam might have been telling the truth about there being no Roman armory down here."

Gordon tossed down the last of his second cupful and grinned. "Hell, I never thought there would be. That old woman wasn't afraid we'd find an armory. She was terrified at the prospect that we'd uncover something much more sinister than Roman history."

"Like what?" Nigel snapped out with a shallow wheeze that sounded like he'd inhaled too much dust. "Are you suggesting another Druid lesson book?"

Gordon stuffed his empty cup and the uneaten half of his sandwich into his paper-carrying bag, stood, and paused before he answered. "I'm not sure. Whatever it was that she didn't want found, I have a feeling we're getting closer. It's down here somewhere. I can almost sense it.

Too many people in this church have gone to a lot of trouble to make sure it stays buried. Let's get back to work and crank that drill up again."

Six hours later, the fading afternoon sunlight threw enough deepening shadow over the open access hole to suggest the possibility that one day's digging might not be enough. Nigel reacted first. "Chaps, I hate to be the bearer of bad news, but we've spent a whole day accomplishing nothing. If we persist in this goose chase, we'll be doing it in the dark. And that's assuming that either no one's become alarmed by our noise or they've decided to leave us alone."

Peter tossed his shovel aside, wiped his bare chest with the shirt he'd tied around his waist, and took a deep breath. "Nigel, I'm with you, except that we've come this far, and I'm reluctant to give up just yet. We have lanterns. This may sound absurd, but I'm betting on Gordon's intuition. Let's take another break, polish off the rest of the iced coffee that doesn't have ice anymore, and push on. What do you say?"

Nigel threw his shovel into a pile of dirt and shook his head. "Rubbish. I'm thinking there's nothing worse than being incarcerated in a dark hole with a stubborn Scot and an over-zealous Yank. Very well, have it your way. I'm going to collapse on one of our dozen or so mounds of dirt and nurse my blistered hands for a while."

Gordon and Peter forced out tired grins. The coffee depleted, they took a breather and sipped from a large bottle of water before they went back to work in the deepening shadows of an advancing evening. They swapped off between drill and shovel in order to plunge deeper. Half an hour later, the hole showed signs of an unaccounted-for change in dirt coloration and texture. The drill droned on for another fifteen minutes until it ground to a thudding stop.

"Nigel, grab your shovel and get over here," Gordon shouted. "We've hit something."

The three men shoveled and scooped with furious abandon until they uncovered a large enough portion of what looked like an oversized coffin for Gordon to wedge a shovel under its lid.

"Light up one of those lanterns and give me a hand," Gordon snapped, sweat pouring from his face.

Their combined attempts to pry open the top produced only frustration and two broken shovels.

"All right, stop!" Gordon barked out. "This is getting us nowhere. Pete, fire up that drill again and let's try this another way. Nigel, I'm assuming this is a burial vault which I thought was made of wood. You're the historic expert on religious interments. What kind of material are we dealing with here?"

Nigel mopped his brow and wiped his hands on the only dry spot on his trousers. "Well, the only authoritative comment I can offer at this point is that we've apparently stumbled upon a Roman-built container of some sort. I'm thinking that this thing must be two thousand years old and would have rotted by now if it hadn't been soaked in some kind of preservative. Maybe it was treated afterward with another layer of wood-hardener, I don't know."

Peter frowned. "Why do you think the Romans did this?"

"Look at the way the wood was cut, Peter. This container was hewn from heavy oak, with axes of the kind used by the Roman army. Then notice the coloration. It's been soaked in some kind of creosote-like substance. Maybe even silica from volcanic ash. Those are Roman procedures. I think Gordon is right. We need to drill an opening and work from there. That's assuming this equipment will work on wood."

"Well, hell," Gordon snarled, "let's get started then." He grabbed the drill Peter had managed to restart and aimed it at the top center. With Peter helping to guide the direction of the boring, the BT-121 ground its way through the top in a flurry of wood shavings until the bit sunk through its own hole.

"Good God Almighty!" Peter shouted. He drew back, turned away, and groped for his handkerchief. "That's the foulest stench I've ever encountered. What is it?"

Gordon and Nigel pulled their shirts up to cover their nostrils. "Damn it," Gordon said with a choking sound, "that's the smell of badly preserved animal meat. I can tell you that for sure. Okay, now if you two guys can stand it, I'm going to drill the whole damned top off and find out what's down in there."

Nigel's guttural cough indicated a successful effort to stifle an urge to vomit. "I'm not sure I really care to know."

"I agree, "Peter said, "but we didn't spend this whole day soaked in sweat and dirt only to quit now. After all, the Romans wouldn't have gone to all the trouble to construct and bury this contraption if there wasn't something pretty important in it."

By the time they had pulverized enough of the container's top to peer down into it, the drill had announced its demise with a sputtering whine, and Nigel's resistance had surrendered to his mounting compulsion to throw up his lunch. Lantern in front of his face, Gordon leaned into the blackness of the mysterious box, groaned, and then jerked himself back. "That's the ugliest human corpse I've ever seen. Take a look."

Peter elected to peer over the edge in lieu of leaning in, but took more time as he swung the lantern back and forth. "Gordon, your definition of human must be different than mine." He pulled back. "This is an animal. I'm guessing a very large goat, judging from the remains of what appears to be a pair of horns. What frightens me are the multiple rows of razor-sharp teeth on both the lower and upper jaws of the creature. This is one savage-looking beast of satanic proportions!"

Nigel soaked his shirt in the leftover water and wrapped it around his nose and mouth. He grabbed the lantern and thrust his head and one arm into the blackness of the heavy tomb. He emerged a few seconds later shaking his head. "Look what I pulled out of there," he said, and handed a parchment scroll to Peter. "What do you make of this? Can you translate it?"

Peter and Gordon huddled, stretching the short, bloodstained parchment out close to the lantern and scanning it. Peter shrugged before he spoke. "I'm afraid I have no idea what kind of writing this is or what it says. All I can tell you is that it starts out with some kind of narrative, presents a list of thirteen items, and then concludes with another short narrative. If I can keep it from crumbling, I'll scan it for Courtney to have a look. Hang on a minute while I take a few photos. Nigel, hold the lantern down into the box a bit, will you?"

"Fair enough," Gordon whispered in a tired-sounding voice after Peter had finished. "Let's pack up and you two go back to the motel. I'm staying here for the night and I'll meet you here bright and early in the morning."

Nigel spun around and glared at him. "What in the bloody hell are you talking about? You're planning to spend the whole night alone in an unearthly hole like this? What if our adversaries—and there must be plenty of them by now—come back to finish what they started?"

"No choice," Gordon said. "It's a chance worth taking. I need to do what I can to guard this place until we can reinter that beast tomorrow, and at least make some effort to refill all our holes. This find is going to be so monumental that I don't want anyone else jumping in on it until we can review the scans and make sense out of this whole affair. This is going to be ours and no one else's. So, get the hell out of here, take the drill back, and bring a new set of shovels tomorrow. Bring better gloves and some salve or something for our blisters. And bring me some breakfast and clean clothes."

"You don't mind being alone all night with that satanic beast?" Peter asked.

Gordon grinned. "I've decided to call him 'Mortimer.' Mort and I will be fine keeping each other company. I'll think of him as my guard dog. Now go."

"You're daft," Nigel growled. "Come on, Pete. Let's go before it rubs off on us."

\* \* \* \* \*

Drenched in sweat again by four o'clock the next afternoon, the three exhausted men could only lean on their shovels, guzzling water while they stared at each other with blank expressions. Peter broke the silence. "I'm not one to use foul language, but I'm for getting our asses the hell out of here. We've filled the holes in as best we can, they don't look pretty, and anyone who comes down here can tell that someone was digging up a storm. Frankly, I don't care. My principal aim in life right now is never to pick up another damned shovel."

Nigel licked the sweat off his lips and pointed a finger at Gordon. "Mr. Marston, that grotesque creature we unearthed last night bloody well better have some world-shaking significance." He turned to Peter. "Pete, I forwarded to Courtney a scan of that parchment we found, along with the photos you took of that satanic-looking beast. If he sends back a note saying this whole thing is nothing but a hoax, I'm personally committed to the assassination of both of you for destroying my hands and wasting two days of my life."

102

Gordon flashed one of his patented grins and patted Nigel on the head. "Not to worry, old boy. What we dug up here will rock the world, trust me. Okay, I agree with Peter. Let's…how do you Yanks say it? Get out of Dodge while we can. Keep your fingers crossed that no one knows for sure just what we were up to."

"Well, Miriam surely must know," Peter replied.

"No. She suspects," Nigel countered, "but she doesn't know."

After Gordon returned what was left of their equipment, they piled their tired bodies into the Mercedes, stopped long enough for Peter to say goodbye to Robin, and began the three-day trip to Selçuk.

# Chapter 7

## Selçuk (Ephesus)

Sam, Courtney, and Roger could have made better time on the road from Konya if Sam hadn't insisted on a few detours to scour the countryside for ancient ruins. The combination of the delays, a late night's work on his thesis, and the dull, empty expanse of road took its toll on Roger. His head slumped forward, and the Hyundai wandered off onto the shoulder.

Courtney lunged over Roger's shoulder, grabbed the wheel, and maneuvered the vehicle back on course. Roger's head snapped up. "Damn it! I'm sorry. I'm sorry. Thanks, Courtney. I've got it now. It won't happen again, I swear." He reached down for a Coca-Cola, popped the top, and took an eye-opening gulp.

Courtney leaned back in his seat and spoke calmly, as if nothing had happened. "Well, if Roger can keep this car on the road, we'll be in Ephesus in time for supper."

"So I take it this is a significant place," Sam said, ignoring the incident. "Am I right, Dr. Stickney?"

"Yes. It was once the fourth-greatest city in the world, right after Rome, Alexandria, and Antioch. It was the gateway to Asia, and the most favorable seaport on that continent. For all travelers, it was the highway to Rome. The Roman ruins here won't produce any findings because they've been gutted, but there's an old museum that has a basement filled with stuff the curator hasn't even sorted out yet. Thanks to Nigel's influence, he's willing to let us poke around. Are you with us again in the world now, Roger?"

"I think he needs to trash the cola and pour down some good, thick, Turkish coffee," Sam said with a broad grin.

"It won't happen again," Roger snapped.

Sam stuffed his architectural ruins notes in his pocket and yawned. "Anyway, Courtney, now that I'm almost awake and ready to indulge once again in this fourth dimension of yours, feed me the next chapter. You know, the one about why you think this God of yours created our world, when the best scientific minds in the business have proof that the universe really began 13.7 billion years ago under the Big Bang theory. I mean, since we don't have anything else to do until we get to Ephesus."

Courtney lowered his head, as though his patience had begun to run thin. "Sam, you're stuck in the temporal world again. Look, whatever begins to exist has a cause. God is the cause, and he is timeless. He entered into your temporal world at the moment your universe was created."

Sam nodded. "Yeah, I keep hearing that stuff all the time. The rhetoric is delightful. Except that no one has ever explained, in rational terms, just how this divine superpower of yours actually got the ball rolling 13.7 billion years ago."

"That's part of the reason you seem to be having so much trouble with the very concept. In fact, the same scientists who traced the universe back 13.7 billion years have yet to come up with a plausible explanation of how it got started then. Some of them have simply thrown up their hands. Some of them hypothesize it's part of a multi-universe configuration, while many have conceded that one kind of super force or another must be the only rational explanation."

Sam shook his head. "I see where you're going. So you're telling me that Charles Darwin was wrong about life beginning with little creatures crawling out of the primordial swamps?"

"I wouldn't say wrong, simply out of sequence. Once again, intelligent life could not have formed without God. Statisticians tell us that the star formations that occurred after what you would call the Big Bang—and without which the planets could not have formed—had less than one chance out of ten to the tenth power to the 129th power of occurring under natural circumstances. At least not in any universe that was randomly structured by physical forces that shaped the galaxies, and intelligent life needed the existence of the planets."

Sam put his hand over his eyes. "How about rephrasing that without the exponential jargon?"

Courtney tilted his head back and closed his eyes, as though he could think better in that posture. "Okay. Stated in a different way, the 13.7-billion-year-life of this universe is not enough time to allow its components to produce precisely the right combination of ingredients to create a living cell from which intelligent life could begin based on random chance. That required the intervention of God. So, to make a long story short, Darwin simply tuned in to the whole process of evolution in midstream."

"So, are you saying his theory of evolution didn't amount to all that much after all?"

"No, his Origin of Species was a tremendous breakthrough in our study of how humans evolved. However, it was entirely dependent on his premise of gradual evolution from a central source. Like branches of a tree sprouting from a single trunk. Unfortunately, the Cambrian explosion 450 to 490 million years ago blew his argument out of the water."

Sam tilted his head back and stroked his chin. "You mean the little invertebrate fossils they discovered in the late nineteenth century in Canada?"

"Right. They all sprang up during the Cambrian period without any discernable ancestry. As one paleographer put it, 'When gradualness is eliminated, you're left with miracle.' Darwin himself couldn't explain where those bug-like creatures came from. He'd be the first to admit that no one has found a way to create the living cell from scratch. In fact, he said so."

Roger took his eyes off the road long enough to glance at Courtney in the rearview mirror. "What do you mean, 'said so?' "

"I mean that, in his second and subsequent editions of *On the Origin of Species*, he wrote, in reference to the Book of Genesis, 'There is a grandeur in this view of life with its several powers, having been originally breathed by the Creator into a few forms or into one.' In other words, even Darwin realized the impossibility of life without a creator."

Sam chuckled. "Okay, Courtney, I'll let that stand for now, only because I'm hungry for supper. Our makeshift lunch didn't do much for me. Roger, how close to Selçuk are we?"

"I think I can see it coming up right past those aqueducts with the big birds perched on them. What are those birds, Courtney?"

106

"They're storks, symbols of birth and fertility. Better park the car over there beside the edge of that market. The downtown streets here are pedestrian only, I'm told."

Roger parked the car in an out-of-the-way cul-de-sac, and they walked to a kiosk that offered a variety of unfamiliar-looking foods.

Courtney grinned. "Come on, we'll dine on *pide*, or Turkish pizza. I'm sure you'll love it. Roger, you order for us while I retrieve my Bible from my bag and try to figure out what the old priest was almost telling us about Revelation. Then after we eat, we'll check in someplace for the night."

"Guys, in case you might have forgotten," Roger reminded them, "the old church where that priest found those original Scriptures was right here in Ephesus. I think we ought to give it a look while we're here. What do you say?"

Sam nodded. "Agreed."

"Definitely," Courtney added. "Jolly good idea. I should have thought of it myself."

The food, still only marginally acceptable, showed some improvement over the previous meals. They chose beer over coffee by unanimous vote, and dessert never came up for discussion. Not wanting to pass up an opportunity to take in the sights of nearby Ephesus before it got dark, the three travelers settled the bill, ignored their fatigue, and walked out into the cool quiet of the evening. They strolled along Arcadian Way, now Harbor Street, to Curetes Street, named after the Curetes—said to be an ancient college of priests committed to the service of Artemis. Inscriptions bearing the names of emperors Diocletian and Constantine stood as silent reminders of the historic prominence of this, the fourth-greatest city of antiquity. While they surveyed the remnants of the lost world around them, Sam allowed his thoughts to wander in directions more familiar to historians than to theologians. After they'd taken in the sights and shared their impressions of a vanished world, the three travelers checked into a hotel and made preparations for the night.

Sam stayed awake long enough to make entries in his diary, with parenthetical notations he planned to unleash about an international wake-up call preserved in a two thousand-year-old letter written by a dying Roman centurion. Roger stayed up even later to assemble the data for his thesis. His Blackberry's memory card absorbed and recorded each stroke. He tapped out facts, observations, and opinions in no particular order under his recently selected title: Interaction of Roman and Early Christian Values – A Crucible for Contemporary Western Cultures. He added a brief summary, turned out the light, and went to sleep.

\* \* \* \* \*

Excavations in recent years had confirmed that the bare-bones remains of structures surrounding Ephesus had survived the Neolithic Age, the Bronze Age, the Hellenistic and Roman periods, and the subsequent Dark Ages. Yet there was nothing about the rolling hills or the protruding ruins that would lure even Sam's imagination back that far. He found himself still grappling with the puzzle of Father Trazerri's Book of Revelation itinerary. At Courtney's insistence, Roger pulled the Hyundai to a stop in front of the Protestant Church of Ephesus.

"Why are we stopping here, Courtney?" Sam asked. "I thought we were going to explore Trazerri's old church."

"We are, as soon as I can find it. None of the locals I talked to knew anything about it. They suggested we start here with Reverend Steen, who they thought might help us." Roger turned the engine off and turned to Courtney. "Has either of you figured out what Trazerri meant when he suggested we pay particular attention to the number seven?"

"No, except that Revelations contains letters written by the Apostle John to seven churches…Ephesus, Smyrna, Pergamum, Thyatira, Sardis, Philadelphia, and Laodicea. I'm afraid that's too simple. I have to believe there's more to the number seven than that. And as to the old priest's comment about Satan's domain, I haven't the slightest idea what he meant. I've sent a text message to Peter asking if he has any suggestions. He's probably a better theologian than I am when it comes to New Testament matters. I also received a transmission I haven't had time to read yet, from Nigel. My homework for tonight, I guess."

They walked into the church and introduced themselves to the office assistant. She led them into an anteroom that offered even fewer amenities than the conference room at MOLAS. As soon as Reverend Steen entered, Courtney made the introductions. After a few moments of small talk, the Reverend led them into his office where he listened to their story while his secretary served tea. Paintings by various nineteenth-century French impressionists adorned the walls.

More likely prints than originals, Sam surmised. His first impression was that this tall, ungainly, and professorial-looking gentleman was not particularly interested in their mission. Sam figured the man would have preferred not to be bothered, but out of professional courtesy, probably felt obliged to accommodate them.

After Courtney finished his summary of the sequence of events that led them to Ephesus, he sipped his tea and the three travelers waited for a response. The Reverend lifted his long, Ichabod Crane-like frame slowly out of his chair and walked over to a table cluttered with tea-serving vessels. He poured a cup and returned to deposit his gangly body back into his chair before he spoke.

"Gentlemen, as captivating as your quest seems to be, I'm afraid I can't help you. I'm not familiar with the priest you referred to as Father Trazerri. The church he referenced no longer exists here as a Catholic church. The property has, I believe, been sold to the Greek Orthodox Church about a mile from here. That's where I think you should go next."

"Any chance the documents we're looking for might still be there?" Sam asked.

Steen shook his head. "Probably not. Nonetheless, a visit there will be worth your time. The head priest is a fellow named Karalekas. I'll ring him up to let him know you're coming. I think you'll find him an interesting character, to say the least. He's kind of a church historian, a real researcher who can probably help, provided you can tolerate his somewhat heretical perspective. However—and please don't take this the wrong way for I don't intend anything personal—I happen to be a very traditional preacher. There have been all sorts of non-canonical writings promulgated over the centuries, many of them forgeries, and many written simply to make a statement in opposition to accepted doctrine. Thus I believe you may be chasing your tails on this whole business of an original Bible, or any parts of it. You must know the New Testament is a compilation of Scriptures accumulated over a number of years, all of which would seem to cast considerable doubt on the validity of what this Roman centurion of yours seems to be saying in his letter."

The comment sparked a lively discussion on the position of the centurion's letter within the timeframe of the scriptural writings. At the end, Steen stood and reached to shake their hands. "Anyway, I wish you success in your search. By the way, as to the number seven you mentioned, I'm not sure it has any real significance since it could conceivably relate to any number of things, such as the seven days of the week, the seven heavens, the seven Sleepers, the seven-branched candelabra...even the seven combined angles of the pyramids. Good luck on that one."

Courtney reached to shake his host's hand and grinned. "I think you missed the seven deadly sins."

Steen frowned and Sam smiled at the thought that Courtney's facetious remark might have burned a bridge behind them. By the time they reached the car, Sam's expression had turned serious. "I think we've wasted our time. Let's move on."

Under Courtney's guidance, Roger maneuvered the Hyundai carefully through the streets of downtown Selçuk, past the food market, around the hostel-style buildings of shared rooms, and out onto a main road. Courtney motioned for him to pull over to the side.

"Why are we stopping here?" Roger asked. "I thought we were going to hear the Greek version of modern religion?"

Courtney cradled the Blackberry in his hands. "We will as soon as I read over Peter's response to my question. It looks like a long one, I'm thankful to say. Maybe he's going to shed some light on this mystery."

"Or maybe add a few more unhelpful applications of the number seven," Sam countered.

Courtney grinned. "No, listen to this, guys. Pete's done his homework on it. He says that each of the Apostle John's letters to the seven churches contains seven distinct components—give or take one or two:

* A correspondent, meaning the pastor referred to in the letter as an 'angel'
* The name of the city
* A reference to the church itself
* A commendation remark
* A condemnation of some sort for the people's misbehavior
* A command to repent or change the people's behavior
* And finally, some counsel as to what specifically the church should do next.

"So, how does that help us?" Roger asked, accompanied by a nod of agreement from Sam.

Courtney put his finger to his forehead and paused before he responded. "I don't know, but I think we need to examine, more closely, the contents of those letters to the seven churches. Maybe the Greek priest can offer a new perspective."

"Yeah, and maybe he can't," Sam said. "Either way, before we visit the Greek, it occurs to me we don't have enough manpower here if we're going to follow Trazerri's itinerary to the letter."

"What do you mean by that?" Courtney responded with a look of surprise.

"I mean, at the rate we're going, it'll take us at least three or four more weeks to visit the next six churches on that list, and we haven't even finished this one yet. Maybe we ought to ask Pete's group to visit a couple of those churches to help out."

"I don't know," Roger interjected. "For the purpose of my thesis I'd kind of like to see them all. So what if it takes us a few extra weeks?"

"Sam's right," Courtney said. "We don't have that much time. We're going to need to split this mission up a bit. I'll send Gordon a message and find out how close they are to finishing at their end. Okay, let's go interview Father Karalekas."

"Courtney, do we address him as 'Father' as a gesture of respect for his position?" Roger asked. "Or is that the official title of all Catholic priests?"

"The term isn't for him. It's an affirmation of the relationship in Christ he has for all people. Symbolically, he becomes our father when he brings us to birth in Christ at baptism, and then he nurtures us with Christ himself."

Sam turned to Courtney. "I still haven't bought into all your rhetoric, but I've been thinking about it. I'll have to admit one or two of your answers make more sense than a lot of the religious garbage I've heard over the years. Now I'm anxious to hear what a Greek priest has to say. Let's do it."

The Greek Orthodox Church of Ephesus looked more like a mosque than a Catholic church, although it was impossible to discern what structural modifications might have been made since the transfer of property from the Catholic Diocese to the Greek Orthodox Church. A

111

tired-looking old building in need of a good refurbishing, it showed stains of stork droppings, courtesy of the large birds that had elected to build their nests along the edges of the roof.

A lower-ranking priest welcomed the three travelers, ushered them through the arched entrance, and told them to make themselves comfortable in a large library complete with all the furnishings their previous location lacked. He smiled and said it would only take a few more minutes for head priest Karalekas to finish his preparations for the upcoming service.

Courtney nodded and turned to his companions. "I'm going to change our approach to one of probing more and telling less this time, in case we encounter another disinterested reception. Everyone okay with that?"

Sam and Roger nodded. Before anyone could speak, the gigantic frame of a man in dark robes completely filled the doorway. Dimitri Karalekas wore two layers of black cassock—the rasson underneath and the exorasson exterior with flowing wide sleeves. A traditional chimney pot hat, which he quickly removed, only partly covered his long, tied-back hair and served to complement his thick, black, untrimmed beard. The three visitors stood up in awe to greet this larger-than-life figure who, Sam figured, could easily have been a linebacker on any NFL football team.

"So," the large, robed figure bellowed, "you have a story to tell me. Good, I like stories. I have one too. Come, we will exchange them while we eat."

Courtney, Sam, and Roger remained silent, mesmerized by the persona that matched the man's immense size. They watched while a young choirboy brought in abundant servings of bread and cheese. He placed them on a table, along with four glasses of what appeared to be an alcoholic beverage.

"Please help yourselves, gentlemen. The bread is psomi, the best kind, and the drink is Metaxa, a blend of brandy and choice wine. They're far superior to what you can get in France or even California." He looked at them with a menacing grin. "The cheese is almost like your feta cheese, but much better, which in Greece means stronger."

112

They exchanged introductions, devoured the food and Metaxa, and did it all while Courtney offered his abbreviated version of their mission, followed by his first probe.

"Well, to make a long story short, Father, we'd like to know your reaction to what Father Trazerri claims he found in the basement of this church. We're hoping you can provide some assistance in our search for all or parts of the original version of the New Testament. And, if it wouldn't be an imposition, we'd like to have a look at the basement here, where Trazerri said he found pages from the original Scriptures."

The priest tilted his head back to drain the last few drops of Metaxa from his glass before he spoke. "Gentlemen, you're welcome to examine our basement whenever you like. I must tell you it was gutted and the stone walls were replaced with concrete blocks several years before we obtained the property. The stones and everything else down there were, I understand, trucked away for landfill somewhere. Now that you mention his name, I recall having met Father Trazerri a number of years ago, but he never said anything about this discovery of his."

Sam guzzled his drink and turned to the priest. "Well then, do you think Trazerri's story is even plausible?"

The priest nodded. "More than plausible. In fact, it's perfectly logical, once you accept my theory of backward causality."

Courtney frowned. "I beg your pardon?"

Karalekas leaned forward as if to emphasize the importance of what he was about to say. "It's simple. Our universe has a destiny. Given that fact, it was simply a matter of time before science demonstrated that the final state of the universe is set and has reached back in time to influence the early events in its history."

"Father Karalekas," Sam said, "as an historian who doesn't believe in God, I'm probably less willing to accept your concept of predestination than is my religious colleague here. I'm not sure we're all following you. How does backward causality affect Father Trazerri's claim? And who said science has ever supported your theory?"

"Ha!" the priest grinned, pointed a finger at Sam, then motioned for the boy to bring in more Metaxa. "Dr. Wykoff, scientists in your own country—California and Arizona, I believe—have conducted a long series of experiments that have confirmed my theory. Tollaksen was one of the scientists. You should read the findings of your own countrymen."

Sam ignored the jibe and pressed the issue. "I'm still not seeing the connection between predestination—a concept of doubtful merit to begin with—and our search for the original version of the New Testament."

"Ah, you question my perspective. Good. I enjoy a challenge. Let me put it to you this way. Even if you rolled the dice for fourteen billion years you would not have enough time to create a universe as conducive to life as ours. Pure random chance would not let you be that lucky. Therefore life, like our universe, was predestined, and our ultimate destiny, quite logically, reached back into time to shape earlier events. Therefore, it's logical that events which took place centuries after the time of Jesus Christ required his pronouncements to be rewritten. Otherwise, they would not have survived the forces that militated against them during the centuries following his death."

The three visitors looked at one another in stunned silence. Several anxious moments passed before Roger broke the hush. "Father Karalekas, if you believe in a universal reset, then how can you believe in God, let alone preach on the subject?"

The priest served a second round of Metaxas. He smiled at Roger, fixing his gaze on him as though Roger were the only person in the room. "Ah, Mr. Denault, you are young but your insight belies your age. That was the kind of question your father would probably have asked, God rest his soul. I read his works. Someday perhaps I will read yours, yes?" The mountainous man's boisterous laugh echoed in the quiet chambers.

Sam and Courtney observed the look of discomfort on Roger's face. It was as though the hapless young man had found himself confronted once again with his father's crowning achievements, which seemed designed to haunt him like the Ghost of Christmas Past.

"Listen to me, Roger," the priest continued. "God and backward causality are not necessarily mutually exclusive. It was God who designed the universe. So, please don't misunderstand me. Of course it was his will that Jesus's original commands be heard throughout that universe. He also recognized the importance of carrying those pronouncements forward in a way that would preserve them from destruction by their enemies. Christianity almost didn't survive the Dark Ages. In fact, it wouldn't have if certain modifications had not been made to the Scriptures."

114

Sam leaned toward his host. "Father Karalekas, have you any idea when, and how, those modifications were made? This is crucial to our search."

The priest rested his chin on his cupped hands. "I wish I could be more specific about that. I strongly suspect that the changes were made sometime between the second and fourth centuries, prior to the Council of Nicæa. What you must remember is that, by the beginning of the fourth century, the Roman form of Christianity had become dominant, following the conversion of the Roman Emperor Constantine, and I believe it was the Roman Catholic Church that determined the future course of Christianity."

Courtney set his Metaxa on a small table next to his chair and leaned in toward the priest. "So, what Trazerri found must have been an original first-century excerpt from original Scriptures, do you agree?"

Karalekas clapped his hands together and grinned. "Yes, and for that reason I would have to believe at one time there was an original version of at least some of the twenty-seven books of the New Testament. However, I must add, with no intent to discourage you, your chances of finding any of them are virtually non-existent."

"Why so?" Sam persisted.

"Because twenty centuries and the overwhelming power and resources of the Roman Catholic Church have combined to erase all traces of such documents." He leaned forward toward them, lowered his voice, and, for a while longer, rambled on about the statistical probabilities relevant to theological research. Then, as if to preempt any further discussion, he stood, indicating that the conversation had reached its conclusion.

"Gentlemen, I have much to do today, so I must bid you goodbye and wish you success on your journey." The priest shook their hands with an iron grip that left their fingers numb. He motioned to the choirboy to show them to the door, and walked out.

On their way to the car, they turned for one last glance at the old church that had changed Trazerri's life. Roger shook his head. "Courtney, this thing has taken another weird turn." The frustration in his voice was unmistakable. "So what's your opinion? I mean, first we thought a New Testament alteration would make world headlines. Now

I'm hearing that the inevitability of it should have been obvious. What do you think?"

"Relax, Roger." Courtney's confident grin came as a soothing balm. "Your thesis is safe. It just has a new dimension now, that's all."

"How do you mean? And how did you know I was worried about how the Greek priest's theory would affect my paper?"

"It was written all over your face. Look, we're all well aware of the pressure you're feeling to live up to your father's reputation. By the way, no one else thinks that doing so is at all necessary. Given that you do, I can tell you that no matter how many bizarre turns this mission takes, they will all work to your advantage."

"Why do you say that?" a somewhat more comforted-looking Roger asked.

Courtney patted him on the shoulder. "Everything that's happened so far, or will happen, is going to be revolutionary in the eyes of the world. And that's what makes a good thesis."

\* \* \* \* \*

With Courtney's guidance, a not-particularly reliable GPS, and their makeshift map, Roger navigated the car back onto the road toward the next destination on Trazerri's recommended itinerary.

Sam settled back in the passenger seat next to Roger, cupped his hands behind his head, and flashed a wide grin as though he'd found a new ally in support of his views. "I don't know about you and Roger, but I saw some sense in what the big Greek said. Aside from what you told Roger, what's your take on it, Courtney?" He reached down, opened a napkin, and pulled out the last of the psomis Father Karalekas had given him.

Courtney pulled his notes from his pocket, glanced at them, and stuffed them back in. "Well, believe it or not, I was okay with everything except the guy's strange concept of God's flexibility with regard to Jesus's original pronouncements. I'm a bit surprised, though, to find a skeptic like you so accepting of it. Are we perhaps seeing a change in Dr. Wykoff's perspective here?"

Sam rolled his eyes. "I don't know, Courtney. Truth be known, I think what you're seeing is a lot more of my confusion about this God thing. I mean, the skeptic in me still marvels at how the original Scriptures seemed to have changed. All you Bible-thumpers claim these writings are the authoritative word of God. So, how could they suddenly become, like Karalekas said, whatever the Roman Catholic Church wanted them to be?"

"I think Sam has a point," Roger chimed in. "What the priest said is consistent with the thesis I'm developing. The rewrite of the original Scriptures seems to represent a critical link between the evolution of religious doctrine and historical events prior to, and during, the Dark Ages. Wouldn't you agree?"

Courtney shook his head. "I'm afraid it's not all that simple. There were many forms of early Christianity which, for various reasons, did not—and could not logically—survive. For example, the Ebionites were very influential at the time. They supposedly had a gospel in harmony with Matthew, but they were not known for issuing any substantive writings. Later, the Marcionites saw Jesus as the representative of a God who delivered people from the law-giving God of the Jews. Then—"

"That one seems too narrow to survive, anyway," Roger interjected.

Courtney smiled. "Probably so. Then again, the Gnostics, a name which derived from the Greek word for knowledge, took a broader view. They believed the world was an evil place from which one could escape only by acquiring secret knowledge about where people came from and how they got here. As if that weren't enough, the subsequent Coptic gospel of Thomas, the gospel of Peter, and the secret gospel of Mark all threw more controversy into the long search for a sound, acceptable doctrine."

"Like I surmised before," Sam said, "this whole thing seems to be setting itself up to be whatever the Catholic Church ultimately wanted it to be."

"No, not really." Courtney held up his hand in protest. "It was finally decided that, in order for a canonical book of doctrine to be acceptable, it must meet four criteria: it must be ancient, meaning written not long after the time of Jesus; it must be apostolic, meaning written by an apostle or one of his companions; it needed to be orthodox, avoiding anything that advocated a false view of religion; and it must be widely recognized throughout the church. Needless to say, the debate went on for centuries, until the New Testament was finally accepted late in the fourth century."

After a few long moments of contemplative silence, Sam said, "Courtney, in the final analysis, doesn't this whole Christianity thing depend entirely on the premise of the resurrection of Jesus?"

"Yes, I think that goes without saying."

Sam held both arms out, palms up, as if to underscore his closing argument. "Well then, unless it can be proved that his resurrection actually occurred, this whole discussion about original Scriptures versus altered ones becomes purely academic, does it not?"

"No, the discussion is always real because the entire Christian community would be startled to discover a significant difference between the New Testament as we know it and whatever might exist in an original version—assuming we ever find one. The validity of Jesus's resurrection is beyond question for anyone who takes the time to examine the circumstances surrounding it, irrespective of what happened to the Scriptures after the resurrection."

Sam spun around to face Courtney. "Whoa! Hold on. What do you mean beyond question? I, for one, vehemently question it, as do many others. So, what are you offering as proof in rebuttal?"

Courtney glanced out the window, as though Sam's challenge was simple enough that it could be answered without having to make eye contact. "Well, let's begin with the empty tomb. And by the way, what I'm about to tell you has been articulately endorsed by several authorities in the field, including current ones like William Craig, to whom I've already referred you. To date, there have been no naturalistic explanations that would outrank the biblical one. Additionally, there were accounts of people who experienced, in one form or another, the presence of Jesus afterward. Then, too, it's plausible in the sense that it confirms the claims made by Jesus while he was alive, and there's nothing either contrived or ad hoc about it."

Sam shook his head. "You theologians sure live in a world all your own."

Courtney couldn't suppress a grin. "Perhaps, but let's not forget that a divine resurrection does not conflict with the perfectly rational belief that people do not naturally rise from the dead. In short, I defy you to find any rival theories that meet the tests I've just summarized. And because Jesus was raised from the dead, God exists. Hopefully, you and Roger will now realize the importance of scanning the centurion's letter currently being worked on in London. That letter represents an irrefutable eyewitness account."

Sam grumbled. "An eyewitness account yet to be determined, of course, but I'll concede your point for now, pending subsequent events."

"Good. Then our first subsequent event will be to continue on to Bergama, formerly a remote city called Pergamos, and the third church on the Revelation itinerary."

"What happened to the second one?" Roger cast a surprised look at Courtney through the rearview mirror. "I thought Smyrna was next."

"It was, until Sam wisely suggested we split the rest of the journey with Peter, Gordon, and Nigel to save time. I received a text reply from Gordon saying they found nothing in Perth, so they're on their way to the city of Izmir. From there, they can try to uncover something in both Smyrna and Sardis, now known as Izmir and Sart, respectively. Thus, tomorrow we head for Bergama. By the way, I had a chance to read that strange message I told you about from Nigel. I think you guys ought to know about it."

"Fire away," Sam mumbled. "Nothing could be much stranger than what we've been through already."

"Don't count on it. Listen to this. Nigel sent a photo of a parchment scroll he says his group extracted from a grave under a church in Chester. He thought I could translate the wording on it. I can't, so I sent it on to London for MOLAS's ancient language guru to have a go at it. Now get this. Nigel also sent four photos, taken by Peter, of what he claimed to be an evil-looking beast buried with the parchment. However—"

"Great," Sam interjected, shaking his head. "That's all we need right now to round out this charade. Okay, let's have a look at them."

"Well, that's the peculiar part. The photos are blank."

Roger frowned. "He sent four photos with nothing on them?"

"No, he said they had clear images of this so-called beast on them. Something must have happened during the transmission because this is all I received." Courtney held out his iPhone for them to see it. "What do you guys make of it?"

Sam yawned. "Hell, maybe Pete's camera screwed up. Or bad resolution. Anyone can mess up a pictorial transmission."

Courtney put his hand to his chin and paused in a gesture of thoughtful contemplation. "No, I don't think so. Pete and Nigel are pretty conscientious about things like that. They would have known before they sent the photos if the resolution was bad. And this isn't simply a case of undecipherable pictures. Those shots were completely blank."

"What did you say the subject of the photos was?" Roger asked.

Courtney chuckled. "Well, Nigel called it 'an unidentifiable satanic beast,' and I'm quoting."

Sam straightened up in his seat and gave Courtney his full attention. "Satanic, like how?"

"I'm not sure. Nigel said it was large, had spiral goat-like horns that had partially disintegrated, and probably weighed—so he said—somewhere in the range of eight or nine hundred pounds. He claimed it had a rather horrible-looking animal-type mouth, with several rows of long, sharp teeth. You tell me what kind of beast that is."

Roger's expression suggested an attempt to suppress a laugh. "Come on, you two guys. If this is your idea of a joke it isn't working."

"No, Roger, I'm serious, and I believe Nigel is, too. I think we're dealing with something here which, oddly enough, might just be consistent with the other biblical contradictions we've had to confront so far. What has my hair standing on end right now is the question of what happened that made those photos disappear."

"Yeah, and if that creature looked anything like the one Courtney just described, I can tell you it's no damned goat," Sam said. "So what's the next step?"

Courtney stuffed Nigel's message and the blank photos into his carrying bag and looked down at Roger's map. "Well, as soon as our London expert responds, we'll decide. In the meantime, we need a place to sleep tonight. My itinerary instructions say there's a roadside inn a few miles ahead. Let's head that way and call it a day."

They found the inn and ordered dinner based on Courtney's recommendations from a menu that consisted mainly of foods neither Sam nor Roger had ever seen. Aside from a brief discussion as to how Roger should present 'the beast' in his journal, they ate in silence, each apparently deep in his own thoughts. Then it was another late night for Roger, the only quiet time he had available to record his observations, and assemble the data he had collected for his thesis. Once again, the soft

120

tapping on the Blackberry was the only sound that could be heard as he typed in relevant events from Ephesus's history.

# Chapter 8

## Izmir (Smyrna and Sardis)

The Mercedes twisted its way through six of Izmir's twelve metropolitan districts and the city's international festival before Nigel conceded they were lost. They had planned for a relaxing evening meal and a good night's sleep before the next day's meetings with the director of the Ataturk Museum and the priest at the Saint Polycarp Church. Instead, they found themselves gridlocked in a flood of traffic through the housing projects, the industrial area, and the jammed southern corridor.

Gordon studied the map while Peter scanned the surroundings for something resembling a recognizable landmark.

Peter shook his head. "The streets are too narrow and the buses too wide to see around. I don't find anything that matches our original set of directions."

Gordon tapped his finger on the map. "Tally ho! I think I see where we are on this route. Take the next left and keep going straight for about a mile. We're closer than we thought."

Daylight had already surrendered to the advancing shadows of evening, by the time they finally parked in front of their hotel and settled down at an adjacent restaurant. The Tarhana soup—a concoction made from yoghurt and dried tomatoes—combined with a kumru sandwich of cheese and sucuk to satisfy their growing hunger.

"Peter, I know you told us once, but I'm not sure it registered," Gordon confessed as he poured a glass of after-dinner wine. "Why are we going to the Saint Polycarp Church before the First Anglican, which is even closer?"

"Polycarp is the oldest. It was constructed in 1625, making it the most likely repository of ancient records. Furthermore, the Romans established a rather dubious connection there when they burned Bishop Polycarp alive for refusing to blaspheme the Lord's name. I think Nigel was right that our battlefield search for the original Bible has produced about all it could."

"I agree with Peter," Nigel said. "I think it's time we turned our efforts to helping Courtney and his group explore the churches on Paul's itinerary."

Gordon threw him a skeptical glance. "Yeah, but we're not following Paul's route. Courtney has us tracking the churches in the book of Revelation, apparently at the suggestion of some has-been old priest with a fixation on the number seven. Has anyone figured out why?"

Peter's expression turned glum. "No, I'm afraid we haven't. According to Courtney, the priest also added a warning about...I think he called it Satan's territory or something. No one's figured that one out either. At least not in a way that's relevant to our search. Anyway, let's have a run at it tomorrow, with open minds and a lot more energy. I promised Courtney we'd visit Sardis after we complete our due diligence here in Izmir."

Gordon shook his head. "From what I've heard, Sardis is now called Sart, and it's a barren no-man's land. Visiting it would be a waste of our time."

Peter nodded. "Yeah, I know, but I promised we'd do it. I'm going to bed. See you guys tomorrow."

Gordon looked at Nigel and grinned. "You'd think he'd be more anxious to shorten the journey rather than lengthen it, so he could get back to a certain romance he's started."

Nigel returned the grin. They paid the tab and walked to the hotel.

\* \* \* \* \*

Ekrem Yilmaz had been curator at the Ataturk Museum long enough to know what its contents were. The short, stocky man with a neatly trimmed, dark black, ear-to-ear beard that flowed carefully around his sharp jaws shook his head. "I can assure you the artifacts we have on display are not what you are looking for. Ours is one of the world's most complete exhibitions of ancient Roman weaponry, domestic equipment, and assorted paraphernalia. We have collected the pieces from all parts of the former Roman Empire. This museum, however, is not a storehouse for religious writings. You're wasting my time and yours here."

"Even so," Peter replied, "we'd hoped that you might allow us to peruse the museum's basement." He extended his arm toward Nigel. "Dr. Patterson represents the Museum of London Archaeological Service, so our purpose is official, not recreational."

Nigel produced a handful of credentials which seemed to remove whatever suspicions the man might have harbored.

"Very well, come with me, but I can allow you only one hour, and my assistant must be with you at all times. Of course, you are absolutely forbidden to remove anything from its storage compartment. That must be clearly understood."

They nodded in agreement.

Problems arose from the beginning. The basement was poorly lit, the assistant didn't speak English, and there seemed to be little or no organizational structure to how the artifacts were sorted. Gordon threw his hands in the air. "Guys, I don't think God himself could figure out what's down here. This stuff is numbered, but the numbers don't make any sense. Look here. This compartment is numbered 12-475 and the one next to it is numbered 12-122. We could probe forever and not decipher this system."

"Wait a minute," Nigel said as he pulled out and carefully examined two differently numbered boxes at the same time. "I think the first numbers before the dash represent a category of artifact, while the three- and four-digit numbers after the dash are dates."

"You can't be serious," Gordon exclaimed with an arms-outstretched, palms-up gesture of disbelief. "Why would two dates, centuries apart, be grouped together?"

Peter examined another set of boxes and grinned. "Nigel, I think you've hit on it. For example, category 12 seems to be a type of weapon. So, it looks like 12 followed by 122 indicates that this type of weapon might have been used in a battle that took place in the year 122 A.D., although I have no idea which battle that might be. So, if we knew what number referred to what category, we could narrow down the search considerably. We're obviously not interested in looking for weapons."

When hand-waving and sign language failed to produce any meaningful communication between the excited trio and the uninterested assistant, they summoned the curator for help. He grumbled, frowned, and in the end provided an index that explained the bizarre numbering system. On the positive side, the number 47 referenced documents, the topic of most relevance. On the downside, there were only two boxes in that category.

Nigel scratched his head. "Peter, you're the religious expert here. What are these papers saying?"

Gordon and Nigel waited while Peter donned his white gloves and flipped through the pages of ancient documents.

"These parchments date back to the first century," Peter muttered. "Yet they're in fairly legible condition. Whatever the museum might have lacked in organization, it made up for in preservation."

"Yes, but what do the documents say?" Nigel asked with mounting impatience.

"I'm having trouble with the Latin." Peter's eyes darted back and forth between documents. "The writings of Polycarp seem to dominate these files. Unless I'm mistranslating, I'd say he's having a vehement argument with the Romans about doctrine."

"Well, if the Romans burned him alive for refusal to blaspheme, then I'd say the arguments must have become intense," Gordon said.

"I'm sure they were. However, these letters don't seem to be about blasphemy. It looks more like they're about Polycarp's view of Christianity, versus what appears to be a different interpretation by the Romans. By the way, just for your information, legend has it that the burning didn't work, and they ended up having to stab him to death."

"Sounds like no one bothered to tell the Romans you can't execute a person twice for the same crime," Gordon added with a wry grin. "So, where do we go from here?"

"I'm not sure, but I'd like to take it up with the head priest at our next destination, the Saint Polycarp Church. What do you guys think?"

"Works for us," Nigel replied. "Peter, I see you have your camera working again."

"Yes. The curator said we couldn't remove any exhibits, but he didn't say we couldn't take pictures of them."

Ekrem's assistant, who hadn't stopped glaring at them, exploded into action. He waved his hands back and forth and shouted something that sounded like, "No, no" in Turkish, while Peter's camera continued to snap away. The commotion brought the curator rushing to the scene. "Stop this! I told you nothing is to be removed!"

"We're not removing anything," Nigel replied as Peter's camera continued to click away. "We're simply taking pictures."

His face now red with rage, the curator shook his fist at them. "I will call the police! I will have all of you arrested! I was warned about this scheme of yours. I should never have allowed you to enter."

The dispute raged on until Nigel's reference to his personal connection to higher authorities in the world of archaeology forced the curator to surrender. Still furious, the agitated man allowed the photographic exercise to run its course. He then accompanied them to the exit, where he made sure he had the last word by waving his fist as they departed and by shouting something in Turkish the trio took to mean, "Don't come back again."

Nigel turned for one more glance at the still-gesturing and cursing man. "I do believe he's madder than hell that we actually found something, after he swore up and down we wouldn't."

During the drive to their next destination, Gordon gazed out the window in silence, still not sure they had accomplished anything in Ekrem's dungeon.

\* \* \* \* \*

Father Polovski's warm welcome to the Saint Polycarp Church came as a pleasant contrast to the trio's experience at the Ataturk Museum earlier that morning. "Please come in. Word of your quest has preceded you, and I have a sincere interest in it."

The robed man ushered them into his small but immaculate study, with its uncluttered desktop and everything that was not shelved stacked in neat little piles. The fastidious priest maintained eye contact as he listened to each one's introduction, as though that person were the only one in the room. Then he listened attentively to their story.

"Father," Peter began, after Nigel had offered a concise summary of their itinerary, "we realize this whole effort may seem to you like an

126

exercise in futility and, in fact, it may well be. As Nigel pointed out, however, we are confronted with some regrettably incontrovertible evidence that an original, presumably unabridged, version of the New Testament existed. Believe it or not, our findings support our suspicions that the original version might have been in book form, and we hope we can find at least some small part, if not all of it."

The priest studied Peter for a moment before he responded. "And what would you do if you found some portion of it?"

"I think at this point we'd be so delighted we'd treasure it. We are in possession of certain facts which strongly suggest the original Scriptures were rewritten prior to acceptance in their present form. We believe this happened sometime during the first three centuries after Christ's death. We would appreciate any help you can give us, because right now, we've run into a dead end."

The priest stood, removed his outer robe, slipped it over the back of a corner chair, and walked to a bookcase that spanned the entire length and height of the wall. "I see your dilemma. You have rather convincing circumstantial evidence, but you don't have proof in case the centurion's letter doesn't stand up to scrutiny." They nodded.

Polovski, a short, bald, almost rotund man, seemed to fit the classic image of a plump, well-fed monk, much like Robin Hood's Friar Tuck. He rose up on tiptoes and ran his index finger along a row of books until he plucked out an old notebook. He opened it and scanned the pages until he found what he was looking for.

"I had occasion, a couple of years ago, to meet the curator you saw this morning," the priest said, as he withdrew one of the papers from the notebook. "He's an excitable fellow with a rather abrasive personality, but I've appreciated his thoughtfulness ever since. He was kind enough to bring me a pile of old documents the museum didn't want, dating back, oh, I don't know, to about the second or third century, I suppose. The papers were mostly Hebrew correspondence, some of them addressed to the senate in Rome. I sent them over to the Beth Israel Synagogue here in Izmir. But I did extract one document, a letter written by the Bishop Polycarp. It references a collection of original Scriptures, much like the one you seem to be looking for. Here, you can look at it if you like, providing you can read Latin. I've done the best I could to protect it since it's in the old parchment form, fragile with age, and was almost falling apart when I received it."

"I think I can decipher it," Peter assured him, without touching the faded document. "I never cease to be amazed that history can still speak so clearly and so persistently to us across the centuries through documents such as this."

Quiet settled over the room for the next five minutes while Peter's eyes followed his index finger across each line, as he mentally translated the ancient words of the martyred bishop.

Peter broke the silence. "Father, maybe your Latin is better than mine. My reading of this document is that the bishop sent his only copy of the original Scriptures on to a destination which doesn't make any sense to me. Perhaps I'm completely misinterpreting what he meant. Look here, I mean, please tell me what you think this last sentence means." Peter handed the letter back to the priest, pointing to the passage.

Polovski grinned. "I don't need to see it." He turned to place the document back in the notebook. "I've memorized what it said, and I, too, have questions about it."

Gordon glanced with raised eyebrows in Peter's direction. "Either of you guys care to share this mystery with the rest of us?"

"Of course. My apologies." Father Polovski's expression turned serious. "The last sentence reads, and I quote, 'I send these Holy Scriptures to the pitiable, blind church that claims to need nothing, since it still remains naked to this day.' It refers to the Laodicean Church, Book of Revelation. However, I'm not sure why Polycarp wrote it, or how the letter ended up in the Ataturk Museum."

Nigel stood and raised his arms in disgust. "As hard as it is to believe after what we've accomplished so far, I'm afraid this has all the earmarks of another dead end."

"Or maybe not, oh ye of little faith." Peter pulled out his digital camera and showed three of the photographs he'd taken. "Look at this one, for instance. It talks about the Apostle John, I think, and was probably written by someone who knew him, or knew of him. Then this one says, 'He wrote what he saw, and sent it to the last, which among them all, was afflicted the most.' It doesn't say who the author is, but I believe he's talking about John. Perhaps there's some connection there between John, Polycarp, and the original Scriptures. What do you think, Father?"

"Well, I'd be inclined to agree were it not for the fact that none of us has any idea whether he's referencing John or someone else. As I'm sure you know, Polycarp lived from A.D. seventy to one hundred and fifty-five. He was a disciple of the apostles, particularly of John. After he was converted to Christianity and consecrated a bishop, he communicated with many of those who claimed to have seen Jesus. For that reason, I've studied the Gospel According to John in the New Testament over and over.

"I still see no firm connection with respect to this writing. I'm afraid the only suggestion I can offer you is to continue your journey in the hope that you might come across something which will help bring all this together. Now, gentlemen, I'm meeting an historian friend of mine for lunch in about fifteen minutes. Would you care to join us?"

Peter put up his hand. "We appreciate the offer, but we're on a tight schedule. I'm afraid three surprise guests might be an imposition on your friend."

The priest smiled. "Very well. I'll bid you all goodbye with hopes that we might someday meet again under conditions of greater certainty. You're welcome to stay for as long as you like here in my study. There's a pot of coffee on the table, and my bookshelves are at your disposal— as long as you don't remove anything."

The trio continued the discussion until the coffee ran out. Gordon pressed the connection issue. "Well, chaps, we seem to be always on the brink of a discovery on this quest only to find ourselves at another dead end. Peter, you sent our other team a message the other day, something about the number seven. Was that about the seven churches we've been instructed by that strange old priest to visit?"

"No. It was about the seven common components of the letters sent to those churches, as set forth in the Revelation section of the New Testament. I'm still trying to make some sense out of why the old priest emphasized the number seven, and I've about given up on his mysterious reference to Satan. Maybe that was simply his version of a generic 'be careful' kind of parting remark. I don't know."

"Not to change the subject," Nigel said, "but let me offer a possible reason for this Polycarp to have gotten himself in such a mess with the

Romans. If he was a follower of the Apostle John, and by definition a devout follower of Jesus, then isn't it possible that his scuffle with the Romans was actually because he was trying to stop the Roman Catholic Church from doing a rewrite of the original Scriptures?"

Nigel and Peter looked at each other in silence for a moment before Peter responded. "I guess anything's possible. If it was the Roman Catholic Church that pushed for the rewrite, as Father Karalekas seemed to think, then it probably would have been a century or two after Polycarp's death that it happened. I'm not sure we can make a connection there. In the meantime, we have two hours before we meet Reverend Carlen Pirtl at First Anglican, so let's have lunch at the Anatolia. I hear it's a great seafood place. I'll meet you there as soon as I run a quick errand. Order for me, and I'll have whatever you guys have. See you shortly."

\* \* \* \* \*

The specialties included barbun fish, octopus, squid, perch, gilthead bream, sea urchin, and cydonnia, all cooked with a variety of side orders. Nigel and Gordon agreed upon grilled perch with black pepper, carrots, potatoes, and onion pivazh. The restaurant service was slow and, as it turned out, Peter and the meal arrived at approximately the same time.

"Well, Pete," Gordon asked, "are you going to tell us what you bought or let us guess?"

Peter sat and rubbed his hands together in a gesture that implied satisfaction with his purchase. "I struck a good deal on a belly-dancing skirt, complete with a book of lessons. A surprise for Robin."

"You're joking, right?" Gordon's facial expression turned from curious to incredulous.

"No. Izmir is the world center for belly dancing. The lessons include a video. I think she'll enjoy the novelty of it, don't you?"

There was a long pause before Nigel put up his hand to interrupt Gordon's spontaneous outburst of laughter. "Peter," he began in a slow, serious tone while Gordon made every effort to wind down, "notwithstanding your obvious lack of experience with members of the opposite sex, have you stopped to consider how a woman you've only known for such a short time might react to such a…well, shall we say, intimate gift?"

"Why, yes. I think Robin will probably use it. After all, if you've ever seen Turkish belly dancers, you'll remember that the best ones are shaped very much like Robin. I mean, a little bit on the slightly well-fed side, and still quite sensuous." This time both of his companions rolled their heads back in laughter.

"Fair enough, Pete," Gordon said, still trying to contain his laughter. "Whatever you say. Only, when you present the gift, I'd leave out the well-fed part."

They took their time and savored the meal, becoming well fed themselves, then paid the waiter and headed out the door, with Gordon and Nigel still shaking their heads and grinning.

\* \* \* \* \*

The stone walkway of the First Anglican Church climbed gently toward two large red entrance doors that flaunted their gaudy color in deliberate defiance of everything surrounding them. It was as though the pale surrounding walls, on which delicate green vines clung during their gradual ascent, had been designed with the intention of highlighting the doors. Inside, a long carpet ran the length of the sanctuary between rows of old wooden pews. It stopped at the chancel, lighted only by two candles and a few muted sunbeams that managed to force their way through stained glass windows at the rear.

Peter basked in the warmth of the place long enough to imagine the kind of sermon he might offer here. He knew, somehow, it would be different than any he had given before. The three visitors were allowed only a few moments to scan the interior before Reverend Carlen Pirtl emerged, shook their hands, and led them into his study. The lanky pastor eased his frame into the high-back wooden chair behind a cluttered desk and took a moment to look them over before he spoke. "Well, gentlemen, you said you hoped I could help you, and I certainly will be glad to if I can. What might I do for you?"

While Gordon went through his summary, Peter and Nigel could see the good reverend's facial expression gradually turn from warm and welcoming to stern and borderline angry. At the outset, his arms rested loosely on the arms of his chair in a mode of relaxed anticipation. By the time Gordon had finished, Carlen Pirtl sat upright and rigid with his hands palms-down on his desk.

"By God in heaven." Pirtl growled, with his eyes now narrowed in a cold glare. "I can hardly believe the blasphemy I've just heard. How dare you! Men of your intelligence and stature bringing such vile nonsense into the house of God. Good grief. Do the Holy Scriptures mean nothing to you? Do you see The Bible as your own personal diary which you can interpret in whatever way happens to please you? Or are you perhaps looking for a shocking newspaper headline that'll sell enough copies to bring you international notoriety?"

The long, following silence that seemed to beg for relief ended with Peter's calm response. "Reverend Pirtl, I'm as much a servant of God as you are, and I can assure you we all wish to find ourselves as wrong in our theory as you seem convinced we are. However, what we have uncovered in a legitimate excavation under the streets of London is an authentic finding. Although many of the specifics of that content have yet to be translated, we are nevertheless faced with historic evidence which seriously questions existing Scriptures. In fact, our discovery even casts doubt on the very concept of Jesus and God which these Scriptures have presented for over two thousand years. We believe these findings, as disturbing as they might be, demand further investigation, and that's precisely what we're doing. We meant no offense to you, the Scriptures, or anything else. With all due respect, we had hoped that you might be able to provide some assistance in our search for the truth."

"I wouldn't help you even if I could," Pirtl snapped, as though he were addressing the devil incarnate. "You say you're searching for the truth. Very well, let me give you some truths which have been well summarized in a document by Josh McDowell entitled 'The New Evidence That Demands a Verdict.' I think that the evidence in this document is far more authentic, as you call it, than whatever muck you've dug up under the streets of London."

They looked at one other in silence while Reverend Pirtl dug into his desk drawer. Gordon opened his mouth to speak, but Nigel raised his hand to stop him.

"You damned well better listen to this," the agitated pastor snarled as he raised himself to a stiff standing position behind his desk. He began reading from the document, 'We have in our possession today only eight copies of Herodotus's historic works whose originals were written circa 480 B.C. Also, only five copies of Aristotle's writings from circa 384 B.C. and ten copies of Caesar's writings from about 100 B.C.' "Now this alone—"

"Excuse me, Father," Gordon said. "We're talking about two different types of documents here. With all due respect to your collection, ours is an original letter—"

"Let me finish," the priest snapped. "The time lapses between the date the originals of these were written and the dates of the earliest copies, ranged somewhere between one thousand and one thousand four hundred years. Yet, despite such an enormous time gap between the original writings and their subsequent reproduction, no one has ever questioned their authenticity. The New Testament, on the other hand, was written between 50 and 100 A.D. with a time gap of only fifty years between the original writings and the A.D. 114 date of the earliest copies. And today, we have in our possession five thousand three hundred known Greek manuscripts of them, another ten thousand Latin Vulgates, and nine thousand three hundred other early versions. This gives us twenty-four thousand six hundred manuscript copies which all say the same thing. And now, you think the ramblings of a deranged priest and one Roman letter dug out of the mud in London are going to change all that? Gentlemen, I consider this discussion over. I can only pray that you manage to come to your senses before this gets out of hand. Good day."

In a solemn procession to the door, he ushered them out. They reached their car before Nigel broke the silence.

"Well, I don't think I've been scolded like that since I stole a box of candy from the store when I was six years old, ate it all, and threw up on the new carpet in our parlor."

Gordon nodded. "I'm afraid we've accomplished nothing here except to rattle the chains of tradition a bit and waste some time."

"I'm not entirely convinced that we really wasted our time." Peter put his finger to his forehead and closed his eyes, pausing to wait for a reaction which wasn't long in coming.

Nigel asked the obvious question. "How do you figure that, Peter?"

"Well, the man seemed surprisingly well prepared for what we were going to say, despite the theatrics of his change in demeanor from nice

133

to nasty. He had that rebuttal paper at the tip of his fingers, ready to pounce with it. The intensity of his defensiveness reminded me of the old saying that the more adamantly an idea is defended, the more likely it is to be wrong. Also, did either of you take note of his parting remark? I mean the one about 'before this gets out of hand,' which makes me think he's afraid we might open a can of worms."

Nigel grinned. "Only you Yanks could come up with a term like can of worms. I think I see where you're going."

"I agree, more or less," Gordon added. "So, let's move on to the next place you promised the other team we'd go. Which is what, by the way?"

"Sardis," Peter replied, motioning for Nigel to take the driver's seat again, a tacit acknowledgement that, despite his previous performance, he hadn't lost his status as designated driver.

"Oh yes, the no-man's land." Nigel rolled his eyes and started the Mercedes on its short journey to the nearby town, now known as Sart.

They checked in at a small bed and breakfast several miles from their destination and enjoyed a quiet dinner. Peter stayed up to write the log he'd promised Roger, summarizing the history of Smyrna for Roger's thesis. After he commented on the highlights, he included a section in which he related his own personal observations, readings, and the results of the interviews. His last thoughts before he fell asleep were about Robin.

\* \* \* \* \*

Sardis spread out before them in a panorama of pastures, wild flowers, a few huts left by Yuruk nomads, partly restored Roman excavations, and small shops for tourists. Nigel fixed his gaze on what was left of the old Roman road known as The Marble Way, while Gordon shook his head in disgust.

"Peter," Gordon said, "this is a wasteland, and if we spend ten minutes here, it'll be too long. Let's move on."

Peter nodded. "I'll have to agree with you. However, it's the site of one of the seven churches in Revelation, and any of them might be able to give us information we're looking for about the original Scriptures."

"Yeah, but this is a wasteland with no existing churches, no archaeological repositories."

Peter flipped through the last pages of the New Testament. "I'm giving Revelation another look to see if there's some way I can connect this place with anything we've discovered so far."

Nigel shifted his eyes from the road to Peter. "Are you expecting to find anything different about Sardis?"

"No, I suppose not, except that the Apostle John called it a dead community. Apparently they were such a loose-living bunch of reprobates that even the pagans looked on them with contempt. The number seven appears here several times, but I still can't figure out why that old priest wanted us to focus on it. I sent a text message to Courtney asking if he thought the old man knew more than he told them. He responded yes, but said they couldn't drag anything more out of him."

"So, we're agreed that this place is hopeless, right?" Gordon's question came more in the form of a request for unanimous confirmation.

"Not entirely," Nigel said. "Courtney reminded me before we left London that Melito, Bishop of Sardis, preached very authoritatively in the second century after Sardis became the capital of the revived district of Lydia. Some of his sermons have been preserved, and I've asked my office in London to forward a copy of them. Since the bishop preached relatively soon after the original Scriptures were written and, hopefully, before any alterations were made, I figured his words might give us some insight. I should be getting a reply soon."

"Well done, Nigel." Peter clapped him on the back, then added, "Oh, one more thing. "You'll notice the ancient remnants of a Christian church on that hill over there." He pointed to a grassy hill, with the ragged remains of an old stone structure protruding like a broken tooth. "That church was constructed adjacent to the Sardis Temple of Artemis, a center of pagan worship of Artemis, the goddess of hunting. Thus, that remnant sort of symbolizes that the church either won out over pagan worship or had better architects."

# Chapter 9

## Bergama (Pergamum)

Once again on its journey, their Hyundai became the venue for Sam's ongoing probe into the mystery of a divine creator. He glanced at the map on the seat between him and Roger, then turned to continue his interrogation of Courtney.

"As much as I enjoyed your rhetoric on the history of the universe, I still don't see how you can infer the existence of God from it, as you seem to have done. Stated a different way, how do you know there weren't multiple universes which could have substantially increased the probability of supporting intelligent life without the help of a divine creator? I mean, unless we know exactly how many conditions there were in total that could have produced intelligent life, we really can't deduce that it could not have been generated by random chance."

Courtney paused and rested his chin on his hand as though he needed time to construct a response. "Sam, I'm pleased about your progress in challenging your own atheist theories. Your arguments are not without merit. You're quite right, and I can't dismiss the possibility that there are other universes. I can only offer you two considerations. One, scientists have never been able to support the existence of other universes. Two, they can clone, but they've never been able to create a living cell from non-living material. Nor could they explain how it could have been accomplished randomly. Therefore, even the expert statisticians have concluded, there had to be some other explanation above and beyond random selection in order to account for the development of intelligent life. That should be deduction enough for anyone, don't you think?"

Sam leaned back in his seat and gazed at the passing scenery without answering the challenge. His thoughts drifted back to his life with

Martha. He knew his images of her death struggle would hold a grip on his subconscious for years to come. He felt a twinge of guilt that his transient thoughts of her had become fewer during the past weeks. The events of their biblical search had consumed him, just as Pete had predicted. The search had now risen to the level of extreme importance. Perhaps it was, he reasoned, forgivable that he hadn't nursed the memory of their time together more diligently.

*What would she think of all the logic that seemed to roll so easily from Courtney's tongue?* Sam wondered why he'd never thought about the living cell phenomenon before. Even so, if God had a monopoly on human creation, he should have done a better job of it. The gentle rocking motion of the car combined with the monotonous hum of the wheels to lull him into the kind of anesthetic slumber that mercifully erased pain. He slept better than he had in a long time—until he felt an elbow in his ribs.

Roger's poke jarred him from his thoughts. "Wake up, Sam. We're here."

Sam straightened up, rubbed his eyes, and stared out at Bergama. "Hell, this is nothing but a tourist trap. All I can see are men with short pants, white socks, and bill-caps. I've never seen so many damned T-shirts with geographic logos that make no sense unless you'd already been to one of those places."

Roger flashed a sly grin. "The women are dressed a little better, though."

"Yeah, but not much. With their little cameras slung from their necks, they all seem to know exactly what they're doing and which attraction should be visited next."

"Forget the tourists, lads," Courtney said. "Focus on the Romanization of this religious center of the empire, which you can see from those remnants of temples and theaters. Did you know parchment was invented here when enemies of the city put an embargo on the import of papyrus? That's why the word parchment was derived from the ancient name of the city—Pergamos."

Sam threw Courtney a frustrated glare. "I'll keep that little gem in my notebook of never-to-be-forgotten marvels. Now let's go check into our hotel."

They had already decided on the Berksoy Hotel Bergama, one of only two acceptable accommodations in town. The check-in procedure produced enough confusion to allow them only a brief notice of the well-dressed couple who approached from out of the shadows behind them. The two figures seemed to be waiting patiently to introduce themselves until after the trio completed the registration process.

They stepped forward. The slender man dressed in a sports jacket held out his hand and offered a warm smile. "Good evening, gentlemen. I'm Sar Hoffman, and this is my associate, Lily Frantz. Please pardon our intrusion. We're researchers from the museum in Berlin. We were given your names and were told you'd eventually stop here in Bergama. As you probably know, the German government financed extensive excavations here during the late nineteenth century. Most of the product of that effort now resides in the Pergamon Museum in Berlin, hence our interest in your mission."

Courtney's stunned expression turned into a frown. "What, exactly, do you know about our, as you call it, mission, and what's the nature of your interest in it?"

"Forgive us for not being more explicit," Lily intervened in a soft voice that reeked of condescension. A carefully form-fitted beige dress drew their attention to her sensuous figure. "We know you're searching for an original version of what you believe has been an altered New Testament. Sar and I are in complete agreement with your fundamental premise." She flashed a warm smile which she allowed to linger in Roger's direction.

She turned back to face Sam and Courtney. "We support your objectives and wish to offer all the help we can. Obviously, our museum stands to gain too, thus our interest is not entirely altruistic. Our museum has authorized us to make whatever resources you need available. Of course, it goes without saying, you can count on our complete discretion in this matter."

Sam, Courtney, and Roger paused to glance at one another as though each was waiting for the other to say something. Sam broke the silence. The hardening of his countenance reaffirmed Courtney's own unspoken, but implied, suspicion. "Two questions. What resources, and why?"

Sar's smile turned from warm to forced. "Well, in response to your first question, Dr. Wykoff, I meant whatever funds and archaeological expertise you might need. As for your second question, the answer becomes a bit more complicated. So, Lily and I would like you, Dr. Stickney, and Roger to be our guests for dinner tonight, during which we can explain more fully and more privately. By the way, we're staying at the Iskander Bergama. Dinner will be there at six. May we count on your acceptance?"

After a long pause during which the trio exchanged glances again, Courtney accepted on their behalf. They parted with handshakes— slightly friendly, but still reserved.

* * * * *

The quiet ambience of the restaurant, combined with a special vintage of German wine brought from Berlin, partially washed away some of their mental reservations. At least it made for an easier introduction of Sar's response to the second of Sam's questions.

"You see, gentlemen, Lily and I have, for some time, been in pursuit of the same answers the three of you are so arduously seeking. We, too, have come into possession of an ancient document. To the best of our knowledge, it appears to represent a portion of what we're certain is an original version of one of the books of the New Testament. Naturally we—"

"Excuse me, Mr. Hoffman," Courtney interrupted. "We'll have to see this document before we accept your assessment of it. How many pages of it do you have? How does it differ from today's version? And how did you come into possession of it?"

"Oh, gentlemen, please," Lily intervened, again with a smile so beguiling and a voice so soft it had a mesmerizing effect. "One question at a time. We understand your reluctance to share valuable information with people you've never met before. Let me assure you, we are legitimate, as well as trustworthy." She held out her museum identification card for her interrogators to see before she continued.

"The excavations our country conducted produced, among other things, a letter from the Apostle John to the church at Pergamos. It prophesied a catastrophic end of the human race through the wrath of God. It references the same message for the other six churches in Revelation. This document makes no reference to the biblical doctrine of salvation and it never became part of The Bible we know and follow today. We believe the omission was no accident."

"Do you have this document with you?" Courtney asked.

"Not the original, of course," Sar responded, motioning to the waiter to refill the wine glasses. "Of course, we knew you'd want to see some proof so we brought a photocopy. I'm sure you understand the original must remain under lock and key at the Berlin Museum. I must confess to you that Lily and I are a bit at odds with museum authorities. We believe the original should be made readily available. In fact, we asked that you be allowed to see it."

Courtney cocked his head. "And I'm surmising that the museum didn't agree."

"They refused, saying it will stay under wraps until the need to disclose it arises in the form of something much greater than one party's desire for comfort. Now, Lily and I are convinced their refusal was based on a Vatican mandate, but we can't prove it. You may or may not believe this, but Berlin and the Vatican have been, for many years, silent partners in more endeavors than you could possibly imagine—including German activities during World War II."

Roger broke the silence he'd maintained in deference to the seniority of the other four. "How do you propose to help us?" he asked. That he hadn't been able to take his eyes off the charming Lily all evening hadn't escaped anyone's notice.

Her lips curved in a seductive smile and she touched his shoulder, a gesture from which he made no effort to withdraw. "A very good question, Roger. There are several ways. First, I believe that when the spectral imaging from your awesome discovery is completed, its effect will be earthshaking. MOLAS will encounter immediate attack from virtually all church denominations throughout the world. In fact, you may be faced with opposition from various governments that will pressure you to retract your findings."

Roger nodded. "Yes, that's what concerns us."

"At that point, you will need some authoritative corroboration, at least enough to move the Berlin authorities to come forth with the original document. Then—"

"How about a look at that photocopy?" Sam interrupted in a tone that connoted a still-lingering mistrust of the whole thing.

Sar reached into his briefcase. "Certainly. This copy is as clear as we could make it, considering the age and condition of the original."

Courtney and Sam scanned the photocopy which revealed a jagged tear, indicating its contents had been detached from a larger document

Courtney shook his head while he translated in silence. When he'd finished, he raised his eyes to face his audience. "Well, the wording in this thing follows the style of the Apostle John in the book of Revelation, which I've read more often than I wanted while trying to follow Trazerri's clues. However, this document we're looking at never appeared as part of Revelation, as far as I can tell."

Sar nodded. "True. The narrative in this one threatens worldwide Armageddon as Lily said. It follows John's style, but he never said anything like this in The Bible as it exists today."

Sar and Lily waited, with expressions of irritated impatience, until all three had digested the document's contents. Disbelief written on their faces, Sam and Roger turned to Courtney, as though in silent anticipation of an authoritative opinion.

Courtney shook his head and paused to gather his thoughts. "Look, I really don't know what to tell you. The message in this is clearly anti-scriptural, consistent with what we can decipher in the centurion's letter. The problem is that it's a photocopy, the authenticity of which is still unconfirmed, and the original still not available."

Courtney folded the photocopy, stuffed it in his jacket pocket, and turned to his hosts. "With all due respect, we still don't know enough about you to make an assessment. We know only that you turned up suddenly here in Bergama, and you both seem to know more about our objectives than anyone should. How exactly did you come into possession of all that knowledge about our mission?"

"Dr. Stickney, we apologize for alarming all of you in this manner." Sar's voice was calm and deliberate. "We should have prefaced our entire dialogue by explaining more clearly where we're coming from. Now, please don't repeat this because I'm probably divulging a confidence. One of your archaeologists in London is a friend of one of ours in Berlin. He filled us in. As a matter of fact, we've just finished a dialogue with Reverend Pirtl on another issue. When he asked if we knew anything about you, it sparked a rather heady exchange of information. Again, we ask for your complete discretion in this matter."

Answers followed questions in a thrust-and-parry discussion that took up the remainder of the dinner and the evening. Finally, Courtney raised his hand to bring the conversation to a close. "Okay, it's getting late." He exhaled audibly. "Let's finish our drinks. Lily, tomorrow you and Sar can tell us more about yourselves. Sam, Roger, and I will mull this whole thing over. By the way, before we interrupted, you mentioned there were several types of assistance you would propose. What are they?"

"Oh, we assumed you might need some help on the research as you move to your next site. And Roger, I've become sort of a self-appointed historian on the places you've already visited." She touched his hand in a gentle caress. "I thought I might be able to provide some help on your thesis. Maybe even do some editing for you."

Roger took the bait. "Great. That's an offer I can't refuse. Pending the approval of my two mentors here, you're on."

"Well, what do you say, exalted mentors?" Lily asked. She threw a flirtatious glance at Sam and Courtney.

Sam's face tightened. "It's acceptable to me, providing you tell us more about yourselves and produce some additional identification. We'll, of course, have to clear it with our other team. How about you, Courtney?"

"I'm amenable to it as long as they understand that anything they do must first be approved by us."

"Yes, yes, we agree completely," Sar replied in a tone of renewed impatience.

They shared more background information in an exchange that produced only a moderate clearing in the air of mistrust. Afterward, Roger put in another late-nighter to continue the historic outline for his thesis. He tapped the salient events of Bergama's long history into his little electronic device, until he'd condensed twenty-five hundred years of human struggle into his six-square-inch twenty-first century digital museum. His last entry consisted of an amorous description of Lily.

\* \* \* \* \*

He was tired; she was agitated. Seth knew she'd be irritable. It happened whenever she became excited or depressed—annoying either way, but worse this evening than usual.

"The Supreme Master has presented us with an opportunity beyond our greatest expectations, Seth," she said, "but there are obstacles. Not the least of which will be trying to use those names, which I deplore. Where did you come up with Lily and Sar anyway?"

"It's late, Lilith. The names were necessary." He yawned and stretched out on the bed. "We need the full cooperation of these people. All of them would know right away what our true names represent, and they'd send us packing in a heartbeat. Get used to your new name until we've accomplished our mission. We can discuss any possible obstacles in the morning."

"We'll discuss them now." Her lips tightened, and the soft facial expression that had charmed Roger all evening hardened. Lilith arched her back in a manner that threw her long, raven hair back over her shoulders and made her ample breasts appear even fuller. She paced back and forth and reached under her collar to fidget with the black medallion that hung from her necklace. The Pentagram of Set signified she had progressed through the first, second, and third levels. That achievement entitled her to wear the encircled, point-down pentagram that bore the head of a goat. Fondling it during tense situations had become a habit.

"Lilith, all three of them are practically ours now, and the Illuminati will be well pleased. All we have to do is continue to rein them in. So, how serious can the obstacles be?"

She put up her hand. "First of all, we don't necessarily have all three of them. Yes, Roger is a child, and as malleable as clay. Sam is an atheist who's in this as Roger's mentor and, I'm not surprised to discover, also as a fortune hunter. Thus, he belongs to us as well. Courtney, however, is a problem. He's one of those devout Christians. In itself, this presents no difficulty. However, he's a very knowledgeable one, and this poses a serious challenge."

Seth breathed a heavy sigh and sat up, resigned to postponement of a good night's sleep. "You've missed the point, I'm afraid, Lilith. We don't need to convert Dr. Stickney, or anyone else for that matter. We need only to use them." He cocked his head to one side and offered a condescending smile. "Come now, haven't I spent years teaching you this subtle difference?"

Lilith slumped on the edge of the bed with her hands folded in her lap. "Well, then, what do you intend to do about the other group? They may not accept us as easily as this one did?"

"Probably not. We chose you for this task because of your innate ability to manipulate people and because of your complete devotion to The Enlightened One. Nevertheless, if you are to capture a person's soul, you must learn to discriminate between what a person preaches and what that person really wants. Only then can self-love be used to prevent the development of divine love."

She sprang to her feet again and glared at him. "Don't speak to me as though I don't understand the concept, damn it. I do. You're forgetting that what we have here is a very practical issue. The other group represents three even more knowledgeable people who seem to have aligned themselves very closely with their God, for reasons known only to themselves. I don't think that concept is going to work very well there."

Seth stood and placed his hands on her shoulders. "Wrong, Lilith. Relax a bit and think about it for a minute. As you inferred, five out of the six of them have turned to their God for whatever fulfillment they may derive from that empty gesture. Yet, all of them are betting their reputations that this search will produce a biblical challenge to their God. In fact, they intend for it to be so significant it will echo throughout the world and bring them unparalleled recognition. This is precisely what we must help them do. Once that happens, it will serve to change the world's concept from Jesus as the son of God to Jesus as little more than a clever, but outmoded, earthly teacher. Now, let's go to sleep. We have work to do tomorrow."

\* \* \* \* \*

Kurya Bayhan, curator of *Arkeoloji Muzesi* (Archaeology Museum-Bergama), provided a welcome considerably warmer than expected from a man whose appearance connoted visions of Attila the Hun. His fierce black eyes launched a piercing glare from under the protective camouflage of thick, bushy eyebrows. The man's appearance contradicted his wide, captivating grin. Or perhaps it was the other way around—a pleasant smile that seemed to offer atonement for the rest of his countenance. He reached out to greet his visitors.

"Kurya, you already know Sar," Lily said, returning his smile. "This is Dr. Samuel Wykoff and his brilliant student, Roger Denault. Sam, where's Courtney?"

Sam shrugged. "We're not sure. All I can tell you is he received a text message. Then he said he had to rush off to see some former priest, who apparently ran afoul of the Vatican and now lives by himself in whatever those mountains are just north of here."

"Those are the Madra Mountains," the still-smiling curator interjected, "and I believe the man Dr. Wykoff is referring to was once the head priest at one of the local Christian churches before it was torn down some time ago. Only a handful of people here in Bergama know about him, mostly the older residents. It was a sad story with which I will not bore you. Come, let me show you our museum and its contents. They make up in historic significance whatever they may lack in volume."

A replica of Zeus's altar looked no less impressive than the actual second-century stone horse that had stood beside the original altar nineteen centuries ago and had been preserved intact. Kurya directed their attention to the statue of Hadrian, after which he pointed to a small collection of ancient artifacts. With language that confirmed he'd done this before, Kurya wove the history of the city into his summary of the evolution of its architecture. After he apologized for Berlin's removal of most of the city's historic treasures during the German nineteenth-century excavations, he asked if they had any questions. Sam started to respond before Lily cut him off.

"Yes, Kurya. Roger here is developing his thesis as he visits the seven cities referenced in the Book of Revelation. I wondered if you'd have any objections to my sharing with him some of the little-known history you were kind enough to discuss with me a few days ago. I'm helping him on his project."

She smiled at Roger while she reached to caress the back of his neck. Sam took on the disapproving look of someone who wanted to say something but then thought better of the idea.

"And," she continued while she made a point to avoid Sam's glare, "I'm trying to convince him that the message in his history thesis would attract much wider public attention if he simply focused the whole paper on revealing the truth about The Bible. I'm sure my museum could provide invaluable marketing assistance and worldwide distribution for his final publication."

Kurya nodded. "I have no objections to your sharing with Roger what we talked about, Lily. I would only insist that proper attribution be given to anything in his publication that relates to Bergama. I'm sure you're both professional enough to assure such documentation. Dr. Wykoff, you looked like you wanted to ask a question before Lily spoke up."

"Yes, Mr. Bayhan." Sam paused just long enough to cast a distrusting glance at both Roger and Lily before he continued. "Bergama, as you pointed out, is one of the cities along the Apostle Paul's itinerary. My colleagues and I are searching for anything that might lead to the discovery of all, or any part, of the original Scriptures Paul surely must have distributed. Or even any of his original correspondence documents."

"As strange as this may sound, Kurya," Sar spoke up for the first time since the introductions under the statue of Hadrian, "we have evidence from Roger's research suggesting rather convincingly that such documents might still exist. They're important because they cast serious doubt upon the accuracy of the Scriptures that currently form the basis for all Christian worship."

Sam shot a glare at him. "Well, we're not sure whether they do or don't contradict the Scriptures." He turned with a disapproving glance at Lily. "Either way, we have reason to believe they might still exist and wondered if you could offer any suggestions." No sooner had the remark spilled out than Sam felt a sudden sense of surprise, and a twinge of embarrassment, that he had inadvertently said something which could have been interpreted as a defense of biblical doctrine.

"Ah, my friends," Kurya said, "I would be pleased to help you if I could. You must appreciate that I'm not in the business of ecclesiastic research. My field is archaeology. Or more precisely, I'm an historian who dabbles in archaeology. I believe I can, however, offer you one observation, for whatever it might be worth. Your colleague—the one who couldn't join us today—what is his name?"

"Dr. Courtney Stickney," Sam replied.

146

"Oh yes, Dr. Stickney. Well, you mentioned that he went to see the one I told you about up into the Madras. No one really knows for sure—and this may be pure myth—but the old man your friend is on his way to see was rumored to have, as you put it, run afoul of the Vatican. It was because he absconded with some ancient documents belonging to the Roman Catholic Church. If there's any truth to the rumor, then my guess is that Dr. Stickney is about to find at least a partial answer to your question. I'm afraid that's all I can offer. Would all of you care to join me for lunch?"

Sam shook his head. "I'm afraid we'll have to decline, Mr. Bayhan. Roger and I need to discuss some issues with Sar and Lily. Anyway, we appreciate the offer."

Sam nodded gratefully and nudged Roger and the two Berliners toward the door. His cold stare in their direction left no room for misinterpretation. He reached out to shake Kurya's hand. "I want you to know we're extremely grateful for your hospitality and your information."

"Anytime, Dr. Wykoff. Come back and see us whenever you're in the area. Perhaps I can treat you to a delightful lunch then."

After they stepped outside and walked toward the car, Lily turned to face Sam.

"I can see we've apparently offended you, Sam," she purred softly. "If we did, please know it was purely unintentional. It's just that we're as anxious as you all are to make your mission a success. I apologize and I—"

"What Lily means," Sar said, "is that we realize this is your mission and we are here only to assist. We will, of course, let you take the lead and do the talking in any further discussions. By the way, since Courtney took your car you clearly need a ride to wherever you're going. Will you let us make up for things by providing whatever transportation you need? And may I also suggest that perhaps we all motor up to meet Courtney? I mean, Berlin has always maintained close relations with the Vatican, and I thought perhaps we might be able to shed some light on whatever dialogue Courtney and this former priest might be having."

"No, that won't be necessary." Sam breathed a deep sigh, wondering if he might have overreacted. "However, Roger and I could use a lift back to our hotel. We need to discuss our next step in private. I think it's best to leave Courtney to conduct his interview by himself."

"Of course. As to your next step," Sar persisted, "have you heard anything more on the status of the imaging scans that your London crew is doing?"

"No. Only that they expect to have a legible product sometime late next week."

\* \* \* \* \*

The locals had assured Courtney the old recluse he was looking for could be found no further up the mountain than a mile or two. A relatively easy climb, they said, since the man's little shack was on the gentler slope of the foothills, not on the steep side of the mountain itself. Courtney parked his car at the base of the foothills and proceeded on foot, following an old donkey path that hadn't been used for so long the weeds and bramble brush had begun to overgrow it.

Almost out of breath, after a two-hour hike, he spotted the shack in the distance and decided to stop for a moment to rest before introducing himself. He reached the not-so-difficult conclusion that the locals' definition of an easy climb differed substantially from his own. Grateful for the downhill slope he was on, he'd progressed to within one hundred yards of the dilapidated little dwelling when he heard the screams, unmistakably cries of pain. Courtney sucked in one more deep breath, then broke into a dead run toward the shack, not at all sure what he'd do once he arrived.

A hooded figure stood over the writhing, prostrate form of a man Courtney assumed must be the recluse the villagers had told him about. The attacker whirled to face Courtney as he came through the door. Although the man was younger and probably in much better physical condition, Courtney had the advantage of size and momentum. He crashed into the attacker with enough force to send the startled man backward into a fragile wall, which immediately gave way, breaking his fall. The man leaped to his feet with the agility of youth and readied himself to return the blow. After he'd paused to assess their size difference, he must have decided against it and bolted out the door.

148

Not at all confident of his ability to fight it out anyway, Courtney heaved a sigh of relief and bent down to check the condition of the bleeding recluse. "How badly are you hurt?" he asked while he wiped the blood from the old man's face with his handkerchief.

The man sat upright and pulled back. "He pounded my backside where the kidneys are. That's the only part that really hurts. Who are you, and what do you want? No…, forgive me. I should be thanking you for breaking up the attempt to kill me. Who are you, and what are you doing here?"

"My name is Dr. Courtney Stickney. I'm searching for some historic information of a biblical nature. They told me in town you might be able to help."

The old man cocked his head. "You a medical doctor?"

"No, I'm the other kind. I'm from the Museum of London Archaeological Service. I'm thinking I'd best take you to a hospital. Or at least get you out of here in case that fellow tries again. Do you have any idea why he attacked you?"

"Damn right I do. The Vatican sent him."

"Why?"

"You sure you're not from the church?"

"I'm sure. I'm a theologian but not associated with any entity other than a museum. Why do you think the Vatican sent him to attack you?"

"I don't think, I know. I disobeyed their orders to collect some documents. I mean I collected them, but I was supposed to give them to that young man you bounced off my wall. I had already sent a few of them to an old friend of mine in Denizli a long time ago. Somehow, my attacker knew it. He beat me and would have given it to me good if you hadn't happened by."

The old man struggled to his feet and leaned against a post. "And I'm not going anywhere. This is my place and they can come after me all they want, but I'm not going to let them force me out. I'll be fine, thank you. So you can stop checking me over. Is that why you're here? I mean, about those original Scriptures?"

"Yes. Does your friend in Denizli have the documents now?"

"He did, but he died before he could publish them as I had urged him to do. I inquired but the documents disappeared, and no one knows what exactly happened to them."

They talked for another hour. The recluse answered some of Courtney's questions before finally asking to be left alone. Courtney saw no point in continuing the interview. He bade the old man goodbye, retraced his steps down the slopes of the Madras, and paused on the way down to pray the attacker would be so obliging as to leave the old man alone.

\* \* \* \* \*

Roger and his mentor shared even less conversation during dinner than they had all afternoon. "Roger, what's going on with you and Lily?" Sam finally asked. It was a subject Sam had carefully avoided all day, knowing it would be like poking a hornet's nest with a stick. Sam's determination to avoid the issue finally succumbed to his concern that continued silence might worsen the situation.

"I'm not sure what you mean, Sam. Except that I kept wanting to open the top buttons on her blouse."

"You wanted to do what?"

"No, I didn't mean it that way. I mean, she kept fondling her necklace or something under her blouse. At first I wondered why she would even bother to wear a necklace if she's going to hide it under a high collar like that. Then I thought maybe it was a nervous tic or something. No, there's nothing going on, although I kind of wish there were. She's absolutely beautiful, don't you think? Who knows, maybe as we work together on my paper I can eventually answer your question with more substance."

His coffee cup halfway to his mouth, Sam stopped and glared at Roger. "Good grief, the woman's at least ten years older than you. I still don't trust her motives in this thing. That garbage about wanting to use her doggone museum as a propaganda conduit for your thesis is way out of line. Look, Roger, I'm just your academic mentor in your doctoral candidacy. I'm not your conscience. Listen, you have to stay focused. Your private life is your business, although not to the point where it jeopardizes our project. Do I make myself clear?"

"Yes, sir." Roger lowered his gaze. "Do you want me not to see her? I mean, not let her help out on my paper?"

150

"That's up to you, Roger." Sam finished the last drop in his cup and pushed it aside. "As I said, your personal affairs are outside of my domain as your academic advisor. Still, I'd be careful about what you say and do with Lily. Not to underestimate your skills with women, but she's a very manipulative lady, so watch yourself. And I don't have to tell you, if she gives you any help or anything useful for your paper, you must be sure to acknowledge her contribution in your bibliography and any citations required by the American Psychological Association. I'm sure you know your APA attribution requirements."

"Yes, sir. I'll be extremely careful."

"Okay, good. Now, on another subject, I happened to notice one of the pages you were writing for your thesis last night about Bergama. I wasn't prying. You had it lying out when I picked you up for breakfast this morning. I saw it while I was waiting for you to finish dressing. You referenced that Bergama was… ah… Satan's throne or something. Was that an assessment of your own or does it have something to do with the actual religious history of this place?"

"It's part of Bergama's history, Sam. Or, I should say, the history of Pergamos as this city was called in ancient times. The city became the capital of a large Roman province in 129 B.C. The Romans used to worship their pagan gods at the temples here during a period when there were reputed to be evil doings going on, hence, the reference to the city as Satan's throne. Why? Is that relevant to what we're doing here?"

"I'm not sure. There's something that bothers me about this place, and our maybe-not-so-coincidental hookup with Sar and Lily. I don't know, perhaps it's just me. Anyway, here comes Courtney. Signal the waiter to bring another menu and I'll pour him some coffee." As Courtney took a seat, Sam said, "Welcome back, Courtney. What got you so fired up this morning that you had to rush off into the mountains? And by the way, we found out something about that old guy you met. You might be interested to hear it. So let's all play show-and-tell while you order dinner."

Courtney pointed to his selection on the menu and gave it back to the waiter. "You're not going to believe this," he began, "but you go first. What did you find out at that museum?"

Sam pointed to his pastry dish and his coffee cup to signal the waiter for a refill of both. "Well, aside from my becoming even less enchanted

151

about this sudden relationship with our friends from Berlin, I heard a local rumor. The man you met stole some ancient documents, presumably of a religious nature, and found himself on the wrong side of the powers that be at the Vatican. That's about it. Tell us about this man and what went on in 'the Madras,' as our local curator called them."

Courtney paused as the waiter brought a fresh pot of coffee. "Well, that man on the mountain was in the process of having the hell beaten out of him when I arrived on the scene. I think my size scared the attacker away, but the old recluse looked so bad he almost wasn't human anymore. I rather felt sorry for him. He refused my offer to bring him back to Bergama for medical help. I think he's just given up and wants to die in peace there in his little hut. Anyway, getting back to the subject, he didn't exactly steal anything. As I understand it, the Vatican only recently got wind of his having discovered some original Scriptures. The man who attacked him was sent to recover the documents and bring them back, probably to be destroyed. Instead—"

"What's the name of the recluse?" Roger interrupted.

"Oh, I'm sorry. I got so wrapped up in this I forgot you didn't know. It's Vilosky. Formerly Father Ylnik Vilosky. He said he'd found a number of ancient Scriptures, like the ones Trazerri told us about. He insisted there's no doubt in his mind they were originals or at least second or third century reproductions of them. He didn't steal them. He'd recently sent all but one of the documents straight back to Rome as he was instructed. He kept out one batch and sent it on to a fellow priest in Denizli. He claims it was an original version of the last few pages of the Book of Revelation."

"Why did he hold out that one?" Roger asked.

"And why did he send it to Denizli?" Sam added.

"Ah, that's the interesting part. This brings me to why I went up there in the first place."

Sam bit off a chunk of his pastry and washed it down with a gulp of coffee. "Yeah, you rushed out of here like a bat out of hell."

"I know. My apologies for not explaining, but time was of the essence. I received an urgent text message from Nigel who's been in contact with one of his compatriots in London. Apparently, Bishop Melito, a second-century Christian leader who lectured authoritatively on the various contents of the New Testament, had written a letter just before he died. He quoted directly from one of his earlier readings of Revelation. His letter referenced the passage in Revelation about the thousand years of Jesus just as that passage appears today. The letter also referenced a passage that says six thousand years of Satan must come first. And that passage never shows up in the version of Revelation we read today. Vilosky saw Melito's letter as it was originally written when he went through the stuff he was supposed to send back to Rome."

"So why did he send the stuff to his friend in Denizli?" Roger persisted.

Sam leaned forward with anxiety written all over his face. "And where is it now?"

Courtney paused while the waiter placed the meal in front of him. He watched the man walk away. "Okay, Vilosky claims his friend in Denizli was in the process of writing his thesis on Bishop Melito. Vilosky sent his friend the original version of the last few pages and suggested he should reference those in his thesis. As it turned out, the church refused to accept his friend's thesis. Or even allow it to be submitted in support of his doctoral candidacy unless he removed all the references to those last few pages. He removed them. Vilosky said his friend passed away shortly thereafter—a rather mysterious death—and now no one knows anything about the original version of the thesis or its whereabouts."

"What about the bishop's letter?" Sam asked, settling back into his chair.

"London has it and forwarded a photocopy to Nigel."

"Was it the original letter written by Melito?" Roger asked.

"It was, Roger. The problem is that Melito was close to death at the time he wrote the letter. Our folks in London seem to be convinced that he was senile at the time and have therefore discounted the accuracy of his recollections. They've cautioned us not to pursue the matter further, since the contents of his letter are likely to be deemed questionable."

"By the church, no doubt," Roger muttered, shaking his head.

"Yes, and by everyone else at all familiar with the circumstances."

Sam raised his arms in a gesture of disgust. "Oh, that's just great. I suppose all the stuff Trazerri saw when he turned up that loose stone might have been part of what your friend in the mountains sent back to Rome."

Courtney took another bite of his meal and shrugged. "Who knows? Father Vilosky said he sent everything back, and he didn't mention anything about what Trazerri saw."

"So where does that leave us?" Roger asked. "Are we at another dead end?"

Courtney polished off another few bites and pushed his plate aside. "No, not necessarily. We still have everything our two teams have come up with so far. Although much of it's largely circumstantial at this point, our findings present a strong argument that the New Testament has been substantially rewritten. Now, in that context, I just received a shocking piece of news from London. Our ancient language expert there has translated the parchment photo I sent in. You know, the one Nigel's group dug up in Chester. Well, it turns out—"

"Don't tell me, let me guess," Sam jumped in. "Another original biblical writing that's been since replaced by a Roman Catholic Church forgery."

"No, Sam. It's worse than that. The narrative on the parchment represents a response to some earlier mandate for the murder of the apostles. All of them. The response confirms that, in compliance with the mandate, the twelve apostles were all killed in the same manner. The translator had difficulty with some of the wording, but it seems that—"

"Courtney, I don't see anything unusual about that," Roger piped up. "I'm no biblical scholar, but church history is pretty clear on this. Eight of the apostles died as martyrs, Judas committed suicide, and no one really knows how John, Bartholomew, and Simon died. Your parchment sounds like nothing more than a summary of what we already knew."

Courtney shook his head. "I wish it were that simple, Roger. The parchment says all twelve were torn apart by an animal of some kind. The dates, places, and names are clearly listed, following the narrative. The translator wasn't sure, but he thinks the thirteenth line after the listing references the slaying and burial of an animal by the Romans. I think we're looking at an egregious biblical forgery and subsequent cover-up by the church, here."

"Who issued the mandate?" Sam inquired.

"Doesn't say. And apparently there was no mention of the kind of animal that killed them, or where it came from, but just indulge me for a moment while I try to put the pieces together on this. Nigel's team digs down under a burned-out church to a point just above what the woman they interviewed thought was a Roman armory. Nigel's group never goes down far enough to hit the armory, but they do uncover a badly preserved burial vault containing this ugly beast and the parchment. Then the images of the beast on Peter's photos mysteriously disappear in transmission. What do you guys think?"

Sam scratched his head and thought for a moment. "Well then, allow me to do some fitting together of the pieces. If the Romans killed and buried this beast, they'd position it either beside or under their armory, not above it. And they'd seal up the vault in good, thorough Roman style. This may sound a bit far out, as the saying goes. I'd surmise that someone dug up the vault, opened it, saw what it contained, and couldn't wait to seal it back up again and get it out of sight, out of mind. Hence the lousy preservation job and that woman's objection to further digging that might reopen a religious can of worms—no pun intended."

Roger turned to Courtney. "Okay, this little journey of ours is looking more like Dante's Inferno every step we take. And don't forget, there's still the centurion's letter, which seems like it just might reconfirm all the strange happenings we've encountered. So, where do we go from here?"

Courtney leaned back in his chair and yawned. "Right now, I'm too exhausted to talk about it. We're clearly approaching the upper limits of bizarre. I'll forward the expert's findings to Nigel, along with our suspicions. Anyway, on a different subject, the three of us need to visit Thyatira."

Roger frowned. "Where?"

"Well, Akhisar, as it's known today. Gordon, Pete, and Nigel will visit Philadelphia—Alaşehir in modern lingo. Then the plan is for both our teams to meet in Laodicea. The map shows it as Denizli, our seventh and last location on this long journey. I figure we'll research what we can there, and then we'll all return to London to review the final scans of the centurion's letter. At that point, gentlemen, this journey will be over. We'll either present the world with a whole new concept of Christianity, or we'll all go home with a renewed respect for The Bible in its current form. You, Roger, will end up, either way, with the makings of a fascinating thesis. Any questions?"

155

Sam leaned forward. "Yeah. Roger and I have been discussing Sar and his sexually aggressive partner, the two wanna-be additions to our team. I'm becoming less and less in favor of allowing them to work with us, and I wonder what your thoughts are."

"Interesting you should bring that up," Courtney said. "I wasn't going to mention this, because I didn't think I'd ever have to, but Nigel says we're stuck with them. That is, at least for a while."

Sam frowned. "What? Why?"

"Well, it seems MOLAS feels it's necessary in order to maintain good relations with the international archaeology community."

"You mean with Berlin," Sam snarled. "So, how do we make our self-invited friends happy and still keep them out of our hair?"

Roger laughed. "Well, I think I can keep Lily out of your hair."

Courtney turned to Roger with a quizzical expression. "What do you mean by that?"

"Never mind," Sam growled. "You don't even want to go there. He's joking."

Courtney shrugged his shoulders. "Okay, I'll assume it's a private matter. At any rate, give them only what they insist on and nothing else. Avoid giving them any gratuitous information, and don't mention anything about the parchment mandate to murder the apostles or anything about our other team's discoveries."

Heads nodded in agreement.

# Chapter 10

# Bursa

Seth had booked their reservations at the Açelya Hotel in Bursa, once the capital of the Ottoman Empire and now the center of the Turkish automobile industry. The hotel selection had been based on Seth's conclusion that the Açelya represented the best of the least expensive and marginally acceptable sleeping quarters in Bursa. Lilith's argument against the choice rested on her articulate characterization of the place as "cheap." Seth's counter-argument revolved around his concept of "frugal," but conceded that the unavailability of anything other than single rooms might be a slight disadvantage. Their discussion ended with moderate agreement that, in view of their differences, sleeping in separate rooms might be preferable anyway.

The check-in process completed, Seth nudged Lilith in the direction of the dining room. "The food here is reputed to be exquisite, Lilith. In fact, the view outside is worth taking in after we eat. We're right at the foot of the sprawling slopes of the Uludağ."

"The what?"

"The mountain range. They say it's a popular ski resort in winter."

"Did you notice that man who kept looking at us while we checked in?" she asked, in an abrupt change of subject.

"No. What man?" Her non sequitur brought a frown to Seth's face.

"That emaciated-looking beanpole who I'm sure has been eavesdropping on our conversation ever since we came in."

Seth rolled his eyes. "Lilith, being careful is one thing. Being paranoid is quite another. Come on, let's find a seat by the window and order dinner. I'm hungry. I've a text message that just came in, and I want to sit down and read it."

The short, smiling waiter, whose dark hair contrasted with his light blue sleeveless vest and matching trousers, approached them with an unrequested tray of candied peaches and Turkish coffee, as though consumption of it was the local custom. In deference to Lilith's preference for sliced beef with tomato sauce and yogurt, Seth ordered the iskender kebab for both of them. After the waiter left, he pushed the coffee aside and stared wide-eyed at the message on his iPhone.

"Seth, you look like you've seen a ghost. Is there a problem?" She waited before repeating the question. "Seth, is it that bad?"

He stuffed the offending instrument into his pocket and looked up at her with an agonized expression. "I'm afraid so. The message is from our loyal follower, Miriam McDarren. She—"

"The old woman who burned down the church in Chester?"

"Yes, she—"

"I always wondered why you liked her. She's completely insane, you know. Most arsonists are."

Seth took a deep breath and raised his hand in a gesture of disgust. "Lilith, she burned the church because the city council was about to vote yes on allowing that Scottish firm to unearth those Roman artifacts reputedly buried somewhere around there. It was a damned smart ploy because, by city ordinance, such a disaster blocks construction, exploration, or any other activity until plans to replace the damaged property have been approved. Otherwise, evidence of The Enlightened One's victory over those abominable proselytes might have been found and made public. And Miriam's not insane, by the way."

"So what happened that has you so upset?"

"Miriam says the other half of the team we just met has dug down there, without authorization, and discovered The Enlightened One's devoted animal, as well as his instructions to it. So, it seems that the prospect of public announcement has reared its ugly head again."

"What's wrong with that?" Lilith asked. "Isn't it our objective to destroy sheepish faith in Christianity and its misleading doctrine?"

Seth glowered. "Lilith, you have much to learn. What you don't seem to understand here is that, right now, disclosure of such an unpopular piece of historic fact could work against us. Here comes the waiter with our meal. Let's enjoy the dinner and we'll decide on a plan afterward."

They picked at their kebab in silence, as though Miriam's message had soured their appetites for both food and conversation. The aroma of coffee and Turkish cuisine drifted through the dining room, as the tables filled up, and the buzz of surrounding conversation droned in their ears.

Lilith pushed her unfinished meal aside and broke the heavy silence. "What I don't understand is how that burial vault could possibly have been found. I thought it was buried next to the Roman armory. Did that three-man team from London actually dig down that far?"

"It was, and no, they didn't get that far. Miriam's ancestors apparently found it and moved it after the miners failed to appreciate the significance of what they'd discovered and walked away. Unfortunately, Miriam's ancestors opened the vault and didn't reseal it properly. Thus, a piece of good Roman workmanship was compromised and some damage to the contents occurred."

"And you think that team will publicize its findings in a way that will reinforce prevailing Christian doctrine? How so?"

"Well, I think it was necessary for The Enlightened One to punish the apostles in a way that would send a message. However, I believe that the rather gruesome way he did it will only serve to anger Christians. Left undiscovered, there would have been no problem. Now that the discovery has been made, I'm afraid public disclosure of any kind may reinforce the convictions of the committed sheep and unite the uncommitted ones with them against us."

"What do you propose to do?"

Seth set aside his resistance to Turkish coffee. He poured a cup from the small ceramic pot the waiter had delivered and pondered the question. He filled Lilith's cup without asking whether she wanted any or not. "As I see it, we have several options. We can do nothing and trust that disclosure will actually work in our favor, insofar as it tends to discredit prevailing Christian doctrine…its brutality notwithstanding. Or, we can try to convince the two London teams to conceal their findings on the premise that public awareness will do irreparable damage to Christianity worldwide. Then again, we could put a positive spin on it as The Enlightened One has often done."

Lilith smiled in her most beguiling manner. "Tell me how."

"We create a diversion, one of His favorite techniques. We say the Berlin Museum has done research which reveals a clever Christian plot—using a fabricated beast and forged mandate—to blame the Romans for such a horrific slaughter of the apostles. Christian doctrine already assumes, for the most part, that the martyrdom of apostles was, directly or indirectly, a Roman function anyway."

Lilith clapped her hands and grinned. "Yes! I get it. We thus convert the London team's discovery from a startling revelation to a cheap hoax. You are truly brilliant, Seth."

Seth offered one of his rare smiles. "I'm pleased that you're in agreement, Lilith. It's been a long day. I'll meet you here for breakfast at eight, and then it's on to meet the teams in Alaşehir. Sleep well."

\* \* \* \* \*

Lilith slipped the little plastic card into its receptacle to open her hotel room door. She couldn't suppress a smile at the contrast of modern technology with a place that once represented the heart of antiquity. She stepped into the dark room and flipped the light switch, but she failed to notice the tall man behind her until he'd wrapped one hand over her mouth and positioned the dagger against her throat with the other.

"You satanic bitch." He whispered a low, angry growl in her ear. "Your only hope for staying alive is to give me enough information to publicly denounce this whole antichrist movement you and your fellow blasphemers have going." Eyes narrowed, he put his mouth closer to her ear. "One scream out of you and the sight of this dagger plunging into your evil heart will be the last earthly image your demented mind will process. Do we have an understanding?"

Lilith nodded barely enough to avoid forcing a penetration of the blade.

Reverend Carlen Pirtl released his grip and shoved her against the wall. "Good. Now, let's begin. Exactly where is the other half of the atheist team you're working with?"

Lilith took a small step away from the wall, swallowed hard, and paused to collect her thoughts while she sized up her adversary. She'd seen his type before. Aside from his obvious anger and possession of a weapon, he was just another of the sheep blinded by their god. This one, however, would need to be handled in a different way. "Sir, I've not yet met the other half, and I'm sorry to say I don't know where they are."

She slowly unbuttoned her blouse with one hand and removed it with the other, almost in one graceful, enticing movement.

"What the hell are you doing?" the reverend barked, his eyes now opened wide at the sight of Lilith's full, firm breasts.

She removed the delicate chain attached to her Pentagram of Set so he wouldn't focus on it. She smiled in her unique, seductive way. "It's warm in here, sir, and I'm simply getting comfortable now that I'm alone with a good-looking man." She paused long enough to assure herself that the man's gaze was fixed on her ample bosom, then purred, "You might want to do the same and take off your jacket. Especially if this is to be a long discussion."

"Curse you, I know damned well you know about the letter your friends unearthed in London. I want to know the details. What's in it? And don't try to plead your coy innocence with me again."

Lilith smiled again and cocked her head. She knew it would take at least another few minutes for the man to become seduced, and she sensed that she had plenty of time. "You might not believe this, sir, but—"

"Stop calling me 'sir.' My title is 'Reverend' for purposes of this dialogue, and your seductive little attempts at guile won't work. Now, answer my question, damn you."

Her movements toward him continued to be gradual and unobtrusive. "As you wish, Reverend. What I started to say was that we both may be on the same side. I happen to know that this document you referred to is a forgery. Like you, my partner and I intend to expose it as such." She continued to ease the medallion back and forth and noticed the expected softening in the man's countenance.

"The hell you do. Did you really expect me to believe that, on your say so, God and Satan have become partners?" He wiped a bead of perspiration from his forehead.

"In this instance, yes, as strange as that may sound. Look, my good reverend, we may be on opposite sides of the religious fence, but there's one point we can both agree on...that is, if you're willing to listen carefully."

His angry glare appeared to have eased up a bit. Pirtl tucked the dagger under his belt and placed his hands on his hips, arms akimbo. "And that would be...?"

"That would be the undeniable fact that the so-called discovery of a new religion by those six fortune-hunters you're at odds with would throw a dark, worldwide, shadow of doubt on your position as well as mine." Lilith loosened her skirt and allowed it to slip to the floor around her feet. She felt a familiar sense of triumph at the sight of Pirtl's wide-open eyes locked on the black silk panties that emphasized the soft curves of her hips and thighs.

The reverend drew a deep breath. He lowered his hand to his crotch in an effort to cover the mounting bulge. His face reddened. "So, are you suggesting that I back off long enough to allow you to complete an exposure of their scam?"

In a single motion, Lilith stepped gracefully out of the skirt around her ankles and slipped out of her shoes, exposing her delicately shaped feet. She moved closer to him. "If you want to stop them dead in their tracks, yes. It's late. You look tired. Do you have a room here at the hotel?"

"Ahh, no." His words came slowly, as though her observation had confirmed his fatigue. "I hadn't planned to stay. I think—"

"Good. Then why don't you sleep here with me tonight? We can share the specifics of my plan in the morning when we're both fresh."

"Well, I—"

"Oh, come on," she purred again. She flashed a beguiling smile while she unfastened her hair ribbon, allowing her long, raven black hair to cascade invitingly around her shoulders. "We can forget our differences just long enough to discredit this ugly hoax. We can always become enemies again afterward, if you'd like." She placed her hands gently on each side of the now partially mesmerized man's head and slid them down to his neck in a caressing fashion. "There's room for both of us on this bed." She reached down to caress the part of his body she knew had reached its maximum point of stimulation.

As she expected, Pirtl acquiesced. Lilith watched him undress down to his striped shorts, then turned out the light and pulled him into bed. Confident that Pirtl's fear of a career-destroying scandal would assure his silence and keep him at bay, Lilith savored a sense of satisfaction.

\* \* \* \* \*

Miriam McDarren had been an active participant in the city of Chester's local government meetings ever since the letters of patent from the United Kingdom had conferred upon the officials the status of charter trustees in lieu of city council. The trustees' rejection of Miriam's prior requests to seek out and punish those who burned down her church now served to strengthen her commitment to prevent any further excavation under the charred remains.

The evening's scheduled business having been taken care of, Lord Mayor Duncan MacInnis finally yielded to Miriam's arm waving. "Mrs. McDarren, you have the floor, but only on condition that this isn't going to be another tirade about punishment for what happened to your church."

Miriam pulled herself to a standing position behind her walker and threw her best effort into the fabrication of a smile. "No, sir. What I have to say now is far more important. It concerns the rebuilding of my church. Now, I have here—"

"Mrs. McDarren, we've told you this before. It is not the responsibility of the charter trustees to reconstruct your church. As angry as we are about what happened, we have neither the funds nor the legal authority to act on that."

Miriam straightened up as much as her arthritic frame would allow and waved her copy of the long-forgotten local ordinance in the air. "I understand, Lord Mayor. However, what you must now understand is that a serious legal violation of our city's regulations has gone unattended for many years. I only recently uncovered it. I now ask you to read this document aloud to the trustees and all present here tonight."

One of the trustees walked back to her, took the piece of paper, and handed it to MacInnis.

The Lord Mayor studied it for a moment, passed it back over the isles to Miriam, and frowned. "Very well, I've seen it. Now, what's your point?"

Miriam's mechanized smile disappeared. "The point, dear sir, is that, if you'd read the ruling carefully, you would have noticed that it requires each and every building in this city to have a concrete floor. As you well know, my little church has never had one. As a result, vandals

163

have recently churned up the dirt which constitutes our floor. Why? No one will ever know. Anyway, that sort of thing must never happen again."

Trustee Alistair Daltry leaned forward. "Mrs. McDarren, why did you wait until now to bring this up? You and practically everyone else in Chester has known for years about the dirt floor of your building, although I'm certain no one was aware of this ruling you've just presented."

"I bring it up only because we've now experienced a break-in with intent to vandalize. It's the responsibility of the trustees to take action." Visions of Marston and what Miriam perceived as his self-serving, treasure-hunting companions and what they must have discovered swept through her mind.

MacInnis threw his hands in the air. "Madam, our hands are still tied. We simply don't have the budgeted funding for such things."

Miriam held the document up, shook it, and glared at MacInnis. "Damnation, I'll finance the concrete flooring costs myself. Now, you damn well get busy and approve this action or I will continue to raise hell at each and every one of your damned meetings. My congregation and I will not tolerate another invasion of our building remains or foundation by outsiders who have absolutely no business there, and this meeting will not conclude until a motion for acceptance of my offer has been made and approved."

The trustees looked at each other and then at MacInnis, who swore softly and nodded his approval. Daltry made the motion after which a brief discussion followed. Five minutes later, an angry Lord Mayor announced the unanimous agreement to accept Miriam's offer, and the meeting adjourned.

# Chapter 11

# Alaşehir (Philadelphia)

Rather than waiting for Sar and Lily, who were, by then, half an hour late, Gordon, Nigel, and Peter decided to order without them.

"I see you're still keeping your running log for Roger," Gordon said as he watched Peter tapping away on his Blackberry. "You've put yourself through quite a bit of work collecting and organizing all that data for him this last week."

Peter responded without looking up. "Only because I'd like to see him put this 'I'll-show-'em-I'm-just-as-good-as-my-dad' thing behind him and get a life of his own for a change." After he finished filling in his one-line summary observations on the ancient city of Philadelphia, he leaned back in his chair with returning thoughts about how the history recorded so far on this journey might fit into his sermons one day.

"Peter, you seem deep in your thoughts," Nigel said. "Care to share any of them with us?"

Peter stuffed the electronic library in his pocket and looked at Nigel. "I'm not sure they're worth sharing. Deep in the labyrinth of my mind, I keep picturing a grinning antichrist thanking me for my contribution to the ultimate subversion of the Scriptures. You know what? I think the antichrist is daring me to become a stronger pastor."

Peter turned to Gordon. "Are you a church-goer, Gordon?"

Gordon shook his head. "Only when there's a compelling reason to be there. Nigel keeps hounding me to go. I am a believer, but I've never seen a church that actually met the needs of its flock. Certainly not my needs."

"And what are your needs?"

Gordon leaned back and stretched. "Oh, I don't know. I guess I've never really articulated them. Since you asked, I'd say, for starters, they'd include something like finding out why a document coming out of a two thousand-plus-year-old patriarchal culture could have any relevance to my environment today. Don't get me wrong, I'm not an avowed atheist like your colleague Sam. I just don't see any point in trying to find answers in a church."

Peter closed his eyes and put his forefinger to his forehead in a manner that made it look like his head was resting on it.

Nigel stopped nursing his tea and turned in time to find Peter deep in concentration again.

As though it would help the process, Pete opened his eyes, looked up, and stared out the window while he contemplated. Gordon's assessment of the church's inability to connect with its parishioners was accurate. They come for answers to twenty-first century problems, he thought to himself, and we give them ancient parables. We tell them The Bible is about a covenant between man and God, but we don't convince them it's relevant.

Gordon reached over and tapped Peter on the shoulder. "Hey, I didn't mean to send you into a trance again. Are you still with us?"

Peter clapped his hands together. "I am, Gordon. You've made me think about the church in a way I hadn't considered before."

"Like how?"

"Well, for twelve centuries after Christ's death there was fear and ignorance for which the church alone held answers. Then came enlightenment, scientific proofs, and technology. Soon the church no longer filled the gap. Worse, the obsolete wording of Scriptures began to get in the way. Faith lost its hold on a modern world. Now I'm thinking maybe the solution is somewhere in this mission, if the dots can ever be connected."

"Very well, you two." Nigel exhaled audibly as though he'd hoped for a more dramatic outcome. "As long as we're on the subject of answers, I have a question. Courtney says he's not happy that protocol requires our acceptance of these two folks from the Berlin Museum. Notwithstanding that none of the three of us has ever met them, what are your thoughts?"

The question caught them off guard and, for a few moments, no one said anything.

"Oh, I don't like their names," Peter said, "but otherwise I'll abstain from offering an opinion until they show up and we see what they're like."

"What's wrong with their names?" Gordon asked, while he plunged his English muffin boldly into his coffee. Peter smiled at Nigel's frown, which he took to be an unspoken condemnation of Gordon's lack of etiquette.

"Well, first of all their names are not Sar and Lily," Peter said. "I've been doing some research with a contact of mine in Berlin. It turns out their real names are Seth and Lilith…. Get it?"

"No."

"Well, they're names of Satanic origin. Lilith was referred to in ancient times as night demon, a succubus who haunted men at night and stole their seed. She's also thought of as a sister of Lucifer. Seth was the ancient god of storms and sometimes thought of as 'one who dazzles,' or the lord of demons."

Peter paused to let it all sink in until the belated arrival of Seth and Lilith ended the discussion. Polite introductions were made, no one brought up the subject of names, and apologies for being late were offered and accepted. They discussed how Sar and Lily would fit into the team's next step in the process, and Sar reiterated the benefits that could be derived from Berlin's support for their ultimate findings.

Lily directed her smile at Nigel and Gordon. "When Sar spoke of the contributions our museum could make, gentlemen, he was, of course, referring to the value we could add to your overall mission. Now, in a more intimate sense, a properly structured outcome would do wonders for MOLAS…and you personally, Nigel. As for you, Gordon, there's no doubt in my mind that your association with such an outcome, coupled with a strong recommendation from the Berlin Museum, would make you more than welcome as an instructor at either Oxford or Cambridge."

Nigel and Gordon exchanged glances with no attempt to conceal their surprise before Nigel responded as though he knew nothing about the name deception. "Lily, how in the bloody hell did you come by such private information about our personal aspirations?"

"Don't forget, we're researchers, too, Nigel. We do our homework just as you do. So let's just say we have friends in London, and let it go at that." She flashed a comforting smile. "You may be assured that we will guard the privacy of your personal objectives as carefully as you would. Now, the only part of your mission that we're still completely in the dark about is the status of the spectral imaging in London. We're excited about that centurion's incredible legacy and would like to know more about it. Can you enlighten us?"

Peter offered an insincere smile of his own. "Right now, we don't know any more about it than you do, except we just learned there's been a delay in completing the analysis. On another matter, how did Bergama happen to be the place where you met our other group?" The sudden fading of her smile didn't escape his notice.

"Oh, that's a long story," Sar intervened, "but the essence of it is that we were undecided as to which of your two groups to contact first. When we finally located you both, it turned out the other group was the closest on our itinerary. A simple matter of logistics. By the way, I know the priest at Johannes Church here in Alaşehir. I'd be pleased to introduce you this afternoon if you'd like."

"Well, St. John's Church was our first scheduled visit," Gordon said as he glanced at Nigel, "but I don't see why we can't do them both. Any objections?"

Nods of agreement confirmed the change. The five of them spent the next half hour planning a schedule that would allow time to visit both St. John's and the Johannes Church on the same afternoon. After Sar and Lily left, Gordon, Peter, and Nigel agreed that no one would confront them about their names as long as they could be considered useful. Peter muttered something about keeping friends close and enemies closer.

\* \* \* \* \*

In spite of his doubts about the value of it, Peter had scanned Revelation pursuant to Trazerri's directive to let it guide their course. Now, the only passage in it that he could remember as they entered the Johannes Church was, "…Hold fast to what you have so that no one may seize your crown," from John's letter to the church at Philadelphia.

168

Like the aging woman whose overabundant application of rouge, eyeshadow, and lipstick failed to restore the lost beauty of her youth, the senile Johannes Church seemed to make a pitiable effort to offer its visitors one last glimpse of what it once was. Clumsy attempts to cement over the cracks in its walls and floor had been made by repairmen whose patchwork showed a lack of professional skill. The building's fading luxury seemed beyond restoration, and, as in the case of the aging woman, everyone knew it.

Sar introduced Peter, Nigel, Gordon, and Lily, and provided a concise summary of the purpose of their mission. Father Stanek nodded every now and then while he listened intently. Peter added certain details, particularly those relating to the various unanswered questions he'd accumulated. As agreed beforehand, he made no mention of their discoveries under the church in Chester.

The priest paused thoughtfully for a few moments before he spoke. "Well, gentlemen and very charming lady, your journey so far seems to have produced as many questions as it has answers. I'm not certain how much help I can be, but I believe I can address one of your observations which apparently puzzles you. Peter, you mentioned a letter from Bishop Polycarp in which he said, and I'm assuming your quote was accurate, '…I send these Holy Scriptures to the pitiable, blind church that claims to need nothing, since it still remains naked to this day.' You said the connection of that passage, and its meaning to your search, was still a mystery. Am I correct?"

"Yes, Father. That, and why Father Trazerri seemed to think the number seven would be a key to what we're looking for. I'm afraid we're all clueless about those two items. It's not that we're implying there's any relationship between them, we simply don't see their relevance individually."

Stanek stroked his chin. "Then I would say you haven't read Revelation very carefully. Am I correct?"

Peter glanced at his companions, then back at Stanek. "Well, I thought I had. Perhaps I haven't, although I can't speak for the others. Why do you ask?"

The priest stood and walked slowly to the small library he'd assembled on an oaken bookcase, which looked to Peter like it might be a century or two older than the church itself. He extracted a well-worn

Bible in such bad shape that it might also have predated the church. "Peter, I think you might find the answer to both of your questions if you'll follow me carefully here in the Apostle John's letter to the church at Laodicea, and I quote, 'For you say you are rich, have prospered and need nothing. You do not realize that you are wretched, pitiable, poor, blind and naked.' "

Peter nodded. "Yes, I'm familiar with it. So, how does that answer my questions?"

Stanek returned The Bible to the shelf and turned back to face Peter. "This is clearly the church that Bishop Polycarp referenced in the letter you cited. I'm not certain as to how, but I suspect this passage somehow holds the key to your search. You might also note that Laodicea happens to be the seventh of the seven churches on your itinerary."

"Father Stanek," Nigel finally spoke up, after he and his companions looked at each other in silence for a long moment, "we're a bit embarrassed that we all seem to have missed that, but we are indeed grateful to you for pointing it out. I think you've just brought us one step closer to either confirming or refuting our accumulated evidence that The Bible, as we know it today, has been substantially altered from its original version."

The priest raised his hands and frowned. "That's a very dangerous premise, my friend. Be careful with it."

"Well," Nigel continued, "the answer may come from our visit tomorrow to Denizli, formerly Laodicea. My question now: what is your overall assessment of this entire project we've undertaken?"

Father Stanek leaned back in his chair, eyeing each of them briefly before he responded. Lily started to speak but Sar raised his hand to stop her.

Stanek grinned. "I could make a strong argument that asking a priest a question like that is somewhat equivalent to asking the defendant his assessment of the prosecution's plan to incriminate him. In truth, I'm not sure I even have an assessment. Until your colleagues in London complete the imaging of that centurion's letter, you really have nothing more than circumstantial evidence. I must confess, however, it's strong and rather frightening evidence."

"True, but we have credible substantiation from Father Trazerri and the Greek priest I told you about," Peter replied. So, what are your thoughts?"

Stanek paused to scan his audience. "I've never met either Father Trazerri or the Greek priest you called Karalekas. So I must accept their views at face value. As to that woman in Chester and what happened there, I'm simply astounded. As far as Dr. Stickney's interview with that mountain recluse goes, I'd be highly skeptical except for the fact that it's disturbingly consistent with Trazerri's account of his own experience."

For the next hour, they exchanged speculations about the meaning of the number seven. A brief round of small talk followed, after which Father Stanek rose from his chair, came around to face his guests, and reached out to shake their hands.

"Gentlemen, I'm sorry, I have a parishioner coming in for consultation. So, in closing, I suppose my only assessment is that I'm now waiting with no small degree of apprehension for the other shoe to fall. At any rate, I think it's imperative that you continue with this mission, as you call it, and compare your findings with whatever the scan results in London turn out to be. Please keep me informed. I'm very concerned, as you might expect. You're welcome to explore my modest church if you wish. My apologies again, but I have to leave you."

The five travelers talked for a while as they toured the church and left when Sar tapped his wristwatch to signal they were running late for their next interview.

\* \* \* \* \*

A narrow road slowed them down enough to make their arrival at St. John's ten minutes late. To Peter, the church looked about as he'd expected an old Christian church to look. The sun glistened off a metal cross mounted on high, and the stone replica of the Virgin Mary seemed to offer an unemotional welcome. The greeting they received from Father Chavez covered them with a chill as cold as the late afternoon was warm.

"Reverend Pirtl alerted me that you would be coming," the priest said, his tone brusque, "and he explained why. Against his recommendation I agreed to this meeting purely as a matter of professional courtesy and out of respect for your London museum." He turned to Lily. "He spoke highly of you, madam. Just why I'll never know."

The priest's frown appeared to be a permanent part of his countenance. After his terse announcement, Father Chavez ushered them into a small conference room adjacent to his office and waited until they were all seated around the table; then he folded his hands in front of him and turned to Nigel. "Dr. Patterson, I've read a number of your papers addressing archaeological issues, and I've been impressed by your work. Therefore, I'm at a loss to understand why you chose to associate with blasphemy such as this against God. Or," he glared at the others, "with fortune hunters like these."

Sar didn't act in time to stop Lily, who launched her attack without warning. Her smile seemed designed to taunt the priest. "I've often found it interesting," she said in a voice so calm it almost seemed designed to further irritate the already-perturbed priest, "that the most indefensible beliefs are always the ones most passionately defended."

Chavez drew his head back slightly and glared at her. "What I find indefensible, young lady, is your assumption that God's word needs a defense." The gradual reddening in his neck began to spread upward until it settled in his cheeks.

Lily raised the duel to the next level before anyone could intervene. "It's not God's word we're challenging," she purred. "It's the perversion of his word perpetrated by self-serving priests."

The priest's lips tightened, and the redness in his face began to concentrate in dark purple blotches. "Then perhaps if you could bring yourself to attend our services you might discover how faithful to his word we are. We deliver the messages in Scriptures exactly as they were written."

Lily leaned forward to position herself for her fatal thrust. "Ah, that's precisely why we're here. You see, we have evidence that those Scriptures have been altered to better serve the church at the expense of God's original version."

"Lily, that's enough," Peter snapped. "Father Chavez, we apologize for—"

"Then by all means produce it," the priest continued through clenched teeth, his narrowing eyes locked on his unrelenting opponent.

"In the meantime, don't you dare come into my church asking me to provide documentation for your blasted heresies!"

"Father Chavez," Peter persisted, "we have imposed upon you inappropriately, and we sincerely apologize. We'll be on our way and trouble you no further. Please forgive this intrusion of your privacy." Peter launched himself from his chair and directed them toward the door, turning an angry glare toward Lily.

Father Chavez followed them out, his fiery eyes still fixed on his adversary while he shook his fist and screamed at her. "I can see into your black heart, you whore of Satan! I know you. I know where you dwell, and I condemn you to remain there for eternity. Damn you!"

Sar pulled Lily away from the others as fast as he could and pointed her toward their hotel without further conversation.

* * * * *

Seth and Lilith ignored the hotel desk clerk's obligatory "Good evening" and rushed past him to the elevator. Neither broke the icy silence until they reached the confines of their room.

Seth had often seen Lilith use a carefully crafted expression of regret as a first line of defense against criticism. This time he made sure his angry glare bored through her contrived wall of penitence. "That display, Lilith, was unforgivable. The first rule is to play your prospect carefully without the prospect being aware of it. I'm sure you know the process, and therefore, I'm curious as to why you flagrantly violated it this afternoon. Explain yourself."

She put her hand on Seth's shoulder and smiled. "You're disappointed, Seth, and I can understand that. However—"

He jerked her hand away and rolled his eyes, his voice thick with sarcasm. "Furious would be a better description. Prior to your surprise attack on that priest, we had three Deliverables primed to be turned over to The Enlightened One. Now we may have lost all of them. Even worse, I'm as angry as Peter. As we were leaving, I overheard him comment that your little sparring match with Chavez was more like a battle between God and Satan. Although I'm moderately pleased with the analogy, we can't afford it at this time."

Lilith forced another smile. "Yes, I know. However, as I started to say before you interrupted, I could see we had no choice."

"No choice?" Seth threw his hands in the air. "You made that decision on your own, even before the discussion began? What incredible insight! Please enlighten me."

"Calm down, Seth. Father Chavez is, unfortunately, one of the Intractable Ones. You know, ignorantly conditioned to their faith and consequently immovable. He's articulate and, therefore, dangerous. It was imperative that I end the meeting before the stubborn old ox could derail our whole train. I know it was chancy, but it was a calculated risk."

"Explain 'derail.' And please be sure to include some defensible rationale for your extemporaneous conclusion that he was dangerous."

Lilith placed her hands on her hips and returned his glare. "It should have been obvious, Seth. All three of our Deliverables were on the brink and could be pushed either way. Peter is wallowing in doubts as to his ability—and even his commitment—to continuing to spread the word about his God. He is therefore ours for the taking. Nigel is torn between his desire to make MOLAS, and hence himself, famous and his commitment to his God. However, his commitment is flexible if the price is right."

"And I suppose, in all your infinite wisdom, you're certain of this." Seth held his glare without lessening it.

"Yes. Gordon would sell his soul for any laudable achievement that would bring Oxford or Cambridge universities begging at his feet to join their faculties, with or without a doctoral degree. What bothers me is that the blind faith of The Intractables, like Chavez, can become contagious, as you well know. We can't afford to give them an opportunity to dissuade The Deliverables from their worldly objectives, as I feared Chavez might have done. An extended debate with him would be useless, and possibly counterproductive. Therefore, I had to anger him quickly to end the interview. I'm sure The Enlightened One would have approved under the circumstances."

Seth turned and walked slowly toward the window. He stared out at the courtyard for a few moments before he turned and walked back to face her. "Allowing for the remote possibility that you may be right, what did you have in mind for our next step?"

Lilith flashed an unforced smile and took a deep breath. "Ah, it's good to see we're together again on strategy, Seth. Well, you should be the one to work with Peter. I may have, as you implied, angered him beyond the point where I could guide him effectively. I will consult with Nigel and Gordon, since the mandate from London that our two teams work together will work in our favor with both of them. I'm convinced a successful outcome there is highly probable. I say this because their personal objectives are jointly dependent on revealing the biblical hoax that has swindled the sheep for two thousand years."

Seth nodded. "Agreed, but there remains the matter of the imaging results, Lilith. They could, as I'm sure you're aware, have the effect of confirming the Scriptures rather than discrediting them. The unexpected failure of our associate to apprehend the data in London was regrettable. Had it been successful, we could have screened the information in Berlin and then shaped our public message accordingly. It would have gone far to discredit the great enemy of our Enlightened One. Now we must prepare for possible reversals."

"I've already begun preparations," Lilith said, "and will continue them. First, a consultation with Nigel and Gordon, then a seductive rendezvous with the hapless Roger. And, of course, you're the best one to deal with Courtney."

"Why do you say that?"

"Ummm, because he's very knowledgeable and quite articulate in his religious beliefs. I sensed, even so, that he would treat the imaging results as a strengthening of his position as a theologian no matter how they turned out. He wouldn't hesitate to resolve that through his participation in the discovery process, and you've always dealt more effectively with the Intellectual Ones than I have."

"I suppose you're right, Lilith. You've always been better where charm and seduction are the critical ingredients. Yet, you still haven't answered my concern about the scans. If the results don't go our way, the rank and file of sheep in this world will remain sheep, only more inclined to follow their shepherd than before."

Lilith cocked her head and frowned. "Not necessarily. Consider the situation. If the scans go our way, the disembowelment of The Bible will make world headlines and will be a tremendous boost for our efforts. If they don't, it won't be newsworthy at all—except possibly within the

Forbidden Chronicles of a Roman Centurion | Chaplick

narrow confines of the church universal, which is already showing a decline throughout the Western world. In that event, all we need to do is to convince our Deliverables that their personal needs are best served by emphasizing the publication of what they've already found, rather than on the imaging results. That will be enough to cast a dark shadow of suspicion on their Bible."

Seth settled on the edge of their bed and rested his forehead on his fist while he paused to mull it over. "Marginally effective, perhaps. What they've discovered up until now, however, might be considered somewhat circumstantial. I'm not convinced Courtney and Nigel would be willing to go public with their findings unless the scanning produces irrefutable evidence of significant biblical alterations."

Lilith nestled on the bed beside him. "That doesn't matter, Seth. They can be easily convinced to put a different spin on the whole thing. They can do this by publicly emphasizing their own discoveries and deemphasizing the scans. This will enable them to achieve their objectives very profitably, despite the results of the imaging. Remember, as you've often reminded me, we don't have to discredit their God entirely. We need only to throw considerable doubt upon him. Their findings to date, if published properly, will accomplish that without their even being aware of it. In other words, we win either way."

The more Seth thought about her plan the more he appeared to accept its credibility. His emerging smile confirmed his endorsement of the plan. "Well designed, Lilith. You've shown a level of skill in your craft somewhat beyond my expectations. I think The Enlightened One would, as you said, be pleased. Very well then, we'll proceed in that direction."

* * * * *

Sar found Peter deep in thought when he knocked on the door of his room. The quiet nature of the hotel, unlike many he'd experienced, appealed to Peter's fondness for uninterrupted contemplation. It remained free from the sounds of screaming babies, clamoring kids, and the ever-present late-night drunk who stumbles down the hall, slurring a loud monologue about his everlasting misery. The silence had provided a venue conducive to the articulation of Peter's thoughts. At least, until Sar's intervention.

At first, Peter pretended he didn't hear the untimely knock. He hadn't finished his email to Robin, explaining an exciting plan to recover his congregation. The gentle thumping continued. When Peter reluctantly opened the door, Sar was the last person he wanted to see standing there.

"Peter, I didn't want to bother you, but I felt so ashamed of what happened this afternoon. I feel I owe you an apology and, perhaps, an explanation. I was, and still am, as angry as you were. May I come in for a moment?"

"Sure, but apologies are unnecessary. Your associate is obviously a very strong-willed woman, and she was clearly offended by the priest's opening remarks. Frankly, so was I, although the way she handled it was entirely inappropriate. Hopefully, she learned something from the experience."

Sar shook his head. "She certainly did. I had a long talk with her. Interestingly, I discovered that, believe it or not, she did it because she feared the priest's negative attitude would discourage you from pursuing your mission objectives any further. In her own naïve way, I guess she was trying to protect you."

Peter raised his eyebrows. "Why would she want to protect me? From what?"

"Well, she apparently overheard your comment about needing to connect more effectively with your congregation. She figured your mission findings, regardless of how the imaging results turn out, would produce two favorable outcomes at the same time. One, it would engage your parishioners as they've never been enlightened before. Two, it would, if properly publicized, substantially enhance your status in the religious community. Lily was truly looking out for you, Peter. And, frankly, so am I."

Peter threw him a quizzical glance. "You said, 'regardless of how the imaging turns out.' I'm not sure I follow your logic on that. The scans could just as easily negate everything we've discovered so far. If they do, and simply confirm the Scriptures and the existing concepts of God and Jesus, I'm comfortable with that."

Sar pulled up a chair and leaned toward his quarry. "To be comfortable with that would be a terrible mistake, Peter. The Scriptures, as currently taught, are boring and difficult for lay people to understand. The wording is obsolete and the concepts inflexible. That makes them irrelevant as I suspect you're already discovering with your own congregation. Your findings to date are exciting. Use them to offer your congregation a more complete insight into the concepts of God and Jesus. Think about it. That having been said, I'll bother you no more." He stood and smiled. "Good afternoon."

After Sar made his exit, Peter threw himself on the bed and stared at the ceiling while he pondered what he'd heard. He'd never been confronted with such an articulate counter-perspective before. He didn't trust Sar, but the man could be right. He hadn't, after all, said anything Peter hadn't thought of before. In a way, the man's line of reasoning connected some of the dots with which Peter had been struggling. It would allow an interesting biblical presentation to his congregation with the stiffness of Scriptures removed from the equation. He left the email unfinished, rolled over, and took a late afternoon nap.

* * * * *

It would have been difficult to determine whether Nigel or Gordon looked more surprised when Lily, instead of Peter, showed up to join them for dinner. In contrast to the plunging neckline and off-the-shoulder ensemble she'd worn the night before, the button-down blouse she wore made her look more like a nun who had strayed from the convent.

"Good evening, gentlemen." She offered a warm, but business-like, smile without the seductive look. "I hope you'll allow me to fill in for Peter, who Seth mentioned is busily involved in an email to his girlfriend. I hope I'm not intruding."

"Not at all, Lily. You're welcome to join us if you'll promise to eat only the dinner and not us." Gordon's humor and broad grin came as a warm wave that seemed to wash away the lingering tensions of the day. He motioned for the waiter.

"I promise." She laughed the first hearty laugh either Gordon or Nigel could remember. "I realize what I did was uncalled for. That stuffy priest just made me so damned mad by calling us fortune hunters. We're not. There's certainly nothing in it for Sar and me, as we agreed yesterday, except perhaps some favorable reviews for our museum, and I know your two teams are simply doing due diligence as an archaeological follow-up."

"We understand." Nigel reached out and gave her a comforting pat on the hand. "We've run into that kind of response ourselves several times. It comes with the job, and you just have to grin and bear it."

"On another subject," Gordon began after the waiter had taken their orders, "from your experience at the Berlin Museum, how do you assess the likely public reaction to what we're doing?"

The question came as an unexpected gift without which she would have had to broach the subject herself, thereby risking suspicion as to her motives. She paused before responding, to create the appearance of thoughtful contemplation. In fact, she needed time to calm the sudden rush of excitement that coursed through her.

"Gordon, that depends entirely on how we present our findings."

"What do you mean?"

"Well, I mean, if it's done in a way that simply confirms the Christian community's conventional wisdom, then it becomes just another dry sermon from the church universal. No one will pay any attention, and that would be a shame, because all of the work your two teams have done will fade away with little notice and no reward."

Nigel frowned. "And in what way would you suggest we present our work?"

She paused until the waiter had delivered the drinks and walked away. "If the scans produce what we think they will, then worldwide presentation will not be a problem. In either case, I'm convinced your teams will have to make sure your findings to date are widely circulated in order to assure that all pieces of objective evidence are fully disclosed."

Gordon swirled his martini and tilted his head toward her. "Then what should we expect to get out of all this once we've done what you suggested?"

Lily flashed the same easy smile that usually came when she sensed victory. "If done with proper attribution to each of you personally, I don't have to tell you what that would mean for you, Gordon, in terms of opening up a host of rather delicious teaching opportunities at the best institutions in the world. Or to you, Nigel, in terms of worldwide kudos to MOLAS and, of course, yourself. Otherwise, without that kind of circulation, all of the diligent and very professional research you've done to date will have been wasted."

Heads nodded without any verbal response. Intermittent rounds of small talk and drinks punctuated the rest of the dinner. An exchange of humorous remarks here and there, along with an occasional reference to the more interesting moments of their respective experiences, sealed her success. During the intermittent periods of silence, Nigel and Gordon appeared to be mulling over what she had said.

Lily made every effort to suppress her anxiety as to how well her subversive raid on Christianity had been received. All in all, she knew she had been lucky—Gordon's helpful opening; the absence of Peter, who might have wrecked her entire approach if he'd showed up; and the apparent forgiveness on the part of both Gordon and Nigel. It was now time to deliver Roger.

# Chapter 12

## Akhisar (Thyatira)

Thyatira no longer existed. Centuries before, a wealthy city stood on the southern bank of the Lycus River along the road from Pergamos to Sardis. It spread across the northern part of Lydia in the Roman province of Asia Minor. In its place the modern city of Akhisar overlooked the remains of an ancient church, Christianity's footprint in the sand, the only surviving reminder that the gospel was once preached there.

If Sam hadn't become lost trying to find the Guerta Museum, he would have been on time for his meeting with the curator. Hrand Darkanian didn't mind waiting for a lost American. Sam's text messages had marked him as one who shared the curator's views on the crying need for far more geological excavation than had taken place over the last twenty centuries. The dark-skinned man ignored Sam's apologetic-looking grin when he arrived, and embraced him. "Welcome, Dr. Wykoff. I'm pleased to meet my...how do you say it in America? Writing buddy, I think, yes?"

Sam grinned. "We call it, 'pen pal,' Dr. Darkanian, but 'writing buddy' will do just fine. Thank you for agreeing to meet with me. As I explained, I'm part of a team of researchers looking for documentation we believe still exists. We suspect it would either confirm or contradict the evidence we've uncovered. Our findings so far provide a strong indication that The Bible and some of its major concepts are erroneous in their present form. I'd also appreciate hearing your professional opinions on the subject of, what I think we'd both agree is, the shamefully inadequate historic excavation that has taken place to date."

Hrand nodded. "Very good. And please, call me Hrand. And may I call you Sam? I feel we know each other so well from our letters."

Sam nodded and smiled.

"Now, Sam, if you would be kind enough to join me for some of my favorite Turkish wine, I believe I can show you something that may well address both your mission and your interest in excavation at the same time." He led Sam into a small anteroom and poured them each a prodigious goblet-full.

"That, my friend, would be the first real break we've had in some time." Sam sipped his wine and puckered his lips. "Ahhh, your wine looks black as ink and dreadful, but it's delicious. Thank you. What is it you wanted to show me?"

The curator opened a small wooden box and held it in his lap. His voice dropped to little more than a whisper. "I've saved this for many years without really knowing why. When we began to correspond with each other I realized it might be valuable." He handed the box to Sam and sat back, waiting for a reaction.

Sam studied the lone piece of paper, lying flat in the box, before responding. "Hrand, this thing is so old the writing is hardly visible. I assume the powder is some kind of preservative. From what I can tell, the wording's in Greek, but I don't read Greek. What does it say, and how old do you think it is?"

Hrand took the box from Sam, returned it to a shelf, and turned back to face his visitor. "It's a first century letter, written, believe it or not, by the Apostle John. First, let me give you some background. Thyatira, as you probably know being an historian, was a center of industry and commerce in its day. The waters somehow made for the most brilliant red dye in the whole world. Thus, the dying and sale of fabrics became a primary industry there. Copper and several other industries also thrived and, naturally, all of the artisans belonged to guilds. You know, the equivalent of your labor unions today, except the guilds focused more on craftsmanship and the behavior of its members."

Sam nodded. "So, what does it have to do with this document?"

Hrand flashed a wide grin. "Ah, good question. To be accepted, the guilds were required to practice the pagan religions prevailing at the time. Consequently, they came into direct conflict with the Christian faith which was growing in Thyatira. Not long afterward, the Roman

Catholic Church refused to allow any member of a guild to become a member of the church or to practice Christianity in any way."

Sam threw a quick glance up at the box, as though to make sure it was still there. "Okay, I'm not sure I ever knew that, but I'll take your word for it. So, how is all that relevant to this document…or what's left of it?"

"Well sir, there was a flurry of archaeological excavations done here many years ago before the sponsors ran out of funds. My predecessor observed the digging from time to time, in case they might donate some of their artifacts to the museum. The archaeologists refused to share any of their diggings with him. They offered a lame excuse that all the artifacts belonged, by law, to the agency sponsoring the excavations. However, my predecessor was so persistent that, to get rid of him, they…how do you say it…threw bones at him?"

Sam smiled. "I think you mean threw him a bone. It's an expression, like giving someone a small part of something, as a form of bribe to pacify the person."

"Yes, exactly. So they gave him this document because they saw no commercial use for it. I must say my predecessor didn't either. He gave it to me, and, as I said, I kept it without formulating a rationale as to why. In fact, I never even looked at it again until I received your correspondence. That's when I went out and had it translated."

"Okay, so what does it say?"

Hrand frowned and leaned in closer to his guest. "Sam, this is a most strange thing. It was part of the letter the Apostle John wrote to the church at Thyatira telling the Christians there that God forbade participation in pagan worship, in the guilds, or any other money-making endeavor. It's part of Revelation."

"Hrand, my teammates practically forced me to read Revelation. I don't remember seeing in it any mention of this thing about God and the money-making activities."

"I know, Sam. That's because it isn't there anymore. Nevertheless, my theological resources assured me this is an original document, and it was an integral part of the original version of John's letter. It reads, and I quote, 'And to the angel of the church in Thyatira write: These are the words of the Son of God: I have this against you; you join evildoers in groups formed to make profits which exceed the value of their offerings;

you worship unholy deities which approve the employment of such labor; you have sinned against your God who has warned against the work of storing up profits and gold for yourselves, returning no part of them to God. Those who commit such works will I throw into great distress unless they repent of their doings.'"

"What about the rest of the narrative?" Sam asked.

"The rest of this document reads as you see it today in Revelation. The passage I read was deliberately removed and replaced, as you can see, with a passage about Jezebel. And I'll tell you why. I am certain it was removed because the church, with all its wealth, could not afford to circulate a Scripture that condemns profit-making. Do you not think I'm correct in this?"

Sam shook his head. "It sounds reasonable, but I'm not really qualified to assess it. What do you plan to do with this document?"

"A museum in Berlin wanted me to give it to them, but I refused. They even offered to buy it. I refused. Now that I understand its potential value, I will keep it for our museum here in Akhisar, and I cannot give it to you either. I just wanted you to see it. I have made a photocopy for you, hoping you might use it in your mission. Now, Sam, here is the whole point. I want to emphasize it so you do not lose all the trees in the forest. Did I say that right?"

"Yes, if you meant for me not to lose the forest for the trees, as the saying goes. What exactly is the point, if it's not for my mission?"

"Here it is, Sam. If the limited excavations done years ago could produce documents such as this, plus many valuable artifacts, then imagine the history that could be yet uncovered if the Western World would cooperate in funding excavations on a much wider scale. Do you see what I mean?"

Sam nodded. "Yes, I believe I do. I agree. I'll take all this back to my two teams, along with the photocopy. I'm sure this will have an impact. Hrand, I can't thank you enough for meeting with me and for your helpful coverage of history and excavation. We've already seen too much of our past buried under centuries of accumulated sediment. I promise I'll devote more of my efforts to the excavation problem." Sam stood and shook his host's hand. "Well, I have to go, so I'll bid you farewell. Let's keep in touch, my friend."

\* \* \* \* \*

Neither Courtney nor Sam could say they were happy about the accommodations at Akhisar's Palm City Hotel. Still, as Courtney pointed out, it was either there or spend the night sleeping on the floor at the Jewish Community Center. The few B&Bs they researched didn't seem appealing. The restaurants didn't either. It all came down to trusting Sar's assessment that, whatever the shortcomings of the Palm City might be, they were offset by the food at the little restaurant across the street. The jury was still out on the food quality since Sam and Courtney had agreed to wait for Sar to arrive before ordering. On the plus side, they admitted they were willing to award three stars to the wine they consumed in the interim.

Courtney raised his glass in a toast. "Sam, is that satisfied look on your face a product of this incredible document you found this afternoon, or should I attribute it to the wine?"

Sam raised his glass and clinked it against Courtney's. "Probably a little of both. Anyway, I wanted to share the contents of that document with you before Roger and Sar got here. Somehow I just don't trust Sar, or her either. By the way, where is Roger?"

Courtney sipped his wine and leaned back in his chair. "Last I heard, he's out with Lily for the evening. We can fill him in later. Let's—"

"What do you mean out?" Sam's countenance darkened under a frown. "Out where, doing what?"

"She took him out to dinner and then to a show by one of those belly dancers, as I understand it. Sar said not to be surprised if he doesn't show up until breakfast tomorrow. I guess she has a small apartment in one of the nearby towns where her museum used to excavate. I presume they'll spend the night together there. Why?"

Sam threw his hands in the air. "Christ Almighty, Courtney! Why in the hell did you allow that to happen?"

"Sam, I didn't have any say in it. I got this from Sar after they'd already left. What's the problem? She's probably just helping him with his thesis, as we all agreed she would. If a little romance is involved, well then, Roger probably could use a little maturing. By the way, Christ

Almighty didn't have anything to do with it either, but I'm encouraged to see you finally acknowledge his status."

"Damn it, Courtney, I don't think we're talking a little romance here. She's planning to seduce him. I know it."

Courtney reached over and put his hand on Sam's shoulder. "Hey, calm down. I agree Lily—or whatever she calls herself—is not the kind of girl you'd want to bring home to mother. Look, Roger's old enough to make his own decisions on that subject. I don't think your mentoring responsibilities extend that far. Anyway, here comes Sar, so let's drop it." Courtney handed Sam a glass of wine.

Sar entered, all smiles, and made a bee-line for Sam. "Well, Sam, if I might ask, how did your meeting with the curator turn out?"

"Came up empty," Sam lied, ignoring the surprised look on Courtney's face.

"Well, there's not much history left here, I'm afraid," Sar replied. His forced smile begged the question as to whether or not he believed Sam. Sar sat down, poured a glass of wine, and paused for a moment before he spoke, as though he had something to say but had decided to wait for the right time to say it. He leaned toward Courtney and delivered his message in a resolute tone. "Courtney, I know you have reservations about actively searching for something that might cast some doubt on the validity of the way The Bible presents God, our Father. Let me ask a question. Have you considered another possibility? I mean, full disclosure of evidence, regardless of how contradictory it may be, might be well received by a world full of a growing youth population that already feels uncomfortable with traditional doctrine."

Courtney raised his eyebrows. "Are you suggesting such disclosure would strengthen their faith?"

Sar drew back his head and grinned. "I think you already know it would, if presented properly and in the right context."

Courtney pushed his glass aside and leaned back in his chair. "I'm listening. Explain."

"Well, the Scriptures are chronicles recorded by followers who, the best of intentions notwithstanding, were as prone as we are to misinterpretation and translation errors. As you well know, the early church itself has been known to, shall we say, modify things a little as part of its canonical screening process. Yet none of that really changes the underlying message or the pre-eminence of God."

Sar paused to take a sip of his wine. "So, what I'm saying is that, if we blindly continue to assert the infallibility of chronicles with which the youth of the world are already becoming increasingly uncomfortable, we fail God by turning away one generation after another. On the other hand, if we publicize your two teams' findings with the intent of bringing the chronicles up-to-date, we revitalize the faith of our youth, not to mention all the doubting adults."

Sam shook his head, and Courtney frowned without responding.

Sar paused, as if to give it all time to sink in…and then continued. "We thereby serve God in a way that could never have been possible without the laudable work your teams have accomplished. This will become even more critical in the event the imaging results should have the unfortunate effect of confirming those outdated chronicles." He leaned back in his chair in the manner of an attorney who had decided it was time to rest his case.

Courtney stroked his chin and took another sip of wine. "Well, your smooth rhetoric pours out as though it had been a divinely sanctioned amendment to Scriptural doctrine. As I've told Sam, the basic concept of God would not be changed by divulging our findings, regardless of what the scans revealed. Still, you make a good point. Failure to disclose our findings in their entirety would be professionally irresponsible. I'd like some time together with Sam to discuss these issues, so I'll have to ask you to excuse us for a while. We'll meet here in the morning before we leave for Denizli, which will be our last stop before returning to London."

Sam glared accusingly at both of them. "That's assuming we can retrieve Roger."

"Of course, I understand," Sar said. He downed the last of his wine, threw a backward glance at Sam, and withdrew.

After they'd ordered dinner, Sam produced Hrand's photocopy of the Revelation document for Courtney's inspection, along with Hrand's summary memo as to why he thought the alterations had occurred. Neither spoke while Courtney studied the photocopy. Courtney nodded perceptibly, but still without comment, then handed the paper back to Sam. "You say you inspected the original document?"

187

"Yes," Sam replied, "although I can't say I actually read it since I can't read Latin or Greek. Understandably, Hrand couldn't give me the original. Could you understand what it said?"

Courtney nodded. "Yes. Your curator friend's translation was correct. Sam, this is a significant discovery. I'm a bit surprised you didn't want to share it. Are you still angry about the Roger and Lily connection, or is it that you still don't trust Sar?"

"I don't trust either of them, her least of all. I found out from Hrand that someone from the Berlin Museum tried to buy the original from him. Care to guess who that might have been?"

"Okay, I see where you're going. However, that doesn't mean we shouldn't treat them as partners on this venture. In fact, London made it clear we should. Since they've already disclosed their relationship with Berlin and their purpose here, it really shouldn't come as a surprise that they tried to buy this document. You would have, too, in their position."

Sam leaned back, cupped the back of his head in his hands, and stared at the ceiling while Courtney waited. "Fine. So be it. I don't like it, but I suppose you're right. We'll share it with both of them and Roger in the morning. You think there's any sense in trying to find Roger and his girlfriend tonight?"

"No. Forget it. Let's eat."

* * * * *

The Turkish belly dancers at Club Şamahka took sexual provocation to a new level with the rhythm of their shimmering movements. The club was so secluded it could be found only by those who already knew exactly where to look. Lily ushered Roger into the best seat in the house.

He turned toward her with a look of warm admiration. "I'm impressed. How did you manage such prime seats on a night with a full house?"

"Let's just say I performed a service for the owner the other night," Lily responded without looking at him.

The lights dimmed and a scantily clad woman, billed as "Johara," began her undulating routine.

Lily leaned closer to Roger. "In Turkey," she whispered, "belly dancing goes by the name *Gobek dans*. The French name is *danse du*

188

*ventre*. This translates into dance of the stomach, or belly dance. It traces its origins back to ancient Greece and Egypt, where legend holds that it was a fertility dance. Do you like it?"

Roger nodded. "I think so, but I've never seen it done like this before. Nothing seems to be moving sometimes except her stomach. How does she do that?"

"It's in the muscles of her abdomen." She placed her hand gently on Roger's lower torso and eased it down to his private parts. "They're extremely well trained to combine intricate hip movements to create a flowing sensuality, often done with the accompaniment of props like snakes or, in this case, a sword, and veils. The noise she's making is done with zils, or cymbals. It's all intended to mesmerize and stimulate you." Lily smiled as she caressed the back of his head. As soon as Roger's involuntary response assured her that the stimulus was working, she withdrew her hand from between his legs. Her foreplay had begun earlier that evening with assurance that she would help him structure and promote worldwide acclaim for his thesis. Her low-cut blouse and mini-skirt had set the stage for the after-dinner *danse du ventre*, which turned out to be more of a strip show than a genuine belly dancing exhibition. She knew Roger had reached the limits of his endurance by the time the show ended.

Lily wasted no time escorting her quarry to her hotel room. She assumed that nothing in his limited experience had prepared Roger Denault for her exquisite figure. She approached him with open arms, naked, and proceeded to undress her prospect. She manipulated his hands over the most sexual parts of her body and, in one smooth motion, articulately caressed his genitals. The results were predictable even before she maneuvered him onto her bed. Despite her twelve-year seniority, her energy more than matched Roger's. Their bodies ravished each other. For the next few hours, she moved professionally, confident that Roger blocked out everything in his universe except the sensual enjoyment of their encounter. She could tell the sexual marathon had left him completely exhausted by the time they both fell asleep somewhere between three and five the next morning.

Before the seduction, she'd made it clear that Roger's sexual satisfaction would be contingent upon his agreement to share with her all of his team's discoveries, particularly the ones she felt his team withheld because they didn't seem to trust her. She woke without disturbing his slumber, dressed herself, and left a note on his pillow, reminding him of his commitment. She slipped quietly out the door.

# Chapter 13

## Denizli (Laodicea)

The tension between Sam and Roger seemed to increase by the minute that morning. By the time they climbed into the car and headed for Denizli, the silence had become oppressive—Sam still angry, Roger wrapped in his own quiet resentment. Their unspoken agreement to let the subject evaporate by itself had made sense the day before. Now, trapped within the close confines of the Hyundai, the awkward silence hung like a fog around them.

Tired of finding himself in the middle, Courtney decided it was time to intervene. "Look, you two, given that we're all on the same team, as you Yanks would say, I think you need to reconcile your differences. I can't say I'm particularly enthusiastic about our friends from Berlin joining up with us either, but they are part of this archaeological research effort now, and hiding things from each other is simply counterproductive. Sam, when you first showed me that document from the curator, you seemed at least moderately excited about it. Then when you showed it to everyone else this morning, you sounded like you wanted to suppress it. Why? Given your anti-scriptural views, I would have thought you'd be eager to highlight it. What's going on?"

Sam shook his head. "That's a question I've been asking myself ever since last night. I don't know. I guess I'm having some second thoughts about this whole thing. Look, those two Berliners have been trying even harder than I have to discredit The Bible. I guess I didn't think much about it until their scheme to buy that document from Hrand."

Courtney shrugged. "Why should that bother you? After all, Sar and Lily are, at least ostensibly, in the business of acquisitions for the museum."

"I'll tell you what bothers me. It's the thought of why they want to buy it. Look, both of them seem hell-bent on discrediting the whole foundation of this religion of yours. A development I'm surprised you haven't noticed. Peter sent me a message saying they'd lied about their names and had put some subtle pressure on his team to document our findings publicly—another of their attempts, I suppose, to discredit the Scriptures. Don't take this as a softening of my position, but my gut feeling is something stinks here. An old faculty advisor of mine once told me the harder someone tries to prove something wrong, the more likely it is to be right."

Courtney couldn't hide his grin. "Why, Dr. Wykoff, did I just hear you, of all people, defend Christianity?"

"No. I mean I don't know what the hell I'm defending. I'll tell you this, though. When it comes to those two, I'm about ready to root for any team they're playing against. And another thing. The more I think about it, the more respect I have for that Trazerri guy. I'll bet he wouldn't have caved in to them."

Courtney's grin widened. "Sounds like you're defending something."

"And another point," Sam continued, ignoring Courtney's remark. "That business about the premeditated murder of those apostles. Look, I never put much stock in biblical doctrine, but I'm betting that the people who were trying to shut those guys down are on the same side Seth and Lilith are on."

Roger emerged from his sulk and turned to his mentor with a look of serious conviction. "Sam, I think the false name allegation is probably explainable, and, if this is about Lily, I can assure you she's a fine lady who only wants to make this mission successful for all of us."

Sam exploded. "Oh, come on, Roger, wake up! That woman has all but seduced every one of us. Maybe not like she did you, but those two have been using us. Peter shared with me some interesting thoughts that started me wondering. For example, Bergama is known as the place where Satan's throne is. That's where Sar and Lily approached us from out of nowhere. The names Seth and Lilith—their real names—both have satanic origins. Both of them have been playing mind games with us ever since we met. This whole thing's looking more and more like a propaganda campaign to publicize any anti-scriptural findings we come up with. Can you guys really convince yourselves it's all pure coincidence? I sure can't."

Courtney looked puzzled. "What exactly are you implying? That Berlin sent us a couple of Satan's disciples?"

Sam threw his hands in the air. "I don't know. You tell me. You're the religious expert here. How much do you believe in coincidence?"

Courtney seemed to be mulling the whole thing over, and Roger shook his head, as if to signal disbelief in what his mentor had just implied.

"Sam," Courtney asked, "have you shared this with the other three members of our team?"

"No. Only with Peter, by way of a subtle hint, but nothing overt."

Courtney held out his arms in mock surrender. "So, what do you suggest we do about it?"

"I think we need to make certain one way or the other. And I mean right now."

"How?"

Sam turned a stern glance at Roger. "Well, I know one sure way. We can ask Roger to unbutton Lily's blouse as soon as we get to Denizli."

"What?" Courtney's eyes opened wide with a look of amazement.

Roger skidded the car to an abrupt stop, spun in his seat, and glared at Sam with an uncharacteristic intensity. "Doggone it, Sam! You're my mentor, and I know you can flunk me at any time. But that was a lousy, cheap shot. I think you owe both of us an explanation."

"I'm inclined to agree," Courtney added. "What are you driving at, Sam?"

"It's simple," Sam said. "Lily—or Lilith—has a tendency to tug at a necklace, or something, under her blouse. Anybody care to guess what that well-concealed accessory might be?"

Courtney frowned, as though he found it difficult to withhold judgment. "Please enlighten us."

"Well, based on my discussions with Peter, I would guess it's some kind of satanic symbol. Like a pentagram or one of those inverted stars. And if it is, then I'd say it changes our whole relationship with the Berlin contingent. Don't you agree?"

"If you're looking to me for a comment," Roger said, "I can tell you I saw nothing like that on her last night. True, I did share with you my curiosity as to why she fumbled around with her collar that one time." His lips tightened. "If her blouse is to be opened for inspection tomorrow, it won't be by me."

"Whoa, you two," Courtney intervened again. "This quarrel isn't going to solve anything. Roger, turn off the engine and let's think this through. First of all, we don't know if she'll be wearing this thing or not. If she isn't and we pull a stunt like that, it'll backfire all the way to London. In fact, even if she is wearing something, it's bound to end up a disaster, not to mention the hurtful consequences of the insult itself. Lilith, or whatever she's called, is a human being and, whether we like her or not, she deserves to be treated respectfully. There has to be a better way. Right now I'm open to suggestions."

A prolonged silence followed before Roger spoke up. "Okay, I think I know how we can do it. This is cheap and it stinks, but it looks like there's no other choice. We set a trap that brings them out into the open. And I mean both of them, not just Lily."

Courtney's brow furrowed again. "Okay, Roger, how do you propose we go about bringing Satan out into the open?"

"Well, I'm convinced if there's any satanic effort going on, it's by Sar, not Lily. She would never knowingly be a part of something like that. I'm sure of it."

Sam rolled his eyes while Courtney tried to stifle an involuntary smirk.

"So, in answer to your question," Roger continued, "we offer Seth what he wants. In this case it's a biblical discrediting strategy that would be effective even if the scan results don't support it. In my conversations with Lily—and I'm kind of reading between the lines—Sar's greatest fear is that the scans will only reaffirm the Scriptures as they now exist. Naturally, that won't give him or the Berlin Museum the kind of worldwide status they're seeking in the archaeology community. That's why he wants, more than anything, for us publicize our own findings to date. They're probably enough to accomplish his objectives if they're developed using his methods."

"Okay, Roger, so then what?" Sam asked. "How does that bring Seth out?"

"We set a trap. Upon our arrival at Denizli, I announce that London's discovered the scans to be a hoax, phony documents planted several years ago, and now the whole project is called off. I tell them I have decided to go off on my own in order to get this published, completely disassociated from MOLAS and Wesleyan University. I tell Sar I can't pull it off without the backing and expertise of some occult society and the Berlin Museum. I think he'll take the bait."

Sam drew his head back and stared at Roger with an expression of amazement. "Good grief, Roger, where the hell have you been hiding all this resourceful insight?"

Courtney beamed his approval. "I think this journey has made a first-rate doctoral candidate out of him, Sam. I believe his scheme has possibilities."

Sam shook his head. "Yeah, but giving that guy all our stuff is a little over the top, don't you think?"

"We're not giving him anything, Sam," Roger said. "We're just promising to turn it all over to him, only after he proves he can get me into an occult organization that'll back me. If he's on the level with no satanic motives, then we fess up and they'll be so mad they'll split. We then go on with the project without them, just as we did before they showed up. You admit you were wrong about both of them, and I'll beg forgiveness from Lily. If their motives are demonic, then we have a good reason to fire them, and I admit you're right. You have a better idea?"

Sam smiled and draped an arm around his young protégé. "Okay Roger, that took a lot of guts, especially given your strong feelings about Lilith." Sam lowered his head and then raised it again to look Roger straight in the eye. "Tell you what. I apologize for my comments about her, and I'll leave you on your own in that relationship. Just know I'm concerned about you. I think Lily is a master at manipulation, and I don't want you to get hurt. That's the last I'll say on the subject. I approve of your plan. Are we agreed, Courtney?"

Courtney grinned. "Agreed. Now, be careful, Roger. I don't want to see you get hurt either."

Sam offered an approving smile. Roger revved up the engine, and an air of quiet contentment prevailed during the rest of the journey.

\* \* \* \* \*

Sam, Courtney, and Roger arrived at Denizli to find almost nothing left of the ancient city of Laodicea. Once a prosperous Roman market town, the Laodicea of past millennia had used its strategic position on an east-west trade route to sell enormous quantities of its woolen and cotton fabrics. Now, only a few crumbled ruins remained as a testament to its bustling past. The scarcity of historic structures and artifacts prompted tour guides to explain that the city was almost completely destroyed by an earthquake in 60 A.D. and never rebuilt.

In an effort to hold the tourists' interest longer, the more experienced tour guides made an occasional reference to the Apostle John's letter to the church at Laodicea: "I know all your ways; you are neither hot nor cold. ...Because you are lukewarm, ...I will spit you out of my mouth!" The guides then commented that John's metaphor was meant to rebuke the Laodiceans for their indifference to God's word.

The three of them broke away from the guides and toured for an hour since they couldn't think of anything better to do until Sar and Lily showed up. Roger's mind wasn't on the tour. He dreaded the upcoming confrontation and knew it would have to be his first item of business the moment Sar and Lilly arrived. The contrived directive from London would be difficult to explain. It was a lie, and too many things could go wrong with a fabrication of that magnitude. Roger forced a smile, stuffed the letter Courtney had crafted into his pocket, and headed for his meeting.

\* \* \* \* \*

Roger greeted Sar with a nervous handshake, determined not to let it slip that he knew the man's real name. He handed Sar the letter and managed an exchange with Lily—the kind of furtive smiles that signal a shared secret from the past. The name deception had cooled his ardor, but he tried to avoid letting it show. He watched the two cultists read the contrived document, Lily with eyes opened in an expression of amazement and Sar with a gradually deepening frown. His immediate concern was that they might see through the sham. Until that moment, it hadn't occurred to him this was a possibility for which neither he nor his

196

two partners had devised a credible contingency plan. Neither Sar nor Lily appeared to have figured it out—at least not during their reading of the letter, a welcome relief that made the next step easier.

Sar threw the letter to the floor. "Roger, how could this have happened?" His angry delivery of the question came in sharp contrast with his usual calm. "Why now? Why so late in the process did they discover this?"

Roger shrugged. "We're all as dumbfounded as you are. Believe me, my group has wasted a lot more time and effort on this than you have."

"Oh, the hell it has!" Lily snapped.

"Well, I'm going to tell you something in the strictest of confidence," Roger said ignoring the remark. "Since the project is officially closed, the rest of my team will be packing up and going home. Not me. I need to produce a thesis. Failure to come up with a downright smashing paper is not an option, not with my father's reputation hanging over my head all the time."

Sar threw his hands in the air. "So what is your point?"

"Well, I'm thinking maybe it's not all down the drain. I plan to go ahead and publish our findings to date as an integral part of my thesis. And Lily knows what I mean. I have to disassociate myself from MOLAS and Wesleyan University, because they would never permit it. However, if I could do it under the auspices and backing of some anti-Christian group with a strong reputation for such publications, it might be doable. At least that's what I'm hoping."

Roger took a deep breath while he watched for any signs indicating his audience might have caught on. Absent any, he decided it was time to play his trump card. "Lily, you said you would help me publish my thesis, but now that I've told you how I plan to do it, I won't blame you for changing your mind, and I'll understand completely if you don't want to be associated with it in any way."

The performance had been as convincing as he could make it. Like the playwright waiting anxiously for the critics' assessments in the morning edition, Roger drew another deep breath and turned his head to prevent his face from betraying his mounting anxiety.

"Roger, would you excuse us for a moment?" Lily asked with a calmness that seemed surprising under the circumstances.

Roger nodded and walked into the breakfast lounge to order a cup of coffee. Sar and Lily huddled in the hotel lobby. He watched a stream of tourists pass through with their cameras and funky shirts. The tourists clutched itinerary sheets and little canvas bags stamped with the name of the agency sponsoring their tour. Roger sipped his coffee slowly. Nervous tension made swallowing difficult. He wondered what his father would think if he could see his son now, embroiled in a mess like this. How would his father feel about Lily?

They didn't give him long to contemplate. Lily slipped in from behind him, took his arm gently, and led him over to a secluded corner booth. Sar motioned the waiter away with an impatient hand movement that signaled they wanted to be left undisturbed.

Sar leaned toward Roger and whispered in an angry tone. "Roger, I have misgivings which Lily doesn't share. I don't like this whole thing. I don't believe your teammates are telling you the truth about shutting down this investigation. I think—"

"What are you talking about?" Roger forced as convincing a frown as he could.

Sar glared at him "I think it's obvious. Your mentor has never trusted us. I think he's become convinced you're infatuated with Lily and can no longer be trusted either. Roger, your team has simply decided to dump you as politely as possible and continue with their investigation. Can't you see it?"

"No. Sam and Pete spent half the night trying to talk me into returning to Connecticut with them. I can assure you they've given up. They're going home."

Lily banged her fist on the table. "Damn it, I'm not happy with the outcome either. The fact is, there are no better alternatives. We can't simply let this whole project drop, especially in view of the amazing discoveries you, Roger, and I have made. The world needs to know that religion has been tragically based upon altered documents that no longer reflect the word of God, and that God has been thus shamefully misrepresented."

Sar lowered his head for a moment, then raised his hands again. "All right, here it is, Roger. We happen to belong to a society exactly like the one you need for your backing. It is, in fact, a very large and very old society with membership worldwide, equipped with commensurate resources. We feel it would be the right place for you, given what's happened."

Roger breathed a sigh of relief. "I think I can make a positive contribution to our group."

"Possibly so. Still, I must alert you, our society represents what they—I mean the Ignorants of the world—disparagingly refer to as the occult. After you learn our ways, you'll come to realize that the word occult is simply a euphemism embracing all the truths which they have failed to understand. Our organization's ultimate goal," he continued, "is to achieve a new world order, a one-world government. This will prepare earth's citizens for the coming of The Enlightened One, the leader your people have dubbed the antichrist. You would, of course, be required to take the vows and become a fully-fledged member before we could actually start work on your thesis. Naturally, Lily and I would have to reserve the right to edit your final manuscript. This would be only for the purpose of making its public impact more effective. I'm sure you understand."

Lily leaned over and embraced him. "Roger, you will be such a welcome addition to our cause." She flashed her seductive smile again. "Together we'll produce a document that will shake the foundations of an obsolete world. We will make manifest The Enlightened One as never before." She beamed and hugged him again.

A contingency plan in case they saw through the ruse was no longer necessary. Roger now faced the disturbing realization that he didn't have a plan in response to the success of his charade either. Should he act on behalf of the teams and immediately disown these two disciples of Satan? Or should he slip away quietly and leave that task up to his senior partners? Or maybe London? Or perhaps let them go back to Berlin and simply decline their offer later by email on the grounds that he changed his mind? They probably would never even know that the mission continued on without them until something was published by him or MOLAS. While he observed their warm smiles, indicating that they were waiting for some kind of closure, bizarre images flooded his thoughts.

Convinced the serpent was harmless, he had foolishly embraced her. He'd even vouched for her. At this precise moment, he realized that the venomous creature that now wrapped its coils protectively around him would strike with vengeance upon discovery of the ruse. Roger decided the best course would be a careful withdrawal to avoid provoking it.

"We will, Lily. First, I have to settle things with my mentor, however. I think it's best that you and Sar avoid any further contact with my partners. Give me a few days, and I'll arrange to meet you in Berlin where we can begin my induction."

"Fine, Roger, we'll look forward to it." She leaned toward him and whispered in his ear. "And please, call me Lilith." She glowed with the look of satisfaction that follows a successful conquest. She kissed him, and the deceit of it all made him feel unclean. That he had enjoyed intimate relations with her made him feel even more squalid. She had been a thoroughly satisfying lover who made him feel the full extent of his manhood. He had even begun to entertain thoughts of marrying her one day. Now he shuddered in disgust at the thought of it.

Sam had been right about everything. It was like the childish shame he'd often felt when his father chastised him for disobeying. He'd soon have to report the results of his devious scheme to Sam, Courtney, and the others. He knew the pride of its success would be dampened by the feeling of defeat that would accompany the admission of his gullibility. In the meantime, he could find some temporary solace tapping his summary of Laodicea into his electronic history book.

* * * * *

The two teams hadn't spent much time together since the start of the project in London three weeks earlier. They found the conference room at the First Protestant Church of Denizli barely large enough to accommodate the six of them plus Pastor Aran Shazarian.

After they'd taken their seats, the tall, lanky pastor managed a grin while he groped for an appropriate way to open the meeting. "Well now, I understand you've recently had a brush with some folks from the Hell side of the River Styx."

"We did, but Roger straightened it out," Sam responded, as though he wanted to make his protégé feel better about the whole thing and at the same time prevent any further discussion of it.

Nigel put up his hand and turned to the priest. "Aran, this is our last stop on an itinerary that a very troubled priest in Konya advised us to follow. That particular priest apparently stumbled upon a cache of original Scriptures that differed substantially from today's biblical offerings. The weight of knowledge that he'd been preaching false gospel all his life finally crushed him. So far, our subsequent travels have produced findings that tend to support the priest's belief that The Bible has been altered."

Aran folded his hands in front of his face and rested his chin on them. "What kind of findings?"

Nigel laid out on the table the folder containing their research. "Basically, interviews, observations, some rather convincing documents or copies thereof. However—"

"Not to mention we were attacked a few times," Peter interrupted.

Nigel nodded. "Yes. Well, our research has also raised a persistently puzzling question. The old priest in Konya correctly warned us about what he summarily referred to as Satan's domain. From our recent experience, we now believe he might have been referring to the two antichrist followers who approached us in Bergama, and who Roger so cleverly disrobed.

"The priest also urged us," Peter said, "to consider very carefully the number seven. We're not sure, even yet, what he meant by that. We think it may have something to do with Laodicea, since that's the seventh and last point on the itinerary he gave us. We were hoping you might be able to help us if, in fact, the answer lies here in Laodicea."

Aran passed around a box of chocolates so dark they might have been mistaken for black licorice. "Well, gentlemen, the number seven has nothing to do with the fact that Laodicea happens to be the seventh church in Revelation. The priest you mentioned was Father Trazerri, was he not?"

"Yes, how did you know that?" Courtney blurted out with no attempt to conceal his surprise.

"I knew him," Aran said in a matter-of-fact tone.

"Were you aware of the incident that traumatized him?" Sam asked.

Aran leaned forward in his chair and swiveled it into position so he could reach out to the chocolates on the table. "I surmised something like that had happened, although he never related the details as he did to you." He grabbed a chocolate and popped it into his mouth. "I will say he was an extremely serious man, even to the point of appearing morose at times. He managed, however, to keep his demons well hidden."

"So then, what's the answer to the number seven riddle?" Nigel pursued the issue. "And what makes you so sure it's not what we think it is?"

"Because I know Father Trazerri, and I know his fundamental beliefs which were the sources of his energy and the cornerstone of his faith. I'm a bit surprised he didn't share them with you. I'm curious as to why."

"If you'll tell us what they were," Sam said, "we may all discover that, perhaps in his own way, he did share them with us."

"Point well taken, Dr. Wykoff." Aran shifted in his chair. "That leads directly into my interpretation of the number seven. Biblical mathematicians will tell you that the number seven appears seven hundred and thirty-five times in The Bible, of which Revelation alone claims fifty-four instances. Additionally, it appears in various combinations and spiritual meanings many times over. To Trazerri, the number seven held only one true meaning."

"Which is?" Courtney asked.

"It meant completeness, as in the complete perfection of God. Trazerri believed in the true meaning of the Hebrew word for seven which is sheva. Sheva has trilateral roots: shin, bet, ayin. Those roots carry three fundamental meanings: seven, full or complete, and oath or covenant. And that, my good friends, is precisely why I believe Trazerri wanted you to focus on the number seven."

Courtney countered with a noticeable air of impatience. "Okay, since I think we're all as confused as we were when we started, let's step back to what Trazerri told us. He said he had been, as Sam accurately described it, traumatized by his conviction that The Bible, or certain critical passages of it, had been rewritten, we believe, by the Roman Catholic Church. That appears to be consistent with our own findings on this itinerary. So, how then can his belief in divine completeness and perfection through the number seven be reconciled with his obviously shaken belief in the validity of the Scriptures as they stand today?"

"And, given such a shaken belief," Gordon continued, "why would he ask us to keep searching for documentation that would only serve to cast further doubt upon such credos as completeness or the perfection of God?"

Aran nodded. "A fair question. It brings up the part of his persona I think all of you missed. Father Trazerri, it seems, desperately needed to separate his unshakeable belief in God from the revelation of God in a Bible he no longer trusted."

Nigel stroked his moustache and rose from his chair to pace back and forth. "Okay, we agree the separation was necessary for Trazerri. Now, to follow up on Gordon's question, how do you explain Trazerri's eagerness for us to conduct our search?"

Aran paused, as if to give the whole issue further deliberation. "Gentlemen, I can only surmise he believed your corroboration of his tragic discovery would release his demons. At the same time, he wanted all of you to make the same separation he did and not allow your findings to cloud your vision of the perfection of God. Thus, I'm not surprised that the number seven was the last word he left with you before sending you on your way."

Silence wrapped itself around the room, punctuated only by the monotonous ticking of the wall clock. It was as though a great story had ended, leaving its readers satisfied with the result but sad that it had to end.

To everyone's surprise, it was Sam who summed it up best in his own off-handed way. "You know, I have to admire this guy Trazerri. He had the guts to follow his convictions even when all the facts were against him. It's kind of like he hung on by a thread and never lost sight of the forest for the trees. I think he'll always hold a special place in my mind."

Aran smiled. "As a matter of fact, Sam, the whole Christian faith hung on by a thread there for a while and was almost lost right here in Laodicea."

"How do you mean?" Gordon asked.

"I mean Laodicea was the home of some of the first bishops. And as you may or may not know, a whale of a battle went on between them and many other notable theologians, right here in this place, regarding the relationship between God and Jesus."

"How did it turn out?" Gordon asked.

"Appolinarius, the bishop of Laodicea, asserted that Jesus is fully divine, but not human. It set off a chain of thought by others who asserted that Jesus and God cannot be one. Therefore, Jesus can be neither divine nor human and must be something in between, a claim which would have destroyed the entire basis of Christianity."

"And then what happened?" Sam pressed the question.

"I'll tell you what happened, Sam," Courtney interrupted. "All the events I told you about when we were discussing Christianity's background happened. I explained to you and Roger how Christian doctrine was finally formulated. So, does it all make a little more sense to you now?"

Sam shook his head. "Yeah, I guess so. Damn it, Courtney, you and Trazerri don't leave much room for doubt, do you?"

"Not if we can help it, Sam." Courtney broke into a broad grin, and smiles could be seen all around the table.

"Father Trazerri took a stand in support of his God," Courtney continued. "The people of Laodicea didn't take a stand either way, and for that the Apostle John was harder on Laodicea in Revelation than he was on any of the other six churches. Hopefully, you see a message in that."

Sam's affirmative nod came in sharp contrast with the tightening of his lips, as though he accepted the message but didn't like it. After a much lighter discussion of other issues, amid laughter and more chocolates, the six of them bade farewell to Pastor Aran Shazarian and left for London—except for Peter, who sought out the first transportation he could find to Chester after he announced his plans to propose marriage to Robin.

# Chapter 14

# London

One of the technicians pulled the large white screen down to its full length. He clicked the power button on his remote-control device to fire up the overhead projector. Another techie scrunched behind his computer terminal and logged onto the program that would display the imaging scan results on the screen. The MOLAS conference room, where it had all begun with space to spare, was now filled to capacity with a variety of archaeologists and forensic experts from MOLAS plus Sam, Courtney, Gordon, Roger, and Nigel.

Nigel stepped up to the podium and opened the meeting with a typically concise explanation of Peter's absence. "Gentlemen, we will have to begin without our colleague, Peter Clemens. Confronted by the difficult choice of listening to me drone on about our spiritual research or proposing marriage to an enchanting woman, he succumbed to his carnal desires. Thus, we will be minus one member of our six-person team until he returns tomorrow—hopefully with a smile on his face." One of the techies ramped up the laughter by pointing out that the two teams, because of their dark purpose, had become known among the London office staff as "the six horsemen of the apocalypse."

"I want to make it quite clear right at the outset," Nigel continued on a more sober note, "everything we say and do here today stays here until I authorize any announcement, public or otherwise."

Heads nodded all around.

Nigel turned toward the London contingent and smiled. "I want to thank the London crew for all the work they did on the imaging and production of these scans, and for briefing Courtney and me so thoroughly last night. We were all shocked at the break-in and attempted theft that happened several weeks ago, but the good news is that the injured technician is now well on the road to full recovery."

The group responded with a soft smattering of applause.

"Fortunately, we were able to keep the true facts behind the break-in from the press. So, as far as any outsiders know, it was simply a routine equipment burglary attempt. At least for now, I intend to keep it that way. We've broken down the centurion's letter into four scans. Their legibility is, shall we say, still less than perfect. Nevertheless, we can see enough to interpret them intelligently. I'm relying on Dr. Stickney for theological comment so, Courtney, feel free to intervene at any time."

Nigel looked up at the screen and motioned to the technician to start the PowerPoint presentation. "Now, this first slide obviously references the centurion's recollection of his third day guarding the tomb. It's barely legible, even after our imaging enhancement, because of twenty centuries of wear. It references the name Jesus, but not surprisingly refers to him as the criminal. I think, here, the centurion was referring to Jesus as he saw him at the time of the burial, at which point his attitude might have been simply that of a soldier following orders. Later in his letter, he describes Jesus much more favorably. I presume that reflects his views following his conversations with the Apostle Paul."

"And then what?" a member of the group interjected.

"After that there are several sentences covering some nondescript personal items and other observations. Then the last part, which is also barely legible, seems to be the centurion's account of a bright, almost blinding light sometime around dawn. At first, this sounded biblically consistent until Courtney pointed out that this bright light was more than likely the emerging sunlight, which would naturally be very bright in the environment at that latitude. In short, that's about all we could glean about the tomb from the centurion's account in that first slide."

Courtney stopped tamping the new fill in his Meerschaum pipe and turned to Nigel. "Except that it definitely provides one more witness to the resurrection, notwithstanding the obvious omission of any details."

"Yes, but it doesn't say that he actually confirmed an empty tomb," someone in the audience interjected.

"True, it doesn't," said Nigel. "And that brings up a disturbing item in the centurion's letter. I'll get to that in a moment." Nigel stepped away from the podium and picked up a laser pen. "Now, the next three slides describe the centurion's conversations with the Apostle Paul, whom he obviously admired despite the wide differences in their respective cultures and allegiances. Even with the translation difficulties, we're certain the centurion is now either directly quoting or paraphrasing the words of Paul." He aimed the laser beam to the centurion's first sentence on the second slide.

"How long had the centurion been with Paul?" one of the technicians asked.

"Not sure, but it's clear they were traveling together for some distance, so there was enough time for some lengthy conversations to take place. And Courtney, here's where we're going to need your expertise. Paul appears to describe mankind's oneness with God in the context of explaining that Jesus was sent by God to teach the concept. The shocking part about this—assuming we've translated it correctly— is that any concept of oneness is inconsistent with the prevailing doctrine of God Supreme, and certainly not one with man in any way."

One of the archaeologists raised his hand. "Doesn't The Bible make several references to oneness with Christ?"

"Yes," Courtney answered, "but not with God."

Nigel nodded and paused to take a sip of tea. "Paul then seems to introduce the concept of the church universal. Now this may be simply a categorical expression, or it may be a rather bold recommendation for all faiths to join together as one without any denominational or cultural separations. If so, our world would definitely have trouble with such a proclamation today. Stranger yet, and this may be simply a conversational omission by Paul, but it appears that Paul later referred to Jesus as the teacher and never as the son of God. There's also no mention of an afterlife. Again, this is surprisingly inconsistent with biblical doctrine. Then, as difficult as—"

"Nigel," another attendee asked, "isn't it possible that the centurion simply misunderstood Paul or maybe misquoted him?"

"Yes, but I think we need to take the centurion's account at face value since it's an original document…a rare and extremely fortunate find. Look, there are a number of concepts which we'll find difficult to understand, given what we've been taught to believe. In his letter, even the centurion's tone sounded a bit shocked when Paul presented Jesus's position to the effect that all armies should be disbanded." Nigel motioned for the third slide and aimed his beam at the top of it. "The centurion goes on to state his agreement with Jesus's mandate that food be willingly shared, not only between rich and poor, but between one nation and another."

"Unbelievable," one of the forensic specialists blurted out. "And just how did Jesus propose to do that? I mean from one nation to the other, that is."

"Well," Nigel continued, "you may find it interesting that Paul quotes Jesus as saying, 'God endowed each nation of people with certain unique food-growing climates and skills. Thus, each nation should focus on producing what it does best and make the output available to all other nations.' Sort of a specialized worldwide bartering market, I guess."

"Sounds like some ancestor of Adam Smith must have been running around back then," someone joked, prompting a round of laughter.

"Or maybe John Maynard Keynes," another archaeologist chipped in, evoking a few muffled chuckles.

Nigel straightened his collar, took a sip of tea, and offered an acquiescent smile. "Perhaps, although it certainly isn't at all inconsistent with the emphasis Jesus placed on giving to those less fortunate."

"Not to change the subject," Gordon said, "but was there any further mention of the book that was supposedly given by the centurion to his son and which we never found?"

Nigel nodded toward the technician and raised four fingers, signaling for the fourth slide. "Ah, yes and no. The expression *unius libri*, meaning 'of the book,' appears a couple of times along with the word *scriptiones*, the exact meaning of which has us a little confused under the circumstances." He pointed the red beam at the slide again. "It would seem to corroborate the centurion's reference to the word *biblio* which we discussed at length before this project began."

Another technician raised his hand. "Well, doesn't that confirm the existence of back-bound books at that time?"

"Possibly. Still, I'm skeptical, given the conventional wisdom that back-bound books as such didn't come into being until the third or fourth centuries. However, since both teams discovered evidence that back-bound documents of some kind existed well before then, I'm willing to be a bit flexible on it."

"Okay, but what about the tomb?" A technician repeated the earlier question.

Nigel scowled. "That issue disturbs me more than any other, as I'm sure it does Courtney. The centurion's omission of any reference to an empty tomb, combined with his decision to leave when the women left and post a lower-ranking guard for another day, seems to negate the concept of the resurrection completely."

Roger stuffed a sheet of thesis notes into his briefcase and raised his hand. "So, where does all this leave us in terms of the official position of MOLAS, when we present the scan results to the public?"

"That depends on tomorrow's review of what the six of us found these last three weeks and how we integrate that with these scan results. I don't want to make any decision as to how, or if, we present our findings until Peter returns. Right now, what we have altogether is strong, but circumstantial evidence that the New Testament, as it stands today, differs substantially from the Scriptures as originally written."

Nigel drew his index finger across his throat to signal that the PowerPoint be shut down. He flicked the wall switch to turn the room lights up again. "Let's call it a day for now. And, once again, my heartfelt thanks and congratulations to everyone for a job well done."

The sound of applause concluded the meeting and announced that the research portion of the project had officially ended.

Roger turned to Sam as they walked out together. "I think I have enough documentation now to complete my thesis, Sam." The remark sounded more like a confirmation-seeking question.

"You may well have. You'll need to go through it carefully to bring it up to doctoral quality, though. After you've completed your review and prepared a preliminary draft, I'll have a look at it."

"Where are you going now, Sam?"

"I'm heading for the nearest pub to drown my laments about Martha. You needn't look so sympathetic. I'm feeling better. Don't tell Courtney, but I think my grief is dissipating in an inverse relationship to a growing realization that my complete rejection of God might not have been altogether justified. Anyway, here come Nigel and Courtney, so don't mention what I said."

Courtney wrapped an arm around Sam's shoulder. "A penny for your thoughts, Sam."

"Well, I'm thinking tomorrow's summit meeting might get a bit heated and the outcome equally controversial. What are your plans after this is finally settled?"

Courtney cocked his head. "They'll depend on the results of our meeting. If we decide to publish our findings unabridged, I believe I'll face a two-edged sword. On the one hand, there'll probably be a promotion in the offing for me at MOLAS. On the other, my future as a theologian will be difficult, unless I can bring myself to buy into Trazerri's pragmatic approach."

"And if we tuck our tails between our legs and equivocate?"

"In that case, my personal beliefs will have been compromised, and I may seek a teaching position somewhere." He turned to Nigel. "Since we're speculating on the future, what about you, great leader of MOLAS?"

Nigel smoothed out his suit jacket with a quick hand-sweep that looked more like a nervous twitch. "If the truth comes out, it will ensure my tenure at MOLAS. Regrettably, it will likely set off a chain of catastrophic sociological events in the Western world. Right now I'm beginning to feel a deep sense of guilt for not having aborted this whole witch-hunt before it began, so I'm going home. I'll see you tomorrow."

\* \* \* \* \*

Two days later, the two teams of three reconvened in the conference room at noon, accompanied this time by three London staffers and Nigel's secretary. The size of the MOLAS conference room hadn't changed, yet it seemed much larger with only the ten of them in it, accompanied by a small pot of coffee, a large pot of tea, and two dozen pastries.

"Pete, it's good to have you back," Nigel said with a warm smile. "May we presume your relationship with the delightful Miss Dunstan is progressing well?"

"You may. In fact, we're now engaged. The wedding, to which each of you will be sent an invitation, is tentatively scheduled for early August, before the fall semester begins."

Applause sounded from all around, and ten cups of various caffeinated beverages were raised in a toast.

"And may we also presume that your engagement offering consisted of something more appropriate than a belly dancing video?" Gordon asked, while the others tried unsuccessfully to restrain their laughter.

"Absolutely, but I'm still saving the video and the Turkish outfit for a special surprise."

Nervous laughter resounded in a room designed with such austerity it conveyed the impression that laughter was forbidden. Nigel motioned his secretary to record the minutes of the meeting, and the participants settled into their chairs—anxiety and a general malaise showing on their faces.

"Folks," Nigel began on a more serious note, "I'm convinced we've completed a more significant piece of historic field research during these last three weeks than has ever been done before. Now comes the difficult part. We must review our findings and make what you Yanks would call a gut-wrenching decision as to how we present them. In the manner of a Dr. Frankenstein, we've created a monster. Now we need to decide whether we want to reinter the creature or turn it loose on the rest of the world."

Gordon threw his hands in the air. "Why would we not release it? The news will make headlines all over the world. Wasn't that why we embarked on this venture in the first place?"

Nigel shook his head in the manner of a schoolteacher admonishing a pupil. "We need to take a much longer view of this, Gordon. We're looking at an incendiary which will, at first, only lick at the fragile edges of doctrine. Soon it will become a roaring blaze that'll blow like a firestorm straight into the heart of Christianity."

Courtney strode to the head of the table and stood beside Nigel. He put up his hand to thwart any sudden reaction to Nigel's summary. "Look, before we make any decisions, we need to conduct an item-by-item review of our research in the context of the centurion's letter. Agreed?"

Heads nodded. They all rose to fill their cups, snatch a few pastries, and returned to their seats for what had all the earmarks of a painful assessment of findings.

Courtney flashed a PowerPoint display on the screen of a summary he and Nigel had prepared. "Very well. We begin with an authentic letter from a Roman centurion who risked his and his son's lives to record his first-hand discussion with the Apostle Paul. He includes in the letter his eyewitness account of Jesus's burial, told in a way that seems to deny the resurrection. Because of the letter's time frame, confirmed by our dating process, we must assume the Scriptures he and Paul discussed are originals."

"And," Nigel interjected, "they definitely vary from the ones we see now in our Bibles."

Courtney moved his laser beam to highlight each successive item on the screen. "Yes. The Scriptures the centurion referenced speak of the oneness of God and humankind, ignoring divinity and any mention of the afterlife. They also speak of such concepts as the elimination of armies and a worldwide religion in which food and other life-sustaining goods are shared. Although it may be a bit of a stretch, some of these concepts are consistent with Scriptures as we know them today. However, if you take away divinity and the afterlife, you've torn down the pillars of biblical doctrine. Now, let's—"

"Yes," Gordon snapped, "and Columbus's proof that the world isn't flat tore down a few pillars. Some pillars need to be removed."

Courtney paused to glare at Gordon while he motioned to Nigel for a tea refill. "Perhaps so, but we should hold that decision until we finish, Gordon. Now, as I started to say, let's review our own findings during the last few weeks. First, there's a break-in here and an attempt to destroy the scans. Then someone tampered with our brakes—a clear message that existing doctrine is not to be challenged. Then a devout priest shares with us his discovery of an older and very different set of Scriptures. He's agonized the rest of his life over this finding and blames the Roman Catholic Church for substituting a more modern version that better suited its needs."

Courtney's laser beam moved down the screen. "Later, a Druid follower concurs with the priest's rewrite assessment, another attempt on our lives is made by attackers who have not been identified. We then run across a Greek priest whose 'backward causality' theory supports the biblical alteration allegation."

"Backward causality?" one of the group asked with a frown.

"Yes. A rather strange way to assert that history can be altered by a post-historic event. As if that's not enough, Sam's pen pal produces evidence supporting an alteration of the Book of Revelation. At about the same time, I find a mountain recluse who claims the same. To top it all off, we're ambushed by a couple of satanic cultists who push us hard to publish anything that would discredit The Bible."

"Wow!" blurted out one of the London staff participants. "Are there no clues as to who these culprits are?"

"I'm afraid not," Nigel said.

Aside from Gordon's occasional complaints that the proceedings were moving too slowly, everyone managed to maintain an air of calm while the ensuing debate about what to do with their findings volleyed back and forth for three more hours. In the end, the refreshments were depleted, the participants were exhausted, and no decisions had been reached. A heavy silence pervaded the room. Everyone seemed to be waiting for someone to fashion a delicate compromise between trashing their findings and making full disclosure. Nigel broke the quiet impasse.

"Gentlemen, I move we table the rest of this discussion until tomorrow morning. I think we need to consider very carefully how we handle the results of our findings here. I've insisted that everyone, including my secretary, keep the contents of these discussions confidential. Let's sleep on them tonight. Breakfast on your own, and we'll reconvene here at eight o'clock. Whatever the outcome, I believe these past three weeks have changed our lives forever."

Nods of unanimous agreement closed the meeting, and they went their separate ways.

\* \* \* \* \*

"Damn it, the more I've thought about it, the more convinced I am that we have a reporting responsibility here." Gordon's words opened the next morning's meeting even before he or anyone else had sanctified it with the traditional cup of tea. "I mean, consider what would happen if the public discovered someday that MOLAS was in full possession of such critical information and arbitrarily elected to bury it. Somehow, I doubt the world would accept our excuse that we simply decided the alternative would be worse."

Another excruciating silence offered testimony to the likelihood that everyone present recognized the Hobson's choice. All eyes turned to the only one who could speak for MOLAS.

213

Nigel rose to his full five feet nine inches, this time without any nervous tugging at his clothes or moustache. He took his time to pour a cup of tea. "Gordon, in your own inimitable way, you've brought this meeting to order with a clear statement of our dilemma. I'll summarize even more concisely. We're the only six people in the world who cannot deny the original Scriptures have been altered. We bear full and inescapable responsibility for how we deal with that. I'm open to suggestions."

Peter turned to Courtney. "Didn't you say one of the priests you encountered made a strong case for world disorder or social chaos if we brought our findings into the open?"

Courtney nodded. "He did. The question now is, do we believe it?"

"I never liked that S.O.B.," Sam said, "and I sure as hell don't believe anything he said. Even so, I'll tell you this. There are two satanic scumbags out there—and maybe a hell of a lot more of them—who'd like nothing more than a public skewering of The Bible. I'll be damned if I'll vote for anything that gives them that satisfaction. And Courtney, I'll bet Trazerri wouldn't go for it either."

Peter broke out in a wide grin. "Courtney, I don't know what you said to Sam out on the trail, but whatever it was, I hardly recognize him." Peter turned serious again. "At any rate, I believe we need to analyze how and why the scriptural changes were made. Only then can we resolve this issue."

"Good point, Pete," Nigel said. "I was about to suggest that. Allow me to lay out my whole point of view, and then each of you can support or attack it. Here's how I feel about this—all of you know full well it's a double-edged sword for me no matter what. The entire Western world is now facing a deterioration of its core values. We live in a far more culturally toxic environment than we did fifty or a hundred years ago. Even so, The Bible, with all of its doctrine, has been one of the factors that enables us to preserve some measure of civility. I've considered each item of evidence we've uncovered during our journey together. Although I'm not sure exactly how or when the Scriptural changes were made, I now believe I understand why they were made. Let's begin with—"

"Damnation, Nigel," Gordon bellowed, "please don't tell me you've bought into that backward causality nonsense!"

214

"No, not at all. As I started to say, Jesus faced a twofold problem. He needed to eradicate a lingering epicurean way of life on earth. He also had to establish the concept of a triumphant afterlife based on salvation by grace, rather than merit. I think the original Scriptures presented a compromise by portraying him as a teacher rather than in some divine form. This would account for the omission of any specific reference in the centurion's letter to the afterlife or resurrection."

One of the staff raised his hand. "Wait a minute," he said. "Maybe the centurion omitted the reference simply because he didn't actually see a resurrection."

Nigel nodded. "Possibly so."

"So, why the rewrite?" Sam interjected. "And who did it?"

Courtney walked over to the serving table, picked up a biscuit, and stood beside Nigel, who motioned him to respond to the question. "We'll never know for certain. My best assumption is that the Roman Catholic Church needed a tighter hold on its constituents. It also needed a stronger concept of both God and Jesus in order to establish and grow its form of Christianity.

"Remember," Courtney continued after taking a bite of the biscuit, "the church faced competition from other beliefs about the nature of God, as well as from those who believed in the ancient Roman gods. Christianity's need for growth could also explain the need to establish the acceptability of profit-making by the church."

"What kind of growth are we talking about here?" another staff member asked.

"Well, for starters," Courtney said, "Sam's friend, Hrand, probably had it right. Funding requirements for missionaries, facilities, priests, and the overall infrastructure of the church made it necessary to remove the original non-profit provisions of Revelation and wherever else they appeared."

"Okay, how long did all this take?" Roger asked. "According to my research, it appears to have covered several centuries."

"You're probably right," Courtney answered. "The process must have taken centuries to unfold. Now here we are, six of us, faced with the prospect of deciding what to do with an almost two thousand-year-old second edition. Nigel seems in favor of leaving it alone and burying our findings. Sam, are you going to surprise us all and cast your anti-Satan vote with Nigel?"

All eyes followed Sam as he walked to the serving table, grabbed a biscuit, loaded up his tea with milk and sugar, and returned to his seat. He bit off a chunk of the biscuit, washed it down with an audible swallow of tea, and turned to Courtney.

"Damn right I am."

Courtney grinned, along with everyone else. "I think I will too. How about you, Roger?"

"Well, I guess I've already been screwed once by the Devil's mistress. I don't see any sense in letting her do it again. I'll go along with you guys."

The room echoed with the eruption of laughter, more it seemed to release tension than anything else. It lasted so long that one of the secretaries stuck her head in to see what had happened and quickly withdrew.

Peter patted Roger on the back and grinned. "Good choice. I'll put pressure on Sam to approve your thesis. After that I'll cast my own lot with the preservation of The Bible."

Sam grinned. "Why am I not surprised, Pete? Your allegiance has always been to The Bible, has it not?"

"True, but I'm seeing The Bible from a whole new perspective now that we've witnessed so many challenges to it. I've looked at it too narrowly before...and I think that's one of the reasons my sermons have been so dull. This pilgrimage of ours has broadened my whole perspective. The Bible is more than the pronouncement of God's word in the context of his relationship with the human race. It's also a basic formula for the preservation of humanity. Any discussion of one must reference the other."

Heads nodded, and Courtney turned to Gordon. "What say you, Gordon?"

Gordon shook his head and frowned. "What about that satanic beast that we discovered...and the mandate to dismember all the apostles? Doesn't that offer significant proof of The Bible's alteration?"

Nigel's face drew into an expression of reluctant sadness. "I'm afraid not, Gordon. Regrettably, the supporting photos that Peter took came out blank. Without them, the written so-called 'mandate' doesn't

216

strengthen our evidence one bit. It won't do any good to even mention that horrible beast, I'm sorry to say."

Gordon shrugged. "Well, it appears I'm out-voted. I bloody damn well don't like it, but I'll support whatever written product we decide on. If Nigel can trash his best opportunity for assuring his tenure here, I guess I can forego a piece of my future. The one I really feel sorry for is that poor centurion. He waited two thousand years for his day in the sun and now we've shut him down."

Another round of laughter brought the meeting to an end. They chatted informally for a while longer, finished off the refreshments, and charged Courtney and Nigel with the production and editing of the project's report. They agreed it would be a plausible report, referencing the usual artifacts and a few scriptural sightings—historically significant, perhaps, but nothing not already recorded in the Dead Sea Scrolls. They made their farewells simple and unemotional. They could have changed the world and didn't...a shared secret that would bind them together forever.

Before he closed the door behind them on his way out, Nigel cast one last glance at the empty room. Three weeks earlier, it had bristled with the electric anticipation of a monumental discovery. He caressed his moustache with an index finger and smiled at the thought of the tales the barren walls could tell if they could only talk. He walked to his office, gathered up all the documents produced by the imaging and their three-week tour, and burned them in a bucket. Then he reached into his desk drawer, opened a bottle of Merlot, and consumed it.

# Epilogue

Nigel's office at MOLAS stood out as the only room on the main floor not immaculately maintained. Cluttered from wall to wall with journals, archaeological specimens, and generic junk, it was as though the room had decided, of its own accord, to rebel against Nigel's meticulous behavior everywhere else. With a note asking not to be disturbed posted on his door, Nigel leaned back in his chair with one foot propped up on his desk and the other on an unopened crate of artifacts while he read Peter's letter.

> Dear Nigel,
>
> It's been six months, and Sam, Roger, and I miss all you Brits. I'm thinking we should reunite someday under a banner reading Annual Reunion of The Six Horsemen of the Apocalypse. At any rate, the three of us feel like we've been changed forever.
>
> Robin and I are married and expecting our first child! The good Lord willing, I've managed to breathe new life into my sermons and my congregation is growing. Even Sam attends services once in a while. He's not fully committed yet, but at least he finally acknowledges the existence of God and seems to have found a peace of mind he didn't have before. Roger's thesis earned him his doctorate and has drawn the interest of several publishers. It looks like he may live up to his father's expectations after all.
>
> Well, I've some hospital visits I'd better get to, so I'll sign off. By the way, our report met with mixed reactions on this side of the pond, but was generally well received.

Looking forward to getting together again to renew old friendships. Sincerely,
Pete

\* \* \* \* \*

Three o'clock in the morning and Reverend Peter Clemens couldn't get back to sleep. Robin's pregnancy called for chocolate ice cream. Peter's search-and-rescue mission led him to the only deli in the nearby area that could answer the call at that early hour. One dill pickle and two scoops put Robin sound asleep, leaving Peter with nothing to do than to give Nigel's letter another read.

Dear Peter,

Received your epistle, and I'm delighted to hear you Yanks are faring well in the colonies. The British contingent misses you lads as well. Our report met with approval here, except for a few bodies of the Church of England. They argued that our findings looked like an upside-down triangle—enormous implications at the top, all resting on a small point of fact at the bottom.

I've planned a three-month lecture tour in response to popular demand for a hearing of our adventures. Courtney, to my regret, has left MOLAS to accept a position as professor of theology at Cambridge. He's brought Gordon along with him as an adjunct instructor in history, a post Gordon will hold until he completes his doctorate and achieves the status of professor.

I think often of that Roman centurion and what it must have been like to travel in the company of the Apostle Paul. This may surprise you, but I believe The Bible we searched for actually existed. What we discovered might have changed the world, with or without that document. Still, I'm convinced we acted in the best interest of the human race when we destroyed our findings. Now, here's the irony of it all: when the six of us reach the end of our lives, we will look back and reach the inevitable conclusion that our most significant act was the one we did not commit.

Until we meet again, I remain your friend and colleague.

Nigel Patterson

# About the Author

John Chaplick earned a Bachelor's degree in Liberal Arts from Wesleyan University in Middletown, Connecticut, and an MBA from the University of Michigan. He has served as an Elder in the Presbyterian Church for thirty years during which he has chaired a number of committees. John's biblical studies have included research on the life of the apostle Paul. *Forbidden Chronicles of a Roman Centurion* has been reviewed by two theologians, a pastor, seventeen members of Florida Writers Association, a professional editor, and three beta readers. Relevant parts of the manuscript have been reviewed by a representative of Dr. William Lane Craig, author of several theological works including *God: A Debate Between A Christian and an Atheist.*

Other Titles by John Chaplick:
*The Pandora Files*
*An Enduring Conspiracy*
*The Rivergrass Legacy*
*Bridge of the Paper Tiger*

CPSIA information can be obtained
at www.ICGtesting.com
Printed in the USA
JSHW030027091222
34599JS00001B/69